BREAK THE RULES

JULIA JARRETT

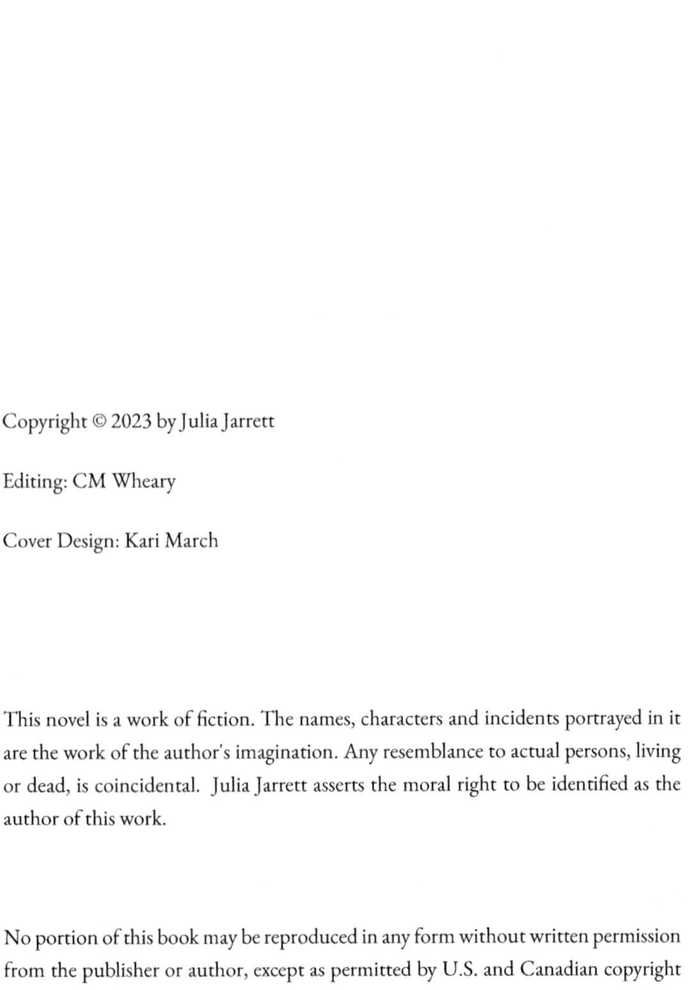

Editing: CM Wheary

Cover Design: Kari March

CONTENTS

Chapter One

September

Willow

My bag is buzzing, and it's not coming from my phone.

Shit. Maybe putting my favourite vibrator in my carry-on wasn't the smartest choice. Oh well, nothing to do about it now. All that stands between me and sun, sand, and relaxation is a five-hour flight. Oh, and the damn security line at Vancouver International Airport, where everyone around me now knows I've got a sex toy in my bag.

"Oops." I shrug at the female guard eyeing the small suitcase. "Sensitive power button."

She gives me a nod, but I see the hint of a smile she's fighting to hide. Picking up my suitcase, she beckons me forward.

After I walk through the scanner, I pass a tall man collecting his items, who if I wasn't intent on dealing with my rogue vibrator, I'd probably give a lot more attention to. *What can I say, backward ball caps do it for me...* His muffled chuckle hits me as my noisy bag passes in front of the plexiglass barrier.

My new friend the security agent opens the bag, and after a quick look inside, reaches in and turns off the toy. She gives me a subtle wink before passing my bag over to me. "Enjoy your trip, ma'am."

I wink back. "I most certainly will."

With my no longer buzzing suitcase in hand, I leave the security area, intent on finding the nearest Starbucks and caffeinating myself. My best friend Tori likes to give me a hard time for my coffee addiction, but I don't care. Ever since university, pulling all-nighters as I balanced working part-time, playing recreational fastball, and trying to maintain my GPA, I've been a three cup a day kind of girly. Maybe four if I have a decaf at night.

The lineup at the iconic coffee shop rivals that of security, making me glance at my phone more than once as the minutes tick by to when my plane will start loading. If I hadn't hit snooze on my alarm clock this morning, I would've been here sooner. Instead, I'm going to be rushing. But the pull of sleep after the chaos of this past season was too strong to ignore. Even with a flight to Hawaii waiting for me.

Coffee purchased, I hurry over to step on the escalator that will take me up to the gate. Lifting the cup of steaming deliciousness to my lips, my gaze drifts over to the escalator carrying passengers back down to the main airport concourse. My gaze locks onto a face that is both startlingly handsome and vaguely familiar. I instantly recognize the ball cap, even though it's facing forward now, and his dark shirt. It's the man from the security line, only this time he's pointing toward me. And oh, what a face.

He's got dirty blonde hair poking out from under his Toronto Wolverines hat with thick scruff covering a strong jaw. The cap hides his eyes, but my imagination fills in the blanks and pictures them being vibrant blue, something with depth and fire in them.

There's no hiding the bulge of his biceps under the Henley he's wearing. And best of all, even on an escalator going the opposite direction from me, it's clear he's a head taller than anyone around him. And there is nothing hotter to me than a guy with some height. After all, I'm five-nine, and I love wearing heels.

His stare meets mine as we pass each other — *blue, I was right* — his lips quirking up into a sexy-as-fuck grin as we pass each other. *Hello, dimples...*

"Who are *you*?" I whisper to myself as I crane my neck around to keep sight of him as long as possible. The only thing keeping my actions from being completely mortifying is the fact that I catch him twisting to watch me as well.

I have a moment when I actually consider abandoning my holiday, getting on the escalator going down, and chasing the captivatingly handsome stranger through the airport. But that's crazy, even by my standards. Although, if there was ever a man worth sacrificing a week in Hawaii, it would be him. There's handsome, and then there's whatever he is. Looking like that, I'm going to say a god among men, guaranteed to be next-level sinful, and a wickedly good time.

But I don't give in in to lust-fueled insanity. Instead, I mentally give my head a shake, step off the escalator, and make my way to the gate. Sure, he was beyond attractive, but there will be an island full of hot half-naked men on the beach where I'm going. I have no doubt I'll soon forget about the escalator god.

Except, I recognize him from somewhere. Or do I? I wouldn't have thought I could forget a man as delicious as him.

Reaching my gate with, thankfully, half an hour to spare, I sink down in a seat and let my eyes flutter closed as I sip from my coffee. Of course, just then, another buzzing starts up, but at least this time it *is* coming from my phone. Part of my job as assistant director of media relations for the Vancouver Tridents professional baseball team is to stay on top of any media leaks. And that means having all the notifications turned on for baseball news headlines.

"Management Shake-Up at the San Diego Devils."

"Free Agent Frenzy: Who's Up for Grabs This Offseason and Who Wants Them."

"Star Pitcher Colt Waterstone Wows Crowds at the World Baseball Classic."

I skim the headlines quickly, and when none of them have anything to do with my team, I heave a sigh of relief and turn on my out-of-office autoreply for the first time in over a year. I am officially on vacation, and any news surrounding the Vancouver Tridents baseball team, possible offseason trades, or player drama will have to wait a week.

Between the ongoing work one of our players likes to make for us with his bad boy ways, and the surprising discovery that our now-retired star pitcher had a secret kid no one knew about, the media relations team was constantly putting out fires this past season.

My work-life balance was nonexistent at times. But the next seven days will be the reset I need and deserve. Some people might hate traveling alone, but I love it. I'm not responsible for anyone but myself, meaning I can just lie in the sun, drinking icy beverages served poolside, and maybe find a holiday hottie or two to have some fun with.

No better stress relief than orgasms.

And if the hotties don't deliver, the toys I packed will.

At that moment, a young family enters the waiting area for our flight. The little boy runs past me wearing a Toronto Wolverines shirt, and I gasp as realization slams into me.

Holy shit, escalator god is Ronan Sinclair.

The first baseman from Ontario caught my eye a few years ago when I was on the field coordinating interviews after a game. Even from a distance, his good looks were noticeable. Especially in tight baseball pants. Not to mention the way he was kind, humble, and respectful toward the media and support staff.

Knowing that my escalator god is a baseball player makes things both easier and harder for me.

I might not see him again today, but I will undoubtedly see him during the season, and now I have to make myself forget the way he made my mouth water with nothing more than an upturn of his lips.

There's an unspoken rule about dating baseball players. As in, *don't do it*. And I take that rule very seriously. With my uncle Mike — my dad's best friend — owning the team that employs me, it would be beyond stupid to mix work and pleasure when I already have to prove I'm more than a nepo hire. I want to be known for my work, not for who I'm related to or who I'm dating.

In an effort to distract myself from the fantasies I really shouldn't be having about the man, I stupidly open my email. Rookie mistake when I want to be in vacation mode, not work mode. Because even with the out-of-office turned on, there's one waiting from my boss, Lydia.

Guilt instantly hits me when I mentally groan seeing her name. When I started at the Tridents, Lydia took me under her wing, mentored me, and helped me get to where I am today.

Here's the thing, though. Lydia's demanding on a good day, insufferable on a bad one. She might have been a powerhouse in the media relations field once upon a time, but these days she seems content to let the rest of us do the work and she just takes the credit. She puts a lot of pressure on me and everyone else. Everyone *but herself* these days. Tori has tried to tell me before that Lydia's not giving me enough credit for what I do, but as much as I love my bestie, she doesn't get it. If I want to prove myself as more than just a nepotism hire, I have to bust my ass.

And kiss Lydia's.

Right now, it's even more important I work hard. Because Lydia's retiring this season, and I want a shot at her job. That doesn't mean I want to see an email from her as I wait for my plane with the subject line "URGENT" in all capital letters. Dread filling me, I open the email.

From: l.hacker@vantri-dents.com
To: W.lawson@vantridents.com

Willow,
Where are the videos of the players' final interviews? They need to be uploaded to the website and I don't have the files on my computer.
Call me immediately.
Lydia

Thank fuck. Not urgent at all. Because it was done a week ago. Which she would know if she read the email update I sent her last night as a handover before my trip. It takes me two minutes to type out a reply. And that includes the time to remember I have to be respectful and not come off as annoyed.

From: w.lawson@vantridents.com
To: l.hacker@vantridents.com

Lydia,
The videos were uploaded along with transcripts of the interviews to the website the day after the game. The web team notified me they emailed you the files and links on Monday.

> You should be able to view them right now.
> Just to remind you, I will be unavailable for the next seven days, but the document I sent over last night summarizes my wrap-up of all necessary projects, and Sheena is on hand to answer urgent questions.
> See you in a week,
> Willow

I hit send and immediately close my email. Won't be making the mistake of opening that up again for a week. Vacation-mode Willow is officially turned on.

A short while later, I'm settled in my first-class window seat and pulling out my e-reader that's stocked with all the books I haven't had time to read these last few months. While the rest of the plane boards, I lose myself in the science fiction saga I've been dying to start. The vivid storytelling sucks me in immediately, and I don't even notice someone sitting down in the seat beside me until the husky rumble of a voice stirs something deep inside of me.

"Seems you are going my way, after all."

I look up. And into the azure blue eyes of my against-the-rules escalator god.

Chapter Two

Ronan

The gorgeous brunette recovers quickly, her open mouth snapping shut as she eyes me. Honestly? When I was rushing back to my gate after retrieving my goddamn cell phone that I left at security, I couldn't stop thinking about the beautiful woman I saw on the escalator.

Not beautiful. Stunning.

Steal-my-breath-away stunning.

Call it fate or destiny or just good old karma that put me in the seat next to her. Whatever transpired to put me here, I'll take it. It's my first vacation ever without my daughter. Ever since my ex announced — while still pregnant — that she had no interest in becoming a parent, thereby leaving me a single dad, vacations have revolved around my little girl. Finding a woman to have fun with wasn't high on the to-do list since I figured I'd be too busy with my friend Eddie's wedding stuff, since that's the entire reason I'm going to Hawaii alone. But it's bumping up in priority as we study each other.

"I'm Ronan," I say, putting out my hand. She takes it, giving me a strong handshake.

"I know who you are." She drops my hand. "And my name is Willow."

Hmm, she knows me. This could go one of two ways. In my experience, when a woman recognizes me, it either means she's simply a baseball fan, meaning no drama, or she's seeing dollar bills. Schooling my tone to be a little more reserved until I figure out which camp she falls into, I reply, "Nice to meet you." Then, I settle back in my seat. But I can feel the heat of her gaze on me.

"You had a good season. Three-twenty batting average, best fielding percentage for a first baseman in your division. Impressive."

A fan, then. Maybe more? Hell, a beautiful woman who can list my stats like that? It's hot. "Let's not forget my RBIs and zone defense rating. You know your baseball."

She lifts her shoulders in a shrug. "You could say that."

Enigmatic. I like it. She knows who I am, knows my game, but she isn't fangirling. There's no ring and no mistaking the interest I saw on the escalator.

"What's taking you to Hawaii?" I ask, lifting my hat off to run my fingers through my hair before setting it back down, tugging the brim down a bit. I may not be as famous as some of my colleagues, but I'd still rather not be recognized right now. People are filing past us, heading to their seats, but I feel as if I'm in a little bubble. It's just me and this woman I really want to get to know.

"Vacation. I just needed to get away for a while." She puts down her tablet and settles against the window to face me. "What about you?"

"Friend from university is getting married." I flash her a grin. "And some time in the sun sounded pretty good before I head into an Ontario winter."

Her chuckle is throaty and fucking sexy. "Yeah, I don't think I could handle the cold out east."

I shrug. "Eh, it's not so bad. It's home, hopefully for a few more years."

Her shoulders relax slightly. Or am I imagining that? Just then, a flight attendant leans down into our space. "May I offer either of you a beverage?"

I glance at Willow, gesturing for her to go first. Her nose crinkles adorably as she thinks before responding, "It's a toss-up. Mimosa or Americano." She taps her chin twice, then nods. "Americano now, mimosa later. Thank you."

The attendant turns to me, but I'm just smiling at the woman next to me. She clears her throat and I realize she's waiting for my answer.

"Just coffee, thanks."

As soon as she leaves to fill our order, I turn back to Willow. "At the risk of sounding like a creep, are you traveling alone?"

She lifts an eyebrow, just one, and goddamn, that's weirdly attractive. "Yes, as a matter of fact, I am. Why do you ask?"

Good question. Why am I asking? It's not like me to be this forward with women. I've got Peyton, my daughter, to think about. Not to mention the built-in complication and drama that can come from trying to pick up women as a somewhat high-profile athlete.

But something's different with Willow. She's beautiful, sure, but there's more to it than just her looks. She's got some sort of magnetic pull that I can't seem to ignore. I pause a second, feeling the simmering attraction between us solidify even further as I figure out how to answer. But what I come out with sounds corny, even to my ears.

"I'm just trying to clarify the situation so I know how best to proceed. It would seem fate keeps putting us together, and who are we to deny that?"

Smothering her burst of laughter with her hand, Willow's eyes dance with amusement. "Fate? Really? That's not what I expected you to say. You don't seem like a believer-in-fate kind of guy."

She's not wrong, but I'm just glad my cheeseball answer didn't turn her off. Which means it's my turn to shrug. "I don't. Not normally. But when I saw you at security, I wanted to run after you, only you disappeared so quickly. Then on the escalator, when I saw you a second time, I cursed my idiot self for leaving my cell phone at security. Even though you were to blame for me forgetting it in the first place." I take a chance and lean in a little closer. "See, I was distracted by the gorgeous woman with a vibrating bag." She laughs again. "If I hadn't needed to go back and collect it, you should know I would have instantly tried to find you. Which brings us to now. Seeing you sitting in the seat next to mine? Definitely a sign that we were meant to meet."

"Ah, so that *was* you at security." Those baby blues scan me from head to toe. "Damn, I knew my instincts were good."

"Instincts?" I ask, raising my own eyebrows.

Willow nods. "I noticed you. I was just otherwise occupied by my vibrator situation..." She trails off, leaving me to fill in the rest. She's bold, and fuck if I don't love that. I noticed it when everything happened at security. Other women might have been embarrassed, but Willow just owned it.

She leans in closer, a faint whiff of citrus and vanilla hitting my nose and making my goddamn dick stir in my pants. "But what if I told you I don't believe in fate. I'm in control of my life and my destiny, not some unseen, all-knowing force."

"Oh, so you're a control freak." I smirk as her eyes narrow. "It's fine, I get it. A strong, independent woman like you has to take care of herself. It's admirable. It's how I want to raise my daughter. But there's something to be said for not knocking opportunity down when it shows up."

I watch closely to see how she responds to my comment about my daughter. If she's a baseball fan, she might already know about my single parent status, but just in case she isn't, her reaction will be telling.

"So you're saying you're an opportunity?" she says lightly, clearly unfazed by the daughter situation. Which means either she already knew or she doesn't care. Both of which suit me just fine right now.

My shoulders lift in a shrug. "Maybe. I could be. We're going to the same small island, after all."

"Well, if that happens, we certainly can't ignore that, now can we." Sitting back, her tongue darts out to lick her lip just before she tugs it between her teeth. "And I suppose I should confess, I almost got on the escalator back down to follow you. Before I realized who you were."

Even with that last sentence being a reason to pause, I mentally pump my fist. It's been a long-ass time since a woman captivated me the way Willow does. I haven't been celibate, but my daughter and my career have come first and second, leaving no time for any romantic connections. Aside from a few one-night stands with women I find at bars on the road, while my mother looks after my kid at home, I've been alone for years. That's never bothered me; there's never been anyone I wanted to get to know. Not until this woman, right here.

"Seems to me you should let me take you out for dinner tonight," I suggest, taking the lead from her bold attitude.

"Hmm. If I say yes, then that's not exactly leaving it up to fate. Maybe we simply enjoy the next few hours as seatmates, then go our separate ways and see what your friend fate has in store for us."

I lean back against my seat with a rueful chuckle. "Alright, you win. Fate it is."

The rest of the flight passes in a blink of an eye. Four plus hours of verbal banter, with only the slightest hint of flirtation, the barest of touches. A brush of her legs when she moved past me to use the bathroom. My fingers grazing hers when I pass her meal to her. For once, I wish I was crammed in an economy seat, simply so we'd be that much closer to each other. But then again, this has been fun.

Do I wish she'd just say yes to dinner? Yeah, I do. She's fascinating, and beautiful, and I want to know more.

When we land on Oahu, I follow Willow off the plane, and we make our way together, but without speaking, to the luggage carousel. It's weird how I don't want to say goodbye to a woman I just met a few hours ago. But even with all the flirting, it's clear she's got some pretty tall walls up. And it's got something to do with me being a baseball player. That was clear from her cryptic comment about following me *before* she knew who I was.

Once we both have our luggage, she turns to me.

"Well, this was fun. Thank you for making the flight quite enjoyable." A warm smile belies her formal words. I take the hand she stretches out and shake it firmly.

"You sure I can't take you to dinner?" I ask, trying not to sound too eager.

I might be imagining it, but I swear a flash of regret crosses her face. "Sorry, no."

There's nothing for me to do but nod, then watch as the most intriguing woman I've ever met walks away from me.

I don't stop thinking about her the entire time while I pick up my rental car and drive it to the beachfront resort where Eddie is getting married in two days. Once I'm checked into my suite, I head upstairs, barely noticing the stunning vista out my window. Instead, I drop down onto the bed and call home.

"Daddy!" Peyton shrieks as her little face fills the screen.

"Hey, Rocket," I say, feeling something settle in my chest the way it always does when I talk to my daughter. "How was your day?"

"Good. Did you find Moana?"

I chuckle. "No, baby girl, not yet. I just got to the hotel." Rising to stand, I cross the room to the open balcony doors and turn the camera around. "But look, the ocean is right there."

"I betcha find Moana at the beach!"

"Maybe. I'll keep my eye out."

"'Kay. And say hi to any chickens."

God, I love my kid. "You bet I will. So, what was the best part of your day?"

I settle back down on the bed for my daily check-in with Peyton. We've never missed it, even when I've had evening games. I always found a way to call her in the afternoon or evening to check in, ever since she started talking. Before that, I'd at least call and wave at her chubby little toddler face. But now, at four and a half, she's a chatterbox.

She's *my* chatterbox, and I'd do fucking anything to make her smile. There's nothing and nobody on this planet more important than my little girl.

Chapter Three

Ronan

I'm coming out of the resort gym the next morning when I come to an abrupt halt and feel the need to rub my eyes, just to make sure I'm not dreaming. Because right there in front of me, wearing a lavender spandex shorts and sports bra set, is none other than my seatmate.

"Willow?" I call out, still not totally sure if I'm imagining things. I'm not ashamed to admit, she starred in a very X-rated dream last night, which should maybe feel weird since I barely know her. But fuck, if she doesn't look like temptation incarnate in workout clothes and a ponytail.

"Ronan?" Her eyes widen and the slightest hint of a smile crosses her face, lighting her up from the inside. "I'd say I'm surprised, but —"

"Fate." I finish for her with a grin. Her laugh is light and easy, and goddamn, do I want to hear it again. "What else could it be? We're staying at the same resort. C'mon, it's gotta be fate."

Willow just shakes her head, but she's full-on smiling now, and I count that as a win. "Or pure coincidence."

"You're not going to make this easy, are you?"

"Why would I?"

"Because I'm handsome and charming, and you're beautiful and intriguing, and I want to spend time with you while we're here in paradise together." Part of me can't quite believe I just laid it all out there for her like that, but something tells me Willow appreciates a direct approach. "But don't worry, I've wised-up. I'm not gonna ask you out for dinner right now."

She arches one brow. "You're not?"

I shake my head slowly. "Nope. Because you'd still say no. You're not ready to say yes. Not yet, at least. But you will be."

"So you're playing a long game?"

I wink. "I'm a good closer. Ninth inning home runs are my specialty."

She leans in, and I hold my breath as her subtly sweet and citrus perfume hits me. But then she whispers, "I don't date baseball players."

I turn slightly, so we're face-to-face, mere inches separating us. "I'm not looking to date you, Willow. Just take you out for dinner."

Her tongue darts out to lick her plump lips as she inhales, then backs away slightly. "Just dinner, huh?" she says, her voice sounding airy and carefree. "Right." She drags that one word out, as if she doesn't fully believe that dinner is my only intention. "Well, we'll see about that. I'm going to go do my workout." She gestures over her shoulder to the gym. "Maybe I'll see you around."

I let her walk away, but she only takes a few steps before I call out, "I think you will. Fate seems to be on our side, Willow."

Her shoulders shake with silent laughter as she waves over her shoulder.

I was already looking forward to this trip, but now? Even more.

An hour later, I'm trying not to think too hard about what Willow might be doing while I'm off with the guys for Eddie's bachelor party day. I've got no claim on her or her time. But fuck if I don't wish I was poolside with her instead of standing at the top of the jetty leading to the boat that will carry me and four other guys out to the ocean for a day of deep-sea fishing.

"Ronan. Dude."

I blink out of my fantasies of Willow in a bathing suit and focus on Jeremiah, my other buddy from university. The three of us were friends all through university. On the varsity baseball team, we were unstoppable. But I was the only one of us to go pro, the guys were content to move on to other things. And right now, Jer, Eddie, and a couple other friends of Eddie's from work are looking at me expectantly.

"Sorry, zoned out for a second."

Jeremiah raises his eyebrows. "Everything okay with Peyton and your mom?" he asks under his breath. I appreciate his discretion. My friends are good about not a big deal over who I am and what I do, but Eddie's other friends aren't quite as discreet. I've emphasized I'm not Ronan Sinclair, ball player, on this trip. I'm just Ronan, Eddie's friend and groomsman, but it still took a bit for them to let it go and treat me like a regular dude.

Since Jer knows I keep my personal life pretty locked down, I'm grateful he's keeping his voice low, even if he couldn't be more wrong about the reason for my distraction.

Instead of a pint-sized brunette pulling my focus, it's a tall, leggy one.

"Yeah, yeah. All good, man. Sorry. What did I miss?" I ask quietly.

"Not much, just the douchebags shooting the shit about who's gonna reel in the bigger fish."

I muffle my snicker at his name for two of Eddie's other friends. I already pegged them as being competitive for all the wrong reasons and have no intention of getting to know them.

"Great." *Not great*. I'm missing out on a day where I could be trying to get to know Willow, win her over, and get her to say yes to dinner. Instead, I'm stuck going fishing on a fucking boat with a couple of cocky assholes.

I hate boats.

The guys all start walking down the wooden pier toward the fishing charter. I lag behind, kicking myself for not at least trying to get Willow's number so I could text her. That might alleviate some of the boredom I suspect I'm in for. Then again, we probably don't have cell service out on the fucking ocean. It's a damn good thing I like Eddie enough to do this.

A couple of hours later, I'm questioning that loyalty. One of the guys caught some big fish, don't ask me what kind, and I joined in a celebratory beer, but I'm over it. My stomach is roiling as much as the waves are, I'm fucking hot as hell on this boat with zero shade, and I swear, if I hear one more bad joke about how I'm striking out on catching a fucking fish, I'm gonna push someone overboard.

"I'm sorry about them, Sin."

The sound of my nickname from college ball makes me smile. Eddie's the one who started it, and it stuck with me all the way to the big leagues. Dropping down onto the bench next to me, Eddie passes over a bottle of water. I take it with a nod of thanks and guzzle half of it down before responding. "Not your problem, brother. It's fine."

"I swear they're not douchenozzles back home. What is it about vacation that brings out the worst in some people?"

I snort. "You mean they aren't always moments away from whipping out their dicks and measuring them?"

Eddie chokes back his laugh, but it's loud enough that one of the other guys looks over. Thankfully, someone's rod starts jerking, drawing the attention away.

"Thanks for coming," Eddie says. "I know it's not easy getting away with Peyton and all, so I just want you to know it means a lot that you're here. Hopefully, you have some fun this week, even if it isn't today."

I chuckle, because he might be one of my best friends, but I'm not about to tell him just what kind of fun I would like to have this week. "Wouldn't want to be anywhere else but here. Even with Tweedledee and Tweedledum over there."

This time his laugh isn't as subtle. "Yeah. To be honest, they're only here because their wives are best friends with Clara. If it were up to me, I'd just spend the day surfing with you and Jer. But she really wants us to hang out and get to know each other, so she planned all of this."

"You could've told her what you wanted," I say bluntly.

Eddie just shrugs, then stands and scratches his chest before looking down at me. "Someday you'll find a woman who makes you realize the whole 'happy wife, happy life' thing isn't total bullshit. When she's happy, I'm happy. It's that simple. And this, fishing with a bunch of guys, is not exactly a hardship."

I nod because what else am I meant to say? He's right, a fishing charter in Hawaii isn't exactly torture, even if it's not where I want to be right now. Eddie wanders over to the other guys, and I watch him for a second.

He *is* happy. That's clear to anyone who sees him and Clara together. And someday, sure, I'd love to find that. A partner, someone to do this life with. But today isn't that day.

Today I'd settle for a dinner date with a beautiful brunette.

Chapter Four

Willow

Okay, fine, I looked for Ronan yesterday. Didn't see him, which is probably a good thing, but I looked. I'd have to be blind not to want to see the gorgeous man. Even if I have zero intention of giving in to his charm and letting him take me out for dinner, the attention is nice. I can't deny that.

I decided last night that instead of heading to the gym again this morning and risking another run-in, I would drive out of town to hike the Maunawili Falls Trail. And I've been told there's an incredible bakery on the way back that apparently has the best donuts I'll ever taste.

An early morning hike followed by donuts, then a session in the shower with my naughty bag-buzzing vibrator? Sounds like heaven to me.

But of course, as soon as the doors to the elevator open, I come face-to-face with temptation wrapped up in a six-foot-plus muscular body with a killer smile and dimples I want to lick.

Nope, no I don't. No licking dimples that belong to baseball players, Willow.

"Well, fancy seeing you here," he says, moving to the side of the suddenly very small-feeling elevator. "Heading to the gym?"

I glance down at the backpack I'm holding. "Not today. I'm going for a hike instead."

"Really? Same here."

I tilt my head at his answer, but there's not even a hint of deceit in his voice. Chalk it up to coincidence, yet again, I suppose.

"Where are you going?" he asks, and I answer automatically, seeing no reason not to.

"Maunawili Falls."

Ronan makes a choking sound and I look over to see him lowering his water bottle. "Seriously?" he asks.

Nodding, I step out of the elevator when it opens on the main floor. "Yeah. Why?" Realization dawns on me when I see his smirk. "No fucking way."

He just nods. "I'm not joking, I swear." Turning his phone around, he shows me his GPS app with the directions to Maunawili Falls already entered. "Want to carpool?"

All I can do is laugh, which makes his smile widen. "You and your friend *fate*," I tease as we walk out into the heat of the Oahu sun. We come to a stop at the waiting valet and he looks at me, not saying anything, even though I know exactly what he's waiting for.

"Okay, you win this round. Let's go." Moments later, we're in his car, a sexy-as-fuck convertible, speeding down the highway.

"I didn't picture you as a convertible kind of guy," I yell across at him, the wind stealing my words. He's holding the steering wheel with one hand, his elbow resting on the edge. It's effortlessly casual but so goddamn sexy. He's hard to resist. But resist I will. *Resist I must.*

I won't fall for a pretty face. Not even a charming one like Ronan Sinclair.

"Yeah, back home I drive an SUV. With the snow and everything, it's necessary. But here? I figured why the fuck not. Always wanted one."

The subtle reminder that he's from the East Coast settles my conscience a little bit. That, and reminding myself I'm just going for a hike. Nothing more, no matter how easy it is to flirt with him.

On the drive, Ronan tells me all about his daughter Peyton. His love for her is evident in the bright smile that's on his face and the adoration in his voice as he describes their tradition of talking every night, the stuffed bear she insists he travels with, and her obsession with the movie *Moana*. It's bittersweet to witness, seeing as it's been almost eleven years since my adoptive father passed away. Not a day goes by that I don't miss him. Hearing Ronan gush about his little girl both warms my heart and breaks it.

My dad was the best father I could have ever dreamed of. I never once felt like I was anything other than everything he ever wanted. The fact that my biological parents couldn't be bothered to raise a kid never bugged me because Dad and Uncle Mike made me feel more loved than I thought possible.

Losing him was like losing an invisible limb.

"Does Peyton get to see her mom when you're away?" I ask, completely unprepared for the glower that comes over his face.

"No," he says in a clipped voice. His hands tighten on the steering wheel. He doesn't say anything else for a second, and the tension grows thick until he exhales. "She signed over full custody and disappeared the day after Peyton was born. It's been just the two of us ever since."

And just like that, my heart melts for his little girl.

"She's lucky to have you," I say quietly, partly hoping the wind will just carry the words away. But he glances over, and I know he heard me.

"Thanks."

Turning off the highway and onto a road that winds through a residential neighbourhood and ends at the start of the trail to the falls, the wind noise dies down considerably now that we're traveling at a slower speed.

We reach the parking lot for the hike, and there's only one other car. "Looks like we'll have the trail to ourselves." I hope I don't sound nervous. I'm not, at least not for any reason that makes sense to me. But being in close proximity to Ronan without the buffer of other airplane passengers or hotel guests has me feeling *something*.

After maneuvering into a parking spot, Ronan hops out while I'm stowing my phone in my backpack. My door opens, and I look up at him in surprise.

"Thank you," I say awkwardly as I climb out. I don't know why the chivalrous act comes as a surprise, but it does.

"No problem."

I stretch my arms overhead, taking in the absolutely luscious view around us. We're in a tropical jungle — well, okay, a forest reserve according to the research I did on the trail last night. Whatever you call it, it's stunning. Green, vibrant, and peaceful.

"Wow," I whisper as we set off on the trail. Ronan lets me lead, and I take my time, just breathing in the spectacular nature. Birds chirp and swoop overhead, and even though the air is humid and fragrant, there's a light breeze that keeps us comfortable.

Unlike the drive, where we fought the wind noise to talk to each other, we're both silent now, just enjoying the experience. Until we hit a break in the trees, and then my gaze locks on the peaks of faraway mountains.

"That's beautiful," I murmur as Ronan comes to stand beside me.

"Yeah." I glance over to see his gaze trained not on the view, but on me. "Beautiful."

There's no fighting back my blush, as his meaning is clear. He breaks eye contact first, turning to face the ridgeline and lifting the edge of his sleeveless shirt up to wipe his brow.

Okay, fine, I drool at the sculpted abs he reveals, covered in just a dusting of light hair. I'm pretty sure I'd be crazy not to appreciate that sight.

"So, what do you do when you're not hiking through tropical jungles with strangers you met on an airplane?"

I have to laugh at Ronan's question, because it just underlines how insane these few days have been. He might be onto something with the whole fate idea, because why else would I be voluntarily spending time with a man who is temptation personified, but also so totally off-limits.

But his question sobers me. Do I want him knowing I work for a baseball team? Making a snap decision, I answer as truthfully as I can. "I work in media relations."

"That must be a tough job sometimes."

Nodding, I take his outstretched hand for help climbing over a fallen log. Chivalry is kinda nice, I have to admit. "Yeah, it can be, but I like the fast pace. My job, where I work, it's everything to me."

"I can understand that."

We share a small smile, then carry on the trail. A short while later, the trail opens up at the base of a small waterfall. "Oh," I gasp, stunned by the sound of cascading water, the sight of dense, tropical jungle foliage, and the tranquility of paradise found.

Next to me, Ronan peels off his shirt completely, and toes off his shoes.

"What are you doing?" I ask as his hand goes to the waistband of his athletic shorts.

"Swimming. I forgot my trunks; are you okay if I'm just in my underwear?" There's no tease in his words, he's seriously making sure I'm good with this and that level of respect doesn't go unnoticed.

Jesus Christ. Am I really about to go swimming with escalator god in his underwear?

I nod, my mouth suddenly dry. For someone who's normally far bolder and more confident in these type of scenarios, I feel weirdly shy. Not that I've been in many situations with hot guys stripping down in front of beautiful waterfalls. It must be Ronan's innate charm and consideration that has me feeling warm all over. He's not like the guys I usually hook up with, where we're both just looking for some casual fun without any feelings involved. Ronan's the kind of guy who's got *feelings* written all over him.

I, at least, am prepared. Lifting my tank over my head to reveal my bikini top, I don't miss Ronan's appreciative grin. Wiggling out of my shorts, I peel off my own shoes and socks before making my way to the edge of the shallow pool at the base of the falls.

"Ooh, it's warm." I wade in slowly. Glancing over my shoulder, I see Ronan studying me. It takes a lot of effort not to let my gaze drop to the bulge behind his black boxer briefs, but somehow I make myself look forward and move farther into the pool.

My foot catches some algae covering a rock and slips out from under me. Just as I figure I'm about to go under, strong arms wrap around my waist from behind and a deep voice sounds close to my ear. "I've got you."

I suck in a breath as Ronan helps me find my footing and try not to think about the disappointment I feel when his strong hands leave my body.

"Thanks."

He just gives me a quiet grin before diving under the water himself, coming up a short distance away and slicking his hair back. "Still think fate isn't involved in our lives right now?"

I simply laugh and shake my head. "You and that damn F-word."

Chapter Five

Willow

It's taken all of my restraint not to open my work email the last couple of days. Even as I laid out on the beach, drinking iced coffee, soaking up the sun, and trying to muster up some interest in the handsome men I saw walking past with surf boards, part of my mind was focused on Vancouver, wondering if everything was okay at work. The offseason might be a lighter workload for us, but it's not nonexistent.

But every time I'd start to rationalize just taking a quick check to make sure there were no emergencies, I remembered the promise I made Uncle Mike the day before I left.

I will relax and enjoy myself, I will not worry about the team. It's early in the offseason, nothing major is happening, and I deserve a break.

The twinkle in his eye as he made me recite that back to him over dinner that night brings a rueful smile to my face. He knows me so well.

Growing up, Uncle Mike was as much a part of my life as my dad. They were inseparable, best friends, just like Tori and me.

I suppose, in some way, I am to Tori's son Cooper what Uncle Mike is to me. Family, the kind that goes deeper than blood.

I knew from an early age that I wanted to work for Uncle Mike's team. Baseball was life, and while I could throw and catch decently well, and spent most of my years growing up playing on a recreational team, there was no future for me as a player. Dad pushed me into media relations, pointing out how much I loved planning events, from birthday parties to team wrap-up parties, not to mention my ability to network and make friends everywhere I went. Combined with how passionate I was about the team, a career in sports media just made sense.

It still hurts that he didn't live long enough to see where I am today. On track to being the next director of media relations. And not because I'm pseudo-related to the owner, but because I've spent a decade busting my ass, working overtime to prove myself worthy of the role.

I don't ever want to be seen as Willow Lawson, niece of the owner. I want to be seen as Willow Lawson, head of media relations. I am my own person, and my accomplishments are because of my hard work. Not because of who I'm related to.

All that stands between me and the position is Lydia's retirement. And her final stamp of approval on me as her replacement. Which is why I know I can handle her overbearing demands, and taking credit for work that I do, for a little while longer.

This morning the skies are a perfect bright blue. Not a cloud in sight. There's a light breeze, and the beach is surprisingly devoid of people. I find a recliner near the water's edge and settle in, my e-reader fully charged, a large bottle of ice water by my side, and my wide brim hat firmly on my head. After slathering a coat of sunscreen everywhere I can reach, I'm mentally debating how the hell I'll reach my back when a deep voice has me looking up. *Way* up.

"If you need some help, I'm happy to oblige."

"You're everywhere, it seems," I reply, the corners of my mouth tipping up. Ronan crouches down, and even though I can't see his eyes behind the reflective sunglasses he's wearing, I'd guess there are little crinkles at the edges, given his grin.

"Or maybe I'm just naturally drawn to where you are."

"Some women would call that stalker tendencies," I sass back. He throws his head back and laughs, and even I giggle at how ridiculous that sounds. If there's any man out there whose intentions seem to be nothing but good, it's this one. Every time we've run into each other, he has been nothing but respectful and kind. To me and everyone else.

"I'll take you up on your offer." I hand him the bottle and turn around so my back is facing him. A beat goes by, then large hands land on my bare skin, making me jump a little.

"Sorry," he murmurs as he starts to smooth his hands over my back.

"It's fine," I whisper back.

"I have to lift your bathing suit straps to get underneath. Is that okay?"

Is that okay? Seriously? Is he waiting for my consent before rubbing sunscreen under the straps of my bathing suit? Belatedly, I realize he really is waiting for my answer, so I nod sharply.

Once again, he's nothing but respectful as he moves quickly. On my lower back, he stills again, but this time stays silent.

"It's fine, Ronan. I appreciate your help." Even though I could technically do that part myself, the touch of his hands that close to my ass feels way too fucking good. I assume he's done, but then his hands come back up to my shoulders.

"Let me just double-check it's rubbed in."

Thumbs start to knead the muscles in my shoulders, and I can't help the moan that escapes me.

"Woman, you're hard as a rock," he chastises gently, and I can't resist a tease.

"Isn't that meant to be my line?" His grip tightens, but just briefly before he lifts his hands off me completely. He stands up just as I turn back around and there's an unmistakable bulge under his shorts. "Sorry, that was inappropriate."

"Nah, you're fine," he says, a little too casually if you ask me. Before I can think of a response, he crouches back down and his hand comes up to grip my chin. "I just didn't want to make it obvious how close to the truth you really are."

Unbidden, my thighs squeeze together as I exhale.

"I gotta go. It's wedding day, and they're probably wondering why I'm not back from my run yet." His voice is gruff, and all I can do is nod. "Don't stay out here too long; I won't be around to reapply."

A strangled laugh sneaks out of me, and his lips quirk to the side in return. Then he straightens up and walks away toward the hotel. And because I apparently have no shame, my eyes remain glued to his perfect ass the entire way until he's out of sight.

I follow Ronan's advice and don't stay at the beach overly long. Knowing he's around today, but busy with his friends, I opt to go to my room for a shower and a change of clothes, then head into Waikiki Beach for some shopping.

But as I stand under the spray of my shower, my hands drift over my skin, teasing my nipples before drifting lower. There's no avoiding the image that is forefront in my mind as I gently glide between the folds of my pussy. What other tall, dark, and very handsome man would I be picturing, if not the one who has been slowly weakening my resolve for days.

I don't date baseball players.

But surely, masturbating to a fantasy of one isn't so bad?

My finger dips inside as I gasp, the heat of the water pelting down on me, one hand squeezing and plucking at my nipple as the other teases between my legs. I have to lean back against the cool tile of the shower wall to steady myself.

As the heat inside of me builds, I can feel that my fingers won't be enough this time. Blinking water out of my now open eyes, I slide the glass door of the shower open and grab the silicone toy that's sitting on the counter. Of course, it's the same toy that went off in the security line. The same toy Ronan knows I have with me.

Bringing it between my legs, I turn it on and let out a low moan as soon as it hits my already sensitive clit. "Fuck, yes," I breathe, leaning back against the tile once more. The contrast of the warm water and the cool tile has all my senses buzzing.

With no one here to witness me giving into temptation, I let my mind fully imagine Ronan down on his knees, holding the toy to my pussy while driving his thick fingers into me. I picture his lips closing around my nipple, biting and sucking.

And when my orgasm overwhelms me, turning my legs to Jell-O, I can't help but cry out his name, letting it echo around me as proof that the man is dangerously close to making me throw my number one rule out the window.

When I return to the hotel after a very successful shopping trip, I head straight to my room to deposit my bags, then return to the lobby, intent on finding a seat at the beachside bar for a cocktail.

But the bar is closed, displaying a sign that reads "private event." As I move to walk away, mentally shifting plans to head into the restaurant and see if they have a seat with a view, I hear my name being called.

I spin slowly on my sandal-covered feet and try not to let my mouth fall open. I've seen Ronan in gym clothes, hiking clothes, casual clothes — hell, I've even seen him in nothing but his boxer briefs. But nothing, nothing at all could have prepared me for Ronan in khaki slacks and a white dress shirt. It's open at the collar, his sleeves rolled up, and his hair is perfectly styled.

He's devastatingly handsome at the best of times, and right now, that much more so. But even if he is the most attractive man I've ever met, and he's kind, and respectful, and the absolute opposite of the douchebags I've dated recently, he's still a baseball player.

But he plays on the opposite side of the country.

But he's a player.

But he has nothing to do with your team.

But he's a player.

But you're both here, away from real life, away from baseball.

But he's still a player.

I don't realize how caught up I am in my internal debate until Ronan's hand lands on my arm, and I register the look of concern on his face.

"Everything okay?"

"Yes, sorry." I nod, then shake my head, then nod again with a small laugh. "Wow. Guess I had too much sun today."

"Shit, do you need to sit down? Let me get you some water." Before I can protest, he's guiding me straight past the barrier across the bar entrance, over to a chair near the edge of the group of people who are obviously celebrating the happy couple.

"Ronan, I'm fine." I find my voice and try to remove his hand from my elbow. "Seriously, I was just distracted. Go back to your friends, to the wedding."

He studies me carefully, and it's sweet, really. How worried he is about me. Except I don't want him to be sweet. I want him to do something awful, something terrible to make me not be so attracted to him.

"Honestly? You're kind of giving me the perfect excuse to get away from some dude-bros that don't understand personal boundaries."

His statement is delivered so dryly, a laugh bursts free from me. Clapping my hand over my mouth, I slowly shake my head back and forth.

"Seriously?" I ask when my mirth is under control.

He nods, his face an expression of complete solemnity. "Yeah. The number of times they've almost outright asked for game tickets or insider info on trades. It's disgusting."

Shit, that *is* gross. "I'm sorry."

His shoulders lift and fall under the slim-fitting white shirt. "Comes with the job, but I'd hoped to escape all that for a bit when I came here. At least my buddy who got married and our other friend know better. They're as pissed as I am at those idiots."

He sits down in the chair beside me, and for a quiet moment, we just watch the other wedding guests enjoy themselves from a distance. Then, shifting in his seat to face me, Ronan holds out his hand. "Dance with me."

"What?" I ask in surprise. He swiftly stands up and moves in front of me.

"Dance. With me, over there." He nods his head toward the small dance floor. "Please?"

I don't even bother trying to hold back my smile this time. Who am I to refuse such a lovely invitation? Standing up, I smooth my hands over my skirt before taking his outstretched hand. "I'd love to."

His answering smile is dazzling as he leads me to the edge of the dance floor before spinning me under his arm, then pulling me into his hold. He keeps a reasonable amount of space between us, ever the gentleman. As we sway back and forth, the sound of the musicians, the ocean waves, the murmur of the people around us, all of it fades away. His captivating blue eyes never leave mine, and the romance of the moment sweeps me up in its grasp.

As much as he's remained respectful and hasn't pushed anything on me, I know without a shadow of a doubt that Ronan's interested in me. He wants me. For what? I don't know.

But finally, right here in this moment, I'm ready to admit to myself.

I want him, too.

Chapter Six

Ronan

Early morning runs are just better when they're on a sandy beach at sunrise. And today, I pushed myself even harder — ten kilometers instead of my usual seven to warm up before a session in the gym with some weights. All to try and outrun the memory of finally having Willow in my arms last night.

Fucking hell, did I ever want to kiss her. But she's like a stray kitten; earning her trust is a long game. And kissing her last night would have destroyed any trust I've already built. Of course, the fact that I only have three days left here in Hawaii isn't lost on me. If anything is going to happen between Willow and me, the clock is ticking.

I'm covered in sweat, my legs aching, but my mind is finally calm when I reach the open-air lobby of the hotel. As soon as I step inside, my ears pick up a familiar voice, only this time, it sounds frustrated. My gym session is instantly forgotten as I zero in on Willow.

"You're telling me there's nothing available? It's not my fault the shower is broken and my bathroom is currently flooded and unusable."

I hurry over to Willow's side at the front desk. "Hey, stranger," I say, touching her arm lightly. Her head whips around in surprise, but she doesn't respond to me, turning back to the concierge who is typing frantically on a keyboard. Her lack of greeting or acknowledgment stings a little, but obviously something's going on that's taken all of her attention.

"I'm truly sorry, Ms. Lawson, but we are fully booked for the next several weeks. I can reach out to a neighboring hotel to see if anyone has room for you. We will, of course, refund you for the remainder of your stay."

"I don't want another hotel. I want to stay here." Willow sounds more than a little disappointed, and I don't blame her. This place is spectacular, and well, I'm here. Not that I'm fooling myself into believing my presence is a factor in her wanting to stay, but it's nice to imagine.

"Willow, you can stay with me." I say quickly before I have a chance to think twice about it.

She pivots slowly to face me. "Excuse me?"

I nod, stuffing my hands in my pockets. "Seriously. I splurged and booked a suite, but it's way too much for just one person. There's plenty of room." I try not to pressure her, but I really want her to say yes. To let me help fix this. "Problem solved, if you're okay with it?" I glance back up at the staff member behind the desk. "And I'm sure the hotel would be willing to compensate you for the inconvenience with a complimentary spa service or something."

The woman assisting Willow nods emphatically. "Yes, of course, Ms. Lawson. I'm terribly sorry we can't do more to resolve this unfortunate situation, but there's just no room at all that we can move you to. If you're willing to share with your friend here —" she gestures to me "— then we are happy to offer you a voucher for a full day of luxurious treatments at our Moana Lani spa."

I see her shoulders lift and fall as Willow takes a deep breath. Her gaze turns up, searching my face for something. "Are you sure about this?"

I nod. "One hundred percent."

"Okay. Thank you." She turns to the concierge. "I'll take that spa voucher, and my friend deserves some compensation for having to share his suite with me as well, don't you think?"

I watch in amusement as the concierge almost fall over themselves trying to offer me restaurant vouchers, free rounds of golf, you name it. I shake my head at all of it. "No, thank you, but no."

The gentleman helping me taps a few keys on his keyboard. "We truly appreciate your understanding with all of this." He hands over a second key card, which I immediately pass to Willow. "And Ms. Lawson, someone will be up to your room to help move your belongings very soon."

Less than an hour later, I've had just enough time to shower, pull on some clean clothes, and tidy up a bit. A knock on my door reveals Willow and a valet with a luggage cart carrying her bags.

"Hi," she says softly. "Thanks again for doing this." She moves to the couch and drops her small bag down. "This is me?"

"Fuck no, you take the bedroom and I'll take the couch," I say emphatically.

"Ronan, you can't give me your bed. I'll be fine on the couch."

I fold my arms across my chest and stare at her. I've got a toddler; patience is my superpower. She won't win this one. "Housekeeping just changed the sheets while I was out for my run. Seems almost as if fate knew you would need to move in here, hmm?" I arch my brow, fighting back a smirk at her adorable huff of annoyance.

"You and that freaking F-word."

I pick up her bag and carry it into the bedroom, not even bothering to see if she follows. Raising my voice slightly, I just keep on as if it's a done deal. "I'll need to come in to grab clothes each day, but other than that, you've got your privacy. Well, that and the bathroom."

"What about the bathroom?" she asks, her voice revealing she's joined me in the bedroom. I glance over my shoulder and grin.

"There's only one. Hope you don't take too long to get ready in the morning."

Her eye roll is impressive, but she's smiling. "You're ridiculous, you know that?"

I just shrug, knowing I've won this round. Shit, it's fun bantering with her. She's got sass and doesn't give in easily.

"Well, damn, this is a step up from the city view in my old room," Willow marvels as she walks over to the large glass doors leading out to the private balcony overlooking the white sand beach. I amble over to stand beside her.

"Yeah, I'm a sucker for a good view."

She turns her face up to me. Only, instead of looking at the beach, I'm staring straight at her.

"You're quite the charmer, Ronan Sinclair."

"When necessary."

She tilts her head to the side, shifting closer to me so our arms are almost touching. "And is it necessary with me?"

"Necessary? Hopefully not. Enjoyable? Absolutely, yes."

"It's not necessary. Consider me charmed." She winks and it's all I can do not to bend down and kiss her right then and there.

"Have dinner with me tonight." I hadn't planned on asking again. Not yet, at least, but between the dance last night and the flirting right now, I can't help myself. Instead of shaking her head in an immediate refusal, Willow's face relaxes into a beautiful smile.

"I'd love to."

My answering grin is massive, I realize, but *fucking finally*. "I'll make a reservation for seven. Do you have plans for today?"

She nods. "Very important ones."

"Well, don't let me keep you from them." I stifle my disappointment. But it's probably for the best. Eddie said everyone is meeting up for lunch before most of the guests head home today. I leave Willow in the bedroom and head out into the main living area to check my phone and see if he's sent any more details. Not that I expect the man to be awake, even if it's now close to 10 am. He did just get married, after all.

Sure enough, there's nothing on my phone except a text from my mom with a photo attached. I open it up, and my heart melts. There's my girl, riding her bike with Gran. There's nothing that kid likes more than the feeling of going fast. Whether she's running, or riding her bike, she loves speed. It's why I call her Rocket.

"Do I want to know what you're looking at that has you smiling like that?"

I turn at the sound of Willow's voice, and suddenly I'm smiling for a *very* different reason. The white bikini she's wearing leaves little to the imagination, even with the sheer cover-up she's got on. "Damn, woman. Need me to do your sunscreen again?" I waggle my eyebrows so she knows I'm not trying to be a creep, and she laughs.

"Thanks for the offer. I don't plan on being in the sun; there's a beach umbrella with my name on it waiting poolside." She lifts her bag and pats the side of it. "I'm going to read and relax."

"That's your very important plan?" I tease.

"Absolutely, it is." She nods.

My phone chimes with an incoming message, this time from the groom. Lifting it to wave at her, I say, "Well, enjoy. I've got lunch with the newlyweds, and then a round of golf with my other buddy. I'll see you later for dinner?"

Maybe my mind is playing tricks on me again, but I swear I see disappointment cross her face. But she schools her expression quickly enough to make me wonder if that's just my hopefulness seeing things.

"See you later," she replies softly, looking at me for another second before whirling away in a cloud of floral and citrus. I watch her go, the filmy fabric of her cover-up hiding none of her alluring curves.

Fucking hell, do I ever want that woman. And tonight, maybe, I'll finally get my chance.

Chapter Seven

Willow

By the time I get out of the shower after a lovely afternoon poolside, I've had plenty of time to question my sanity.

Flirting with a baseball player is bad enough.

Sharing his fucking hotel suite?

Definitely skirting the lines of my *don't date a player* rule.

Then again, I'm coming around to the idea of suspending that rule, just this once...with just this man. After all, it's not exactly breaking it if we don't date, just fuck, is it? I came here wanting a holiday hottie, and maybe Ronan is just the man for the job. Some hot vacation sex, then we go our separate ways to opposite ends of the country.

Opening the door of the bathroom, wrapped only in a towel with my hair dripping down my back, I come to an abrupt halt at the sight of Ronan standing at the dresser, obviously in the middle of getting his clothes.

"Sorry," I blurt out, my cheeks turning pink. His eyes do a slow perusal of my body, but not in a lecherous way; more one of pure appreciation.

"Good shower?" he asks in a low, suggestive rumble.

"Yes," I manage to rasp out before straightening my spine and slipping past him. I feel his gaze follow me, and it's as if I'm wearing nothing at all. I go straight to my open suitcase that I had lifted onto the bed and pull out a purple bra and panty set, tucking them in close to my body as we stand there eyeing each other. My pulse starts to speed up, the heat from my shower, building.

His gaze on me is hungry. Predatory, even, and I shiver. There's an obvious bulge beneath his shorts, but he makes no move toward me, his restraint both admirable and annoying.

"Are you done in the bathroom?" he asks, his voice gravelly.

I nod, holding in my breath until the door to the bathroom closes behind him, and only then do I sag onto the edge of my bed. *Damn, that was hot.*

Once we're both dressed, we make our way to the hotel's main restaurant, armed with the voucher they insisted on giving Ronan as compensation for having to share his suite with me. To my surprise, he doesn't mention my little underwear stunt even once.

"Does it count as you taking me to dinner if the hotel's footing the bill?" I tease as we enter the open-air space. The atmosphere is heavy with a luscious tropical aroma, the firelight from torches lining the walkway adding to the romance. "God, how is everything just so beautiful here?" I blurt out, coming to a stop. The ocean is directly in front of us, and it's so picturesque, I just want to stare at it forever.

Ronan's hand finds my lower back, a light touch, but one I feel down to my toes. "It's stunning. And so are you if I haven't made that clear."

I angle my head to look up at him, once again marveling at how it feels to be with a man taller than me, even in the strappy heeled sandals I'm wearing. "Charmer."

He grins. "Honest."

With a slight shake of my head, I let him guide me over to a table overlooking the ocean, right on the edge of the terrace. He pulls my chair out, something a man has never done for me before, and I'll be damned if it doesn't make me feel good.

A server comes over, holding a tray with two tropical drinks. "Our signature cocktail, compliments of the hotel. We call it 'mango fire' for the slight spice note you'll get at the end. It's a combination of mango and pineapple juice with dark, spiced rum, a splash of grenadine for colour, and our secret sugar and spice mix on the rim." They set the drinks down along with two menus. "Our special tonight is a coconut crusted mahi-mahi with a citrus infused vinaigrette, served alongside rice pilaf and roasted vegetables."

I give them a smile, murmuring my thanks, and Ronan does the same. After the server leaves, he raises his glass, tipping his head toward me. "To beautiful views."

We clink our glasses together and I take a sip. "Mmm," I moan as the cold, fruity, and slightly spiced drink hits my tongue. "That's incredible." Glancing down, I smirk and fish out the neon red cherry by the stem. "These are my favourite."

Ronan's chuckle is relaxed and warm. "I don't think I've ever met someone who actually likes maraschino cherries."

I pop it in my mouth, stem and all, and raise my eyebrows. A few seconds later, I open my mouth, and hold out my tongue.

"Holy shit, did you just tie that with your tongue?" He laughs as I lift the knotted stem off my tongue and nod.

"It's a fun party trick." I set it down and take another sip of the cocktail. Ronan shakes his head, then carefully fishes his own cherry out, holding it toward me.

"Want another?"

I briefly debate taking it from him the normal way, but no. *Let's have some fun.* Lifting slightly out of my seat, I lean over the table and open my mouth slightly. There's no mistaking the flash of heat in his eyes as he places the cherry on my tongue. I sit back down and make quick work of tying another knot before popping it out with a smirk.

"That's a talented mouth you've got there," he says, innuendo heavy in every word.

Lifting my eyebrows and shoulders in unison I give him an impish smile. "I'm a woman of many talents."

Ronan settles back in his chair after the server has taken our dinner order and picks up his drink. With the warm glow of the setting sun behind him, he truly does look like a god. His light-coloured shirt molds to his body, showing off his strong arms. The top two buttons are undone, letting me see the light smattering of hair on his chest. His face is relaxed, but those eyes. Those eyes are full of dirty promises, just waiting for me to say yes to him. To what is feeling more and more like a foregone conclusion.

Neither one of us will be on the couch tonight.

"What do you have planned for the rest of your time here?" he asks.

"Absolutely nothing."

He chokes out a small laugh in the middle of taking a drink and swallows before answering. "Nothing at all?"

I shake my head. "Nothing. For once, I have zero plans, zero commitments, zero responsibilities. I wanted a week of following every whim and only doing what I want, when I want."

"Sounds amazing." Our eyes are locked on each other, saying more than the words we've spoken can do. "Think you'll want some company for following your whims?"

I can feel a smile creeping across my face and don't bother trying to hide it. "I think I might, if the company is good enough."

God, his laugh does things to me. "It'll be better than *good enough*."

After that promise, I barely remember dinner. The food was delicious, I'm sure, but all I can think of is the inferno building inside of me. The moisture dampening my panties with every deep chuckle, every smirk, every peek of the dimple in his cheeks. This man is potent. Devastatingly alluring. I never thought I would let myself get intimate with a baseball player, but the truth is, there's no way I can resist Ronan Sinclair any longer.

When we leave the restaurant, it's unspoken but undeniable that we're going back to the room. It takes a ridiculous amount of self-control to keep my hands to myself the entire ride in the elevator. When his hand finds my lower back again as we exit the elevator and walk down the hall, I want to lean into him, feel more of his warmth. All of it.

We arrive back at the room, and instead of reaching around me to open the door, he slides his hand down to take mine, turning me around to face him. "I want to make this very clear because I feel like we've been dancing around each other all week. But I'm done dancing, Willow. If we go in that room together, I'm going to fuck you. I'm going to devour you and make you see fucking stars. If that's not what you want, if you haven't been growing more wet and more desperate for me with every goddamn minute, I'll stay in my buddy's room tonight and you can have this one, no questions asked."

It's almost laughable that he could possibly think I'm feeling anything other than pure pulsating need by now. At the same time, his restraint, his chivalry, is kind of incredible. But it's not what I want. I want him unrestrained. I want to be devoured. *I want to see stars.*

Plucking the key card out of his hand, I scan it and push open the door, stepping inside. He holds it open, still not crossing the threshold. Is he going to make me say it?

Nah. I can do better. Reaching to my side, I unzip my dress, pull the thin straps off my shoulders, and let it fall to the floor. Stepping out of it, I hook my fingers in the edge of my panties and pause. "Do I keep going, or..."

With what can only be described as a growl, Ronan finally steps inside, slamming the door and locking it behind him.

"You're mine, Cherry. Tonight, you're mine."

Chapter Eight

Ronan

The sound of the door closing behind me is like the gunshot at the start of a race. In two strides, I'm in front of her, and in one second, I'm kissing her upturned lips. I make good on my promise to devour her, plundering her mouth, drinking down her needy whimpers as my hands tangle in her hair. Hands roam my back, gripping my shirt, then releasing it to move to my shoulders, then back down, as if she can't stop herself from trying to touch every inch of me.

I can relate. There's nothing I want more than to spend the next several hours exploring all of her.

Starting right fucking now.

Sweeping Willow up into my arms, I carry her through the suite until I reach the bedroom. Her tits are pressed against me, her long sun-kissed legs wrapped around my waist. I don't want to set her down but it's kind of a fucking necessity for me to get my clothes off. Slowly, I lower her to stand, our lips never breaking apart in kiss after hungry kiss.

I fumble with my buttons but manage to get the damn shirt open and tear it off as her hands make quick work of undoing my shorts. They get shoved down along with my boxers and my cock springs free, already hard. Hell, it's been hard all goddamn evening.

"Ronan," she moans as I suck a mark into the base of her neck. Fucking right, I'm claiming her. I've never felt semi-feral over a woman like I do over this one. We only met a few days ago, but it's as if my body knows exactly what to do to drive her wild. I graze my teeth and tongue over her soft, warm skin, dropping down to her perfect tits that were just pressed against me. Sucking one into my mouth, I pull, then release with a pop as she tugs on my hair. Moving to the other side, I repeat the action before pushing them together in my hands.

"Fucking hell, I could spend forever here," I mutter in between kisses to the soft mounds.

"I hope you don't," comes her reply. I glance up to see that one fucking eyebrow raised again. Goddamn. *Why is that so sexy?* Is it the way she so unabashedly says what she feels, asks for what she wants, and takes no shit? How the fuck do I get all that from one eyebrow? I don't know.

"There's somewhere else I'd rather you focus your attention." She grins, then pushes away from me, hooking her fingers in her panties and sliding them down to kick them off before sitting on the bed. Those long legs spread wide, and there's no holding back my groan at the sight of her glistening pussy, covered in a neatly trimmed strip of hair.

"Look at how fucking wet you are for me. What a good fucking girl," I growl. Dropping to my knees, I kiss my way up the inside of one of her legs. My dick is aching, but there's not a chance I'm doing a goddamn thing about it until I've tasted her on my tongue.

Willow lifts her legs and drapes them over my shoulders before tangling her hands in my hair again. "Devour me, Ronan."

Fucking right. I dive in, and the second her essence hits my tongue, I groan. Swear to fucking God, I've never tasted anything so sweet. My tongue swirls around, lapping her up.

Every drop is like nectar, and I'm addicted. I suck on her clit, drawing out a shriek. Her body bows off the bed when I sweep my tongue up and down her slit, then tug her clit in between my teeth again, this time letting them lightly graze the sensitized nub.

Her breathless sighs guide me just as much as her fingers tightening and releasing their grip on my hair. I add my fingers to the mix, dipping in and curling over to find her G-spot, surprising even myself with how I apparently zero in on it, judging by her reaction.

"Oh fuck. Oh fuck. Oh *fuck!*" she screams as her legs shake, squeezing my head like a vice. I taste her explode on my tongue as my fingers feel the clench and release of her inner muscles. Looking up at her face, I know for a fact I'll never forget how beautiful she is in the throes of her orgasm. The pink flush on her cheeks, her slightly parted lips, the pulse fluttering visibly in her neck.

She's a goddess.

Her legs relax, and as soon as I can move, I surge upward. Holding myself over her, I pause to lift one hand to wipe off my mouth, but Willow levers her upper body to capture my lips before I have a chance. Her desperation is driving me insane in the best possible way.

"I knew you would be good, but did you have to ruin me for any other man?" she purrs as she lowers herself back down. I lean my head in to kiss her again.

"Yeah, sorry."

"No, you're not." She laughs, shaking her head. I lower down onto one elbow, keeping most of my weight off her. But my cock is nestled between us and when she starts to shift under me, I groan.

"If you do that, things are gonna move a lot faster than I wanted them to."

"I'm good with fast. Really, really good. Fast is fun."

She pushes at my chest, and I roll over onto my back, taking her with me until she's straddling my hips. Her hand wraps around my dick, and the friction from her jacking me off has my spine stiffening, my head thrown back onto the pillow. *"Fuck."*

"Yes, please," she says saucily.

"Condoms are in the bathroom." I look her in the eye. "I'm clean, the team tests us regularly. But I've got one kid and don't want another right now."

She hops off and saunters into my bathroom, tossing her hair over her shoulder. "Trust me, a kid is not in my future plans right now, either."

Coming back with the strip of condoms I almost didn't put in my wash bag while packing, she tosses them on the bed beside us before climbing right back on top of me. "Now. Where were we?"

I lace my hands behind my head and just grin. "Wherever you want us to be."

Taking one of the condoms, she tears it open with her teeth. It's such a guy move, I chuckle. "You're gonna be a lot of fun, aren't you?"

She doesn't answer right away, instead rolling the condom down my dick. Lining up her hips, she slowly starts to lower. Then, only then, does she reply. "More than you can handle."

I move to grip her ass, squeezing my fingers, then lifting one hand off and slapping the rounded flesh lightly. "You have no idea what I can handle. Ride me, Cherry. Use me like you'd use that fucking vibrator I know is in your bag."

Her smile is wicked. Sinful, lust-filled, and wicked. As her hips start to rock back and forth, she lowers herself down so that her breasts brush against my chest and her hair falls in a curtain around our faces. Her hips continue to bounce up and down my length. "Spank me again, Ronan. I like it."

My hand rubs a circle over her ass, feeling the muscles clench as she lifts herself up slightly, then slides back down. "Only good girls get what they ask for, and if you make me come before you do, then you'll be a very bad girl."

Willow stills. Our eyes are locked on each other. Heavy breathing is the only sound in the sexiest standoff I've ever imagined. Slowly, I lift my hand off her skin. She lifts her hips. I tilt my head and meet her smirk with one of my own.

"Goddamn it, woman," I grind out as I smack her ass, following through with a push up of my hips that forces her to clench around my cock.

"Fuck, yes, Ronan. Again," she moans, taunting me by rising up again. I shake my head, instead gripping her ass with my large hands and taking over from below, pistoning my hips up into her over and over.

My plan threatens to backfire as I feel my orgasm coming over me, but Willow's pussy is starting to flutter around me, and I know she's close as well. Reaching down between us, I manage to pinch her clit, making her scream my name.

"Ronan!"

"That's right, Cherry. You're mine. I told you. That means I decide when you come, and I say you come right fucking now." The last word comes out as a roar as she squeezes my dick in a vice, that orgasm I've been holding off hurtling through me at max force.

Her cries of pleasure mix with mine as I feel her own release ripple through her, the vibrations making me groan. She collapses down onto my chest, the two of us panting, hearts racing, skin sticky. Somehow, her arms wriggle underneath me so she's full-on hugging me.

Hugging me.

I haven't had a grown woman, other than my mother, hug me in a long fucking time. It should feel weird, but as my arms wrap around her, holding her to me, it doesn't feel weird at all.

"We are *so* doing that again."

I start to shake with laughter at her muffled words. She lifts her head off my chest and quirks her lips at me.

"You disagree?"

"Oh, hell no." Thanking all of my trainers and coaches for the muscles that make it possible, I flip us over so she's spread out underneath me. "I most definitely agree. Again, and again, and again." I kiss her, then pull out slowly and tie off the condom as I stand up. "You're really good at riding my cock; how good will you be at riding my face?"

Willow props herself on her elbows, and she's just so fucking beautiful, sprawled against the messed-up sheets in this hotel room on the other side of the world from my normal life, it makes me feel like I'm in a dream.

A really hot dream.

"You should know I had a horse when I was younger. I'm really good at riding *anything*."

I drop the condom in the waste basket and lunge back over her on the bed, sweeping her up in my arms as I roll onto my back. "How about you find the toy that had every man in the security line imagining you using it and ride away, cowgirl."

Chapter Nine

Willow

Rolling over, a smile already on my face despite the lack of sleep last night, I expect to find Ronan's warm and willing body. Instead, the sheets and pillow are cold. And empty. Gathering the sheet to my chest, I sit up, pushing my hair back as I blink my sleepy eyes open.

Somehow, instinctively, I know he's gone. My brain catches up and I take in the evidence to support my intuition. His shirt that was draped over the chair last night isn't there. An open drawer in the dresser looks empty. His watch from his bedside table is gone.

Leaning over the side of the bed, I grab my panties from the floor and slide them on before I get up and grab a tank top from my suitcase that I pull over my head. Twisting my hair into a messy bun, I walk out into the living area of the suite.

He's definitely gone.

His shoes and sandals are missing, and there's a folded piece of paper staring at me from the coffee table, my name written across it in bold print.

A tsunami-sized wave of mixed emotions crashes over me. At the forefront is disappointment and hurt, but fast on its heels comes anger — at myself for feeling hurt, for feeling anything at all for a man who is, for all intents and purposes, off-limits. Then worry creeps in. What could have possibly made him disappear in the early hours of the morning after our sex marathon last night?

Snatching up the note, I open it and begin to read.

Willow,

I'm sorry to leave like this. I would have woken you up but you looked so peaceful. And after last night, I figured one of us should get some rest. The last few days have been amazing, you made this trip a hell of a lot more enjoyable than it would have been without you. My daughter fell at the playground this morning when my mom was dropping her off for preschool. Apparently, she might have broken her wrist, so I'm headed to the airport to grab the first flight home. I want you to know, last night was amazing. I know it was probably not that easy for you to let me in, but I hope you don't regret it.

Maybe I'll see you on the field sometime.

Ronan

P.S. I'll feel like the biggest dumbass if I don't leave you my number, but please know there's zero expectations. I just figured I'd put it out there and leave it up to our friend fate.

I read it again, and then a third time, still trying to settle the tumultuous emotions swirling around inside of me. I fucking hate that I'm so mixed up over him leaving. I mean, we might not have come out and said it last night, but in my mind, this was a onetime thing. Well, maybe two, since I thought we still had a few days together.

A vacation fling, I could handle. I could rationalize it in my brain, so far departed from real life. He lives and plays on the other side of the country from me; the chances of us crossing paths for more than a few seconds after a game are slim to none.

But if that's all it was ever going to be, then why am I disappointed he had to go early? He made the right call, putting his daughter first. If anyone can appreciate that, it's me. In fact, him leaving to be with her just makes this all the more confusing. Because it confirms what I was already learning.

Ronan Sinclair is one of the good ones. Handsome, sexy, kind, respectful, and fucking amazing in bed.

That must be why I'm all torn up inside. I'm disappointed I'll be missing out on a few more days of orgasms. Nothing more.

But as I go through the motions of brushing my teeth and hair, my memory keeps betraying me. Instead of remembering the intense pleasure of Ronan making me come, it's the sweeter moments that keep popping into my head. The look of reverence in his eyes when he stroked back my hair as I rode him, my vibrator pressed to my clit. The gentleness with which he cupped my face and kissed me. And even earlier, before last night. The way he came to my rescue with the hotel room situation, even if that did turn out to be mutually beneficial.

There's no doubt about it. Ronan made the last few days exciting, fun, and totally unexpected.

So how am I meant to go through the rest of my vacation without him?

The answer to that question is this: by doing whatever I can think of to keep myself extremely busy. So, caving into my guilt, I open the computer I now regret bringing.

Yes, after only four days spent trying to ignore work, I give in, and out of a desperate need to keep my mind occupied, I open my inbox.

But as I sit here at a coffee shop just off the beach in Waikiki, I can't make myself focus on the mountain of messages that came in, despite having my out-of-office message turned on.

And as I keep looking around, my gaze consistently landing on cute, adorable, sickeningly happy couples strolling in the sunshine arm in arm, I just keep getting more and more angry. Both at myself and at the damn man consuming my thoughts.

Slamming my computer shut with a huff, I pack away my things, and stand up from the table. There's nothing pressing for me to do at work, nothing that would distract me from the swirling questions in my mind that won't go away, no matter how hard I've tried ever since waking up and finding Ronan gone.

Will it get back to my uncle that I hooked up with a player?

Is this going to ruin everything I've worked for?

Deep down, I want to believe the answer to both of those questions is no. I want to believe that Ronan truly is a good man and won't be the kind of guy to blab about what we did last night. After all, we were two consenting adults. Nothing bad happened, nothing that we didn't both want.

All the same, the rest of my vacation is nowhere near as relaxing and enjoyable as the first half. And when I sit down in my seat on the airplane that will carry me across the ocean, back to Vancouver and back to reality, I stare out the window at the clear blue skies of Hawaii and force myself to do what I must.

Leave Ronan, and his orgasms, where they belong. Here, in my memories, and far, far away from my real life.

Chapter Ten

January

Willow

"Sources: Ronan Sinclair traded to Vancouver Tridents, details still pending."

My heart stops beating for several seconds as I stare at my newsfeed.

This isn't happening. How is this happening?

For the last several months, I've watched the trade headlines. I've kept my eyes and ears open for anything about my team. And at no point whatsoever did I hear even the faintest whiff of a rumour that we were looking for a starting first baseman.

Let alone the one I had sex with countless times over one night in Hawaii last fall.

Thankfully, my office door is closed, so no one bears witness to my freak-out as I drop my head into my hands and start to mutter. "No, no, no, no, no." My pulse is racing, and I feel sweaty. Is this a panic attack? I think it might be.

Maybe it's not true. I push away from my desk and stand up on shaky legs. Taking several deep breaths, I run my hands down the front of my cream-coloured sweater. I can't let Lydia see me like this, and she's the person to confirm whether or not my nightmare is true.

When I pull open my desk drawer to get out the small mirror I keep there, of course my gaze lands on a folded piece of paper that I tucked way in the back after I returned from Hawaii. It might not have been the smartest move, bringing a note with Ronan's phone number on it in to work, but I told myself it was to serve as a reminder to never give into temptation like that again. Because it never ends well.

Little did I know...

Ignoring the note, I grab the mirror and check to make sure I don't look as freaked-out as I feel. Exhaling once more, I put away the mirror, close the drawer, and stand up, brushing invisible lint off my pants.

I can do this. Everything's fine. Nobody is going to know I slept with our new player... Or that it was the best sex of my freaking life. No big deal. No. Big. Deal.

I let out a silent scream, then take a few calming breaths before going to get the confirmation I really don't want to hear.

Opening my office door, I walk the short distance down the hall to Lydia's office, knock twice, and wait for her response.

"Come in." Her nasally voice reaches me, and I open her door. "Oh good, it's you," she says, her gaze returning to her computer screen. Guaranteed she's playing solitaire on there, not working. I'm no idiot, I know Lydia's checked out and perfectly content to let me do her job.

"Hi, Lydia." I clear my throat. "I, um, just saw a news headline I wanted to check with you, something about a player from

Toronto being traded here?" My voice squeaks a little, but Lydia doesn't seem to notice.

"Hmm? Oh, yeah. That one. I saw the leak."

I nod slowly, willing my heart to stop pounding out of my chest. "Right. So is it true?"

"It's just sources. Nothing's finalized."

I blink slowly at that non-answer. "But are the sources telling the truth?"

Finally, Lydia glances up. "Well, yeah. Of course, they are. That's why I wanted to see you, because I need you to get everything set up for when the player arrives next week to sign contracts. We'll need the usual. Local media, socials, all of it. You can handle that, right?"

Can I handle the job? Yes. Can I handle the fact that Ronan Sinclair is going to be here in a week?

Not so sure about that.

"Of course. That will be fine." I force the words out, even though, no, everything will not be fine. She waves her hand at me and I know I've been dismissed.

Good thing, because if I don't get somewhere private before I lose it, this could get messy. Thankfully, I make it back to my office undisturbed. Closing the door behind me, I lean against the wood and sink down to the ground.

"Holy shit," I whisper.

For all that Ronan and I joked about fate, this feels more like karma coming to bite me in the ass. Fine, we didn't date. But we did do a hell of a lot of other things that night. I thought I could justify it, knowing he would be on the other side of the country, far away from me when it was over.

And now? Now he's going to be much, much closer.

I manage to make it through the rest of my day, fortunately without needing to interact with too many people. I might have one hell of a poker face normally, but today, that skill has abandoned me. Possibly due to the number of times I clicked over to my news feed to see that damn leak and then over to the Wolverines roster to stare at his photo.

I drive home that evening on autopilot. And the second I enter my apartment, I start stripping out of my clothes, leaving them in a messy trail that leads to my bedroom, where I flop down face-first onto my bed in nothing but my underwear. Then, I scream.

After a few seconds, I roll over, lifting my phone up over my head and making a video call. Within seconds, the screen fills with the face of my best friend. When she moved to Vancouver Island last year, I was devastated, more than I ever let her know. She's more than my best friend, she's like a sister. No one knows me better than she does; the good, the bad, and the ugly.

"Are Coop or Sawyer around?" I blurt out as soon as I see her. This isn't a conversation I need her kid or her boyfriend overhearing. Not to mention I'm not dressed...although I do keep the phone angled so Tori doesn't see too much.

"No, they're out at the movies." Tori's face fills with concern. "Are you okay?"

"Um," I start. "Maybe not. Guess who's getting traded to the Tridents?"

Tori's eyes widen. "No way."

I nod. "Yes way. I have to set up everything for the press conference when he comes to sign contracts next week."

"Holy shit," Tori whispers, the rare curse word slipping out of her, proving she gets how monumental this is.

"What am I gonna do, T? The only reason I let myself go there with him was because I thought the chances of ever seeing him again were slim to none. And if I did, it would be from a distance, or brief, like a quick sound bite on the field, at best. Now he's going to be here, in my city, in my stadium, on my team." I'm starting to spiral, but Tori's right there to stop it, thank God.

"Listen to me, Wills. If you're going to let what happened in Hawaii affect your ability to do your job, then we have a problem. You're Willow Lawson. You're a badass, you don't take crap from anyone, and you have more courage and confidence in your pinky finger than most women do in their entire bodies. You're better than this. So what if he's being traded to your team? You had some hot sex with the man, that's all. It was enjoyable and consensual. You're both adults. This. Is. Different. From. Before."

"What if he says something?" I whisper, voicing my biggest fear. "He's more important to the team than I am. If Lydia finds out we have a history, I could lose my shot at the promotion, or worse. Have you ever heard of Vicki Daws?" My voice starts to rise, in volume and in pitch, as my panic grows. "She was the head of HR for the Arizona Flyers. *Was.* Until the player she was dating from the team broke up with her, and she not only lost her job but also had to move away from the city. The players always come first, Tori. If Ronan decides me being here is too messy given our Hawaii hookup, he could seriously ruin my life."

"Okay, but you're the one who said he was a good guy. Do you really think he's going to do that?"

"No," I reply, and even though most of me believes it, the kernel of doubt remains.

"Trust your gut, Wills. It's not often wrong." Tori's face softens. "And I know you hate the idea of nepotism, but the one benefit you don't like to admit about your uncle owning the team is the fact it would take something huge for him to let you go."

She's right, I do hate the idea of getting special treatment just because of my relationship to Uncle Mike. I've worked my ass off to prove I got to where I am without his help. But she's also right. He's got my back when it matters.

I exhale loudly. "It's going to be so weird seeing him all the time."

"Seeing him and not having him, you mean?" Tori's eyebrows waggle suggestively as she smirks, earning a short burst of laughter from me.

"Stop being the romance author and go back to being my best friend."

"I am being your best friend. I'm reminding you that he was nothing more than some good dick. That's what you told me when you got back, and that's what you have to remember right now."

"Nothing more than some good dick," I repeat. "Sure. I can compartmentalize. Easy." *Yeah, I don't believe me, either.*

"And if he's half as decent as he was in Hawaii, I don't think he'll say a thing," Tori soothes. "You said he seemed like a good guy. Not one to kiss and tell. So don't worry about it. Do your job, let him do his, and that's all."

"Okay. You're right. I'm a badass, he's just a player, and there is absolutely no reason why anyone needs to know any different."

"That's my girl."

A week later, dressed to kill in my favourite black pencil skirt, eggplant-coloured blouse, and low-heeled booties, I close my eyes just outside the conference room. "I'm a badass, he's just a player," I whisper to myself once more before turning the handle and entering the room for our preliminary meeting before the media conference that will formally announce Ronan as a Vancouver Trident.

The second I enter the room, my eyes zero in on him. His back is turned to me, his dark blond hair trimmed from when I last saw it curling out from under a hat. The light blue dress shirt he's wearing tapers perfectly into the tailored pants that cup his butt. A butt I'm intimately familiar with. A butt that probably looks even better in baseball pants.

Nope, not going there, Willow. I shake my head and plaster a professional smile on my face as I walk confidently over to where Ronan and his agent stand with my uncle Mike and the head coach.

"Gentlemen, if we're ready, I have everyone waiting for our exciting announcement."

Heads turn, but the only one I care about is his. I hold my breath. This is it, the moment when I find out if he'll keep our secret just that — or if he'll ruin everything. The shock on his face when he registers my presence makes it evident he wasn't expecting to see me here.

Guess that's my fault for not telling him exactly where I worked in media relations, but too little, too late now. His mouth is open, like he's seen a ghost. Widening my eyes slightly, I try to mentally tell him to get it together before someone sees him looking at me like that. Thank goodness, he gets the message. I watch him give his head a little shake before a mask of indifference falls over his face.

And I hate the fact that seeing that mask directed toward me stings.

"Ah, Willow. Thank you." Uncle Mike walks over and drapes his arm over my shoulder, guiding me closer to the others. "Ronan, Gage, this is my niece Willow, from our media relations team. You'll get to know her quite well, as she's very hands on."

Oh God, shut up, Uncle Mike. I manage a polite laugh, shaking hands with Ronan's agent before finally turning to him. Here we go. "Ronan, welcome to Vancouver." I put out my hand, and the second his much larger one engulfs mine, I know I'm in trouble.

Deep blue eyes, eyes that have seen all of me, in every possible way, sweep up and down my body. His tongue darts out and licks his lips. Lips that I still remember feeling whisper across my skin. And when he speaks, the voice that growled out the dirtiest of dirty talk reverberates through me with one simple statement.

"Thank you, Willow. Happy to be here."

Chapter Eleven

Ronan

Happy to be here? Seriously? I guess that's the best I can come up with when faced with the surprise of a fucking lifetime. Holy shit, I was not prepared for this. For her.

Here I am, shaking her hand, probably looking like a complete idiot. But I can't stop staring at the woman who has haunted my dreams for months.

What the fuck is she doing here? Then all the pieces fall into place. How knowledgeable she was about baseball, and just now, the team's owner introduced her as a member of the media relations staff. The little minx never told me she worked for a goddamn major league team. Suddenly her hesitation in getting close to me in Hawaii makes a little bit more sense.

Then the other thing Mike Cartwright said when he introduced her comes flashing back to me. His niece. I fucked the niece of the man who owns me for the next five goddamn years. The man who could make or break my future.

Fucking fuck.

Even as my pulse races and my mind spins in circles, I can't help but steal glances at her, drinking in her beauty. It doesn't take a genius to deduce from her body language and the way she greeted me that Willow doesn't want anyone finding out we know each other on a personal level, and I'll respect that. Honestly, it's probably for the best. But damn, she's more stunning than I remember. Even if she does look so very different from the relaxed, vacation Willow I knew. This version of her in heels and a tight pencil skirt is sexy as fuck.

I only realize I've been ogling her when I get a not-so-subtle elbow in my side from Gage.

"We just need your signature Ronan, then we can go get the circus over with." For a sports agent, Gage hates the media more than he probably should. There's no missing the derision in his voice, and Willow catches it, judging by the slight frown that crosses her face.

A frown I want to smooth away. But I've got no right, and no reason, to do that.

Honestly, of all the teams I could have been traded to, Vancouver wasn't high on my list. Hell, I didn't want to be traded at all, but the offer the Tridents made was one I couldn't turn down. The chance at a long-term contract, one I could possibly extend for the remainder of my career, depending on how long I play, was one I couldn't say no to.

Peyton first, baseball second. That's the way it has been, and the way it has to be.

Which is why I have to push aside this adrenaline rush I'm feeling just from the surprise of seeing Willow again and put on my game face. A mask of cool professionalism with a hint of pro-athlete arrogance the media eats up. We go into the other room where a crowd of reporters are waiting. Questions about my move across the country are thrown at me, and I answer them with ease.

Until one.

"What excites you the most about relocating to the West Coast?"

An innocent question and one I had a ready-made answer for. Except now, that answer is different. I just can't say the *real* reason I'm excited to be out west. Because the truth is, even though I don't have time for a relationship and know I need to keep my distance from Willow, seeing her again was like a jolt of electricity running through my body. Lighting up parts that have been dim for so long.

"The warmer weather, of course," I say with a cocky smirk at the reporter who asked. But my eyes betray me as my gaze darts over to the side where Willow stands, looking at something on her phone.

The press conference wraps up pretty quickly after that, and Willow disappears before I can get free. One of the assistant coaches shows up to take me around the stadium and facilities on a quick tour we didn't have time for before the conference, and I find myself glancing down hallways and into offices, desperate for a glimpse of her.

With spring training starting up in just over a month, there's not a lot of players around. Just the ones who didn't travel for the offseason. But when we enter the gym filled with top-of-the-line equipment, walls lined with mirrors, and a sound system pumping out rock music, a couple of guys notice our arrival.

"Ronan Sinclair. Nice to have you on board." Dan Montgomery, one of the catchers and a local Vancouver guy from what I recall reading through the player roster to familiarize myself with my new teammates, comes over to shake my hand. "Call me Monty. Only my mom calls me Dan."

"And Lark," another guy calls out as he ambles over. He's got a southern accent, deep enough to make it clear he's not from here. "Rhett Darlington. Pleasure to meet ya. Call me Rhett, or Darlin'."

"Nice to meet you both. Call me Sin, or Ronan is fine. And who's Lark?" I ask, curiosity getting the better of me. To my surprise, Monty blushes a deep red as Rhett just grins.

"You'll meet her soon. One of the best trainers out there, the woman can fix just about anything. Unfortunately for our friend Monty, she's very much unavailable. And he very much wishes she wasn't."

"Shut up," Monty mumbles, scrubbing his hand over his face. I glance over at Harvey, the assistant coach escorting me around, but given the smirk he's fighting back, it seems everyone is aware of Monty's crush on the unavailable trainer. In a way, I can relate to the guy, seeing as the only woman I've had any interest in for years has also made it clear she's unavailable.

"Sorry man, that's a shitty situation," I say.

He just shrugs. "It is what it is."

"Someday, you'll get your shot." Rhett slaps his hand on Monty's shoulder, the other man grimacing slightly.

"Moving on." Monty looks up at me. "You got family moving with you? Wife? Girlfriend? Boyfriend?"

"My daughter and my mom, who helps when I have to work. No partner." I shrug. "Never found anyone who could handle the demands of my job and my kid."

Until I met a beautiful brunette that made me wonder if having it all could someday be possible. But I don't share that part with the guys. Instead, I glance down at my watch and frown when I realize what time it is back on the East Coast. "Shit, actually, I need to get going. They're waiting for me to call before Peyton goes to bed."

"That's cool, Sin. Hey, we'll be here again tomorrow for some batting practice if you want to join."

"Thanks, that'd be great." We exchange numbers, and I let Harvey lead me out of the gym to wrap up our tour. But the truth is, my mind is somewhere else, across the country, in fact. On a four-year-old girl waiting for my call.

When I finally get back to my hotel room over an hour later, I have just enough time for a quick shower while I wait for room service to bring up some dinner before I need to call my mom and Peyton.

With my hair still wet, I pull on some shorts and a T-shirt before sitting down in the armchair next to the window that overlooks the water of Coal Harbour. Pulling up my mom's phone number, I hit the video icon and wait to see my girl.

"Daddy!" her excited shriek has me grinning. "Lemme see your hotel room."

Right on cue. Every time I travel, the first thing Pey wants to see is wherever I'm staying.

Standing up, I start to pan the room. "Okay, baby girl, here it is. There's my bed, and the bathroom, and here's the view."

Peyton starts babbling on about the water and the boats she can see, and my mind travels back in time to standing by a window overlooking crystal clear blue water with a beautiful woman by my side.

Damn it, no. I can't go there.

"Can I have a purple bedroom when we get a house, Daddy?" The question startles me out of my spiral. I look down at my phone where Peyton's waiting for my answer. Shit, I haven't even started to look at houses. And they'll be here in a week.

"Sure, Pey," I answer, feeling the overwhelm start to build inside of me. The last time I was traded, when I landed in Toronto, I didn't have a kid. It was easy to just live out of a hotel room until I found an apartment close enough to the stadium.

This time, I need a house big enough for me, my daughter, and my mother. I need to think about school districts. Community safety. Amenities. A backyard. And a purple bedroom.

"Thanks! Oh, Gran wants to talk to you. Love you, bye!" Peyton fumbles the phone over to my mom and I hear her tell Mom about a purple bedroom before my mom's face appears on the screen.

"Hi honey, how did today go?"

I exhale slowly, sitting back down on the chair. "Good. Nothing special, but it was fine. Met a couple of the guys on the team, checked out the facility. It's nice."

Here's the thing about living with your mother as an adult. She learns to read you like a fucking book.

"What are you not telling me, Ronan Sinclair?" she asks, her tone making it clear — answer, or else.

I'll answer, but I'm not telling her everything. "Nothing, I promise. I'm just tired. There's a lot to do before you guys fly out. Is everything set with the movers?"

Mom nods. "Yes, you confirmed it all before you left. Everything will arrive within a week of leaving Ontario. Did Gage get you connected with a realtor out there?"

I shake my head because I forgot to ask him. "No. I'll get going on that tomorrow."

"We can't live out of a hotel forever, Ronan." Mom sounds concerned, and it's not the first time she's expressed her worry over the condensed timeline in which I'm trying to do everything. She might be really fucking great and respect my decisions and autonomy with my daughter, but Pamela Sinclair is also the ultimate mama bear. And if she thinks someone or something isn't in the best interest of her family, she doesn't hesitate to tell them so.

Which is why she tried hard to convince me it was fine if she and Peyton didn't move until after spring training, but I argued. That then, the season will start, I'll be traveling, and it'll be crazy. I want them moved and settled into a house before I head south to Arizona with the team.

Besides, I miss my little girl. Being away from her is the one downside to my career, and I try to minimize the time we're apart as much as possible. Hawaii was the first time we were apart for something other than baseball. And look how that ended. With me on a plane at five in the morning because my daughter fell on the playground at preschool and hurt her wrist.

But their imminent arrival doesn't leave me with a lot of time to find a house and organize the move.

"I know, Mom. Don't worry, I'll find a place soon."

The knock on my door gives me the perfect excuse to end the call before she can make my stress level go any higher. I love her and could never find a way to show her how much I appreciate all of her help, but she still manages to stress me out with what she chooses to fixate on. "Food's here."

"Okay. I need to get your daughter to bed, anyway."

I stand up and move to the door as Mom goes looking for Peyton to say goodnight. After tipping the room service attendant, I sit back down on the edge of the bed this time as my daughter comes back on screen.

"Goodnight, baby girl, I love you. Can't wait to see you next week." Seeing her brings a smile to my face, even with the stress mounting in my head.

"Love you, too, Daddy." She yawns widely. "Give Snowberry a hug from me, 'kay?"

I lean over and pick up the small white bear she gave me a year ago that now travels with me everywhere, squeezing it to my chest. "Done and done. Tell Gran to give you an extra hug from me."

"Night, Daddy." Peyton waves at me, and I wave back before the screen goes black.

The low that always hits when I hang up from a call with Peyton sweeps over me. I miss her constantly.

Midway through eating my now cold dinner, my phone lights up with a new email. From none other than Willow Lawson, assistant director of media relations.

There's no subject line and no content except for a string of ten numbers that I immediately save in my phone. The phone barely rings once before she answers. "Ronan?"

"Hey, Cherry."

I hear her sharp intake of breath and know I've already made a mistake. "You can't call me that."

"Sorry." I run my hands through my hair, stand up, and start to pace the room. "Is this gonna be okay? Me playing here?" Not that I can change anything if she says no, but I feel like I have to ask. "I didn't seek out this trade, but it was one I couldn't turn down. And I had no idea you were here."

"I know, I saw the contract after you signed it. Five years is a long time. I know you probably wanted that stability for your daughter." Her voice sounds too clipped, too formal. I know I've got professional Willow on the phone, not vacation-fling Willow.

"Yeah. It's a hell of an offer."

Silence falls for a minute, which stretches into two.

"No one can know about us, Ronan. About what happened in Hawaii." She rushes the words out, as if they're difficult to say.

I exhale slowly. I didn't expect her to say anything different, and truthfully, I agree. But it still sucks. "I know. I don't want to cause any waves with management. I won't say anything."

Her sigh of relief is audible over the phone, and I feel a bit bad realizing she must have been worried about this all day. "Thank you." The two words are said so softly, I almost miss them. "Well, I should let you go."

"Yeah," I say, clearing my throat. "But, ah, it was good to see you again."

Another second of silence as I wonder if I crossed the line again saying that. Then...

"You too, Ronan."

The call disconnects, and I let my hand that's holding the phone drop down to my side. There might be a huge wall between us now, but some part of me is still drawn to her.

Which is going to be a huge fucking problem.

Chapter Twelve

Willow

"Willow, did you finish the preseason interviews?"

My face scrunches up. Almost made it. Schooling my expression, I turn from the elevators and make my way back to Lydia's office.

"Yes, it all went well and footage has been sent to the social media team already." I try to hide my impatience. I just want to go and eat lunch with Lark, not tell Lydia another thing she should already know.

For a while, I just blindly followed her every instruction, but the more time I spend working under her, the more I become aware of just how easily she passes off every task to someone else — namely me — and manages to skate by on the bare minimum of effort, still earning the maximum credit. It's starting to drive me nuts, but if there was ever a rock and a hard place, I'm in it right now. Because, of course, she's the one determining my future when it comes to taking over her job.

"Good. I'll need the transcripts on my desk before you leave today."

Somehow, I manage not to huff with annoyance. "Already done and in your inbox." I give her my most chipper smile. "I'm going on my lunch break now. See you later."

Pivoting on my heeled foot, I quickly walk away before she can say anything else.

Lark is waiting for me at the end of the hallway that houses all of the admin offices. "What are you doing up here?" I ask. "I thought I was coming to your room?"

She rolls her eyes and grimaces. "I had to drop off treatment reports with Mr. Cartwright."

"You know you can call him Mike," I tease. Even after being a member of the training staff for years, Lark still can't call my uncle by his first name. Doesn't matter how hard he tries to be approachable and accessible to staff, she's got upper management on a pedestal.

"Nope. I can't." We get off the elevator on the lower level that houses the gym, batting cages, and rehab area where Lark has her private room that often becomes our lunch spot.

"Oh my." Lark stumbles to a stop just outside the glass doors that open into the gym facilities. "Is that the new guy?"

"Aren't you in a relationship?" I tease, refusing to turn my head and see what I can all too easily picture. After all, I'm intimately acquainted with how Ronan looks with his muscles bulging, a sheen of sweat covering his skin.

Oh shit, now I'm getting turned on. For fucks sake, this is going to be a problem if I get horny every time I see the man. Or in this case, someone *else* sees him.

"Well, yeah, but I'm not blind. Look at him." Lark gestures behind me, and reluctantly, I turn around. Sure enough, there he is, standing by the weight rack, doing bicep curls that make me remember how easily he picked me up and moved me around in bed.

Gah! Stop it, Willow! Bad girl.

"He's hot. Even you have to admit that."

I shrug my shoulders and take a step down the hall, desperate to get away before he notices us here. But of fucking course, I'm not that lucky. Ronan turns at that very instant, catches us watching, and the fucker winks. Winks!

"Woah. Okay, yeah, we better go before I start having thoughts I shouldn't be having." Lark laughs, shaking her head as she joins me and we continue down to her treatment room where we planned to have lunch. "But really, what was with the wink? That was most definitely directed at you, girlfriend."

I shoot her a glare, silently imploring her to stop talking until we're in private. Thankfully, she seems to get the hint, going quiet until we reach her treatment room and I close the door behind me. I stare at my friend, hoping she realizes the trust I'm about to place in her.

"What I'm about to say doesn't leave this room, got it? Cone of silence."

Lark's eyes grow wide as she sits down and opens up her lunch bag, nodding solemnly. "Got it."

I snatch up the mini package of Skittles that I tossed in with my lunch as a treat, open it up, and pick out the lemon ones, passing them to Lark before I start to pace the small space. "Okay. Remember when I went to Hawaii last fall?" I hear her mumbled agreement and keep going. "Right. So. Guess who sat next to me on the plane."

"No way."

I turn to face her and nod. "Way. And guess who was staying at my hotel."

"Oh my God," Lark whispers, her face lighting up with excitement.

I decide to skim the details of how he charmed me, the time we spent together, and just give her the highlights. "Let's just say I thought I'd never see him again, so I gave in to temptation. I mean, there wasn't even the faintest whisper of a trade for him. I don't know what came over me." Dropping down into a chair, I slump down until my head hits the back of it. "Lark, I fell for a pretty face and then I got dick drunk. We fucked more times in one night than I had in the previous month."

Lark snorts, water shooting out of her nose. Grabbing a towel out of the basket on the counter behind me, I pass it to her, stifling my laugh before tossing a couple more Skittles in my mouth.

"Good Lord, warn a girl before you say something like that," she manages once she's cleaned up. "But also? Damn. Well done. So, are you guys together? Keeping things on the DL? Oh my God, is that why he winked?"

Lifting my hands up to slow down her insanity, my head is already shaking back and forth. "No, no, and I don't know. We're not together, did you miss the part where I said we never thought we'd see each other again? I mean, obviously I knew there was a chance we could run into each other, but I never expected this." My head falls back again. "I can't be with him, Lark, even if we both wanted it. I can't date a player. There's an unspoken rule about it, you know that."

"That rule is just an urban myth, not contractual, and it's a pile of misogynistic bull crap," she scoffs. "So when you say *can't*, do you really mean that? Or do you mean you won't?"

"Both." I sit up slightly. "Anyway. Enough about me and Ronan. Bottom line, there will never *be* a me and Ronan. So let's eat lunch and figure out how you're going to get out of Baron's next family event."

Lark grimaces. "Lord help me, that man's family is next-level insane."

"You realize if you ever take things further with him, they'll be your family." From what I know, Lark's boyfriend has the kind of conservative, snobby family you think only exists in movies. But no, the Hazelwood family brings every rich cliché to life.

"Trust me, that's crossed my mind." Lark sighs, looking down at her salad, poking at it with her fork. "I do love him, but enough to spend the rest of my life dealing with those narcissists? I don't know."

We're quiet for a moment. I might not be as close to Lark as I am to Tori, where we literally know everything about each other, but I consider her a good friend. Which is why my heart aches knowing how conflicted she is. And it seems to be getting worse, not better, every time we talk about her boyfriend and his family.

"Has he said anything else about the future?" I ask cautiously. Lark nods, her eyes still downcast.

"Yeah, he keeps mentioning me giving up my apartment and moving in with him. But come on! His house is on the same block as his parents. We'd see them all the time. He already admitted his mom has a key to his house and comes and goes as she pleases. Do you know how terrified I am of her walking in on us when we're together?"

"Damn. That's some blurred boundaries if I ever heard them."

Overbearing parents are a foreign concept to me, having grown up with a single dad who respected my space and independence. Don't get me wrong, Dad and I were close, and not a day goes by that I don't miss him, but Lark's situation is proof enough of how fucked-up parents can be. Unbidden, my mind darts back to Ronan's situation. Didn't he say he lives with his mother?

All the more reason to stay far away.

"Before you say anything, yes, it's half-caff, but I love you too much to let you have another sleepless night because you drank too much coffee." I breeze into my uncle's office and come to an abrupt stop when I realize he's not alone. "Shoot, I'm sorry. I didn't realize you were in a meeting."

Ronan's blue eyes twinkle with amusement as I stand there frozen, two coffee cups in hand.

"Nonsense, you're fine, my girl. Although, if anyone needs half-caff, it's you, you little coffee addict. Come on in, Ronan and I were just discussing his housing dilemma."

My uncle kisses my cheek and takes the coffee I hand over to him. "Actually, maybe Willow is the perfect person to help you."

I'm already shaking my head, my eyes widening. "What? Me?"

But Uncle Mike just barges on ahead. "Yes. Maybe you can connect Ronan with one of the real estate agents our guys have worked with in the past. Oh, and give him a rundown on the good neighbourhoods since he isn't familiar with Vancouver."

What the actual fuck is happening right now? "Uncle Mike —" But I'm cut off as he keeps going.

"You were just saying how stressed you are about finding the right place for your daughter." He gestures to me. "Willow grew up here. I'm sure she wouldn't mind going with you to look at a few places." He turns to me expectantly, and all I can manage is a dumbfounded nod.

"Great. Well, you'll have to excuse me. I've got a call with the alumni association in a few minutes. Thanks for the coffee, darling." He kisses my cheek again before sitting back down in his seat, and I know Ronan and I have been dismissed. "Ronan, why don't you go to Willow's office and she can get you that contact information for the real estate agency."

Why the hell do I feel like a puppet being manipulated by someone who has no freaking clue what they're meddling with?

I'll get out of it. I have to. Maybe Ronan just didn't want to turn down my uncle's overbearing suggestions in front of him.

I walk swiftly down to my office, and when Ronan follows me in, I close the door, staring at it for a second to steel myself. But before I can say anything, Ronan speaks.

"Thanks for agreeing to help," he murmurs, and I whirl around, my finger already lifted to point at him.

"This can't happen," I say firmly. But my resolve wavers when he smirks and slowly walks over to me, standing close but not too close. I can smell him, that rich, warm scent that transports me back to sunny days and one sex-filled night.

"You made that clear." His voice drops even further. "But I gotta be honest, you're not an easy woman to resist."

I suck in a breath, my eyes closing as his deep timbre washes over me. "Too bad."

"When did you last have a cherry?"

A breathy laugh bursts out of me. "With you. In Hawaii."

"Good answer," he rumbles. My eyes fly open to find he's staring back at me intently. "Fucking hell, I want to kiss you."

"No." My whisper comes out ragged, but I have to be strong. I might have given in to his charm once, but I can't, *won't,* do it again. The sharp sound of my desk phone ringing breaks us out of the staring contest we're in.

Ronan stuffs his hands in his pockets and steps back. "Right. Okay. I'm gonna go. Yeah."

Staying away from that man is proving to be *impossible.*

And now I have to go house hunting with him? Great. Just great.

Chapter Thirteen

Ronan

"You didn't have to pick me up."

"Hello to you, too." I grin at Willow as I approach where she's standing outside of her apartment building, her defensive posture of folded arms and a narrow gaze doing nothing to deter me. Being alone with her in her office, the temptation to kiss her was intense. But she said no, and I sure as hell wasn't gonna ignore that. Still, after punishing myself in the batting cages for an hour, I went back to my hotel and lay on the bed thinking about her.

Thinking about Hawaii.

About the feel of her body against mine, the sounds she made when she orgasmed, the easy smiles and laughter that would come just being around her. Even if she doesn't want to acknowledge anything between us, there *is* something between us. I may not have the time or energy for it, but I also can't ignore it.

She walks toward my rental SUV, and I jog ahead to open the door for her. "Thanks," she says grudgingly. I noticed this in Hawaii, her surprise when I'd do small things like open a door or hold out her chair. This is a woman who's not used to letting men — or probably anyone, if I had to guess — take care of her.

I shut the door and hurry around to my side, sliding in before I say, "I should be the one thanking you. I wasn't sure if you'd actually go through with it, coming with me, I mean. But I do appreciate your help. Your uncle wasn't wrong when he said I was worried about finding a good place for Peyton."

As I reverse out of the parking spot in front of her building, I see her body start to relax. "Yes, well, you promised me lunch."

I chuckle at that. "I did. Wherever you want to go." I pull out onto the street, the GPS already directing me to the first house.

Twenty minutes later, we pull into a long driveway, coming to a stop behind a black sedan. I can see an older gentleman waiting for us, but I look past him to the imposing house behind him. It's tall and dark, almost Gothic in a way, and giving off mausoleum vibes. "Yeah, this is gonna be a no. Can you imagine a kid running around here?"

Willow giggles, the first sign I've seen that maybe she's starting to relax around me. "It doesn't exactly have much curb appeal, does it? Maybe it's better inside. Come on, let's at least meet the realtor."

She climbs out before I can get around to open her door, and when I reach her side, I cup her elbow and lean down. "Next time, you wait until I can open your door. Got it, Cherry?" I whisper before straightening and extending my hand out to the realtor. "Hi, Ronan Sinclair, and this is Willow. Thanks for meeting us on such short notice."

"Not a problem. I'm Ken, lovely to meet you both. Our agency is thrilled to help another Trident family find their home. This first one is just to get us started since it's in your preferred neighbourhood and meets many of your criteria. Four bedrooms, large kitchen, and an enclosed backyard." He unlocks the front door and holds it open. "After you."

As soon as we step inside, Willow comes to a stop, shaking her head. I can tell she's holding back her laughter, and so am I. Black and white marble floors lead to an ornate curved stairway. Huge vases hold what seem to be very dusty fake flowers. There's fucking wallpaper on the walls, and a crystal chandelier hanging down. All of it is very dated in appearance, even I can tell that. This place is definitely not any better on the inside.

"Ken, I can tell you right now, this place won't work. Not with a four-year-old," I say.

"Of course, I had a feeling you might say that but wanted to get a better feel for your tastes. Your child will want something more homey and comfortable. Mrs. Sinclair, would you like to see any more, or shall we move on?"

"Oh, I'm not —" Willow starts to protest.

I, on the other hand, am sensing an opportunity for some entertainment, maybe a way to get her to remember how much fun we have together. "I think we're both ready to see something else."

Ignoring the sharp elbow that lands in my side, I drape my arm over her shoulders. "Come on, sweetheart, let's look at another house." It's hard to keep the amusement out of my tone as Willow walks stiffly beside me to the front door.

Ken locks up behind us as we move toward the vehicles, and Willow hisses at me. "What the hell are you doing? He thinks we're married!"

I just shrug, ignoring the agitation rolling off her in waves. "Just go with it, what's the harm?"

"The harm is that we're lying to a stranger. The harm is that we —"

Once again, she's cut off, and I have to hide my smirk as Ken joins us. "Alright, then. Let's move on to house number two. It's close to the stadium, with excellent schools and a lovely backyard."

"Sounds great, we'll see you there," I say jovially, steering Willow over to the SUV. I open her door, averting my eyes from the glare she's shooting me.

Once I'm in the car, she turns on me. "Seriously?"

I keep my eyes trained forward as I follow Ken down the long drive. "If it really bugs you, I'll correct him when we get to the next house." Chancing a glance over, I can see her lips twitching. "Is that what you want me to do?"

Willow doesn't answer, and the silence sits between us the whole way until we pull up to the second house. This one is much more my style, with a porch, a red front door, and a tidy, well-kept garden that doesn't seem like it would require too much upkeep.

This time, she does the right thing and waits for me to open her door. Watching her closely, I wait to see if she'll give me a sign of how she wants to manage things. To my shock, she handles it by threading her arm through mine and beaming at Ken. "Oh, look at this one, sugarplum, it's so perfect."

Sugarplum? She'll pay for that one later. "Let's see the inside before we get too excited, honeybun," I reply, squeezing her arm to my side.

"Fantastic first impression." Ken claps his hands together as we walk up to the front door. "Now, this one has the three bedrooms you wanted, a lovely open kitchen, and a couple of surprises out back that I think you'll love."

We step inside and Willow audibly gasps. I don't blame her, this place looks like someone plucked the perfect family home out of a magazine and magicked it to life right in front of us. It's warm, full of natural light, and I can instantly picture Petyon running down the hall.

"Ronan, this place is gorgeous," Willow murmurs to me as we move into the living room. Big picture windows look out over the front yard, which has hedges high enough to offer privacy but still plenty of light. I take in the open layout, my head already nodding in agreement. We move into the kitchen, and Willow detaches her arm from mine, only to drape her upper body across the large island in the center of the space.

"That's it, I'm never leaving. This is the kitchen of my dreams."

God, she's so fucking gorgeous.

"Shall we take a look at the bedrooms next, or would you like to see outside?"

I blink as Ken's voice interrupts the fantasy that was playing out in my mind, of stripping Willow naked and eating her out on the kitchen island she's so in love with.

"Bedrooms." Willow winks at me. "Come on, lovebug. Let's see where the magic is going to happen." This is the Willow I remember. Full of life and fun, flirtatious banter, and happiness.

I gotta give Ken credit, he's not batting an eye at our cheese. But when I join Willow, I hold her back a second so I can whisper in her ear. "Lovebug? Sugarplum?"

She turns her brilliant blue eyes up at me. "Your idea, I'm just playing along." Threading her fingers with mine, she pulls me to the staircase where Ken is waiting. "Lead on, Ken, let's see the bedrooms."

After touring the impressive bedrooms and bathrooms, my decision is just about made. This place is damn near perfect, even if it does mean either Mom will have to sleep upstairs with me and Peyton, or I have to find her an apartment nearby.

Maybe Willow will come with me to look for that as well...

"And I saved the best for last." Ken pauses at the bottom of the staircase. "Out back is not only a large enclosed yard, but also an in-ground pool and hot tub, and...a small but fully contained guest house for your mother."

That brings me to a stop. I'd forgotten that in the brief I sent over to his office, I mentioned that ideally, we'd have a separate space for Mom. Honestly? I didn't expect to find it, or if we did find a property with space for her, I'd have to sacrifice something else. But here we are, literally standing in my perfect house.

"Ken, I think you just sold yourself a house," Willow says quietly.

Running my hand over my jaw, I give her a grateful smile for answering while I'm momentarily struck speechless. But I find my voice and turn to Ken. "She's right, you did. Thank you, this was far easier than I expected it to be. How soon can I move in? I'm willing to pay extra for a quick closing."

Ken's eyes light up, no doubt seeing dollar bills, and I don't blame him. "Let's go to my office and work out all the details."

After signing a mountain of paperwork, I take Willow out for the lunch I promised her. She leads me to a little hole-in-the-wall Vietnamese place, where the bowls of noodle soup are bigger than my head.

"This is insane." I laugh when the server walks away. Looking over at her, I see Willow already using her chopsticks like a pro, picking up a piece of meat and laying it in her spoon that already holds some broth.

She slurps it down and then smiles. "It's worth every penny, and the stomach ache, if you actually do manage to eat the whole bowl. Ask me how I know. But they're good about giving you a container to take the leftovers home."

This feels so easy. Being with her all day without the pressure of being around anyone from the team. It's almost like it was in Hawaii, when it was just the two of us flirting and having fun. My hand reaches out across the table and covers hers. But when she snatches hers away, folding them on her lap, I realize my mistake.

I let myself be fooled by the teasing, the laughter, the innocent fun of pretending to be a couple looking for a house together. I let myself forget that Willow has made it abundantly clear there can be nothing between us now. Or that my own life doesn't allow for a relationship.

"Sorry," I mumble, putting my focus back on my food.

"No, I'm sorry," she says quietly. I'm already shaking my head to disagree with her but she puts her hand up in the air to stop me. "Today I let the lines be blurred, but that can't happen again. I think it's because we never got to have any closure after Hawaii. Don't get me wrong, I completely understand why you had to leave, and I guess it saved us the awkward morning after, but it also meant we never set any boundaries for seeing each other in the future. Which was kind of inevitable, I guess, even if I didn't expect it to be like this." She lets out a pained laugh, then sucks in a deep breath. "Like I said on the phone, I need you to promise me that Hawaii stays between us. That no one from the team will know what happened. Today? The flirting? I promise not to let things go that far again. It's not right, and it's not fair to either one of us."

I let her finish, ignoring how every piece of me wants to reject what she's saying, even though my head knows it's for the best.

"Okay," I say simply. "No one will know."

She gives me a sharp nod, then returns to her bowl of soup. The rest of lunch passes quickly and quietly, then I drive her home. And as I pull away from her apartment building, I vow to myself to do as she asked and put it all behind me.

Every perfect, sinful moment we had together. It's in the past, no matter how much a selfish part of me wishes it wasn't.

Chapter Fourteen

Ronan

"Daddy!" Peyton's shriek has heads turning as she barrels toward me, my mom following more slowly behind, pushing a luggage cart piled with suitcases. I sweep my daughter up and into my arms, that piece of my heart settling back into place the way it always does when I'm reunited with her.

"Hey, Rocket," I say, pressing a kiss to her head. "Missed you."

"I missed you more," she mumbles into my shoulder.

I smile. "I missed you the most." Stretching one arm out, I pull my mom in for a side hug. "Hey, Mom, how was your flight?"

"Fine. This one was an angel, as usual."

"Oh, yeah?" I look at Peyton. "How many episodes of Bluey did you watch?"

"Eleventy!" she announces proudly and I just laugh, arching my brow at Mom in mock judgment.

Mom gently swats my arm. "Listen, if a cartoon dog keeps her happy while she's strapped into an airplane seat, then so be it."

"No complaints here. I'm just happy to finally have you both in Vancouver." I smile and set Peyton down before taking over the luggage cart. "Hey, Pey, do you want to go for a swim when we get to the hotel?"

"Yes!"

Her excitement doesn't diminish at all the entire drive from the airport into downtown Vancouver. There's a little bit of melting snow on the ground, and it's grey and dismal outside, but Mom and Peyton eagerly look around at our new hometown.

It's only when we finally reach the hotel suite I moved into this morning to make room for Mom and Peyton that she starts to fade. "Maybe a nap before the pool, kiddo."

"But Daddy," she whines, and I shake my head.

"Nope, you've had a long day. And if we're gonna go out for dinner tonight, you need to be awake so you don't face-plant into your pizza."

That earns me a tired giggle. I take Peyton's special blanket that Mom has already fished out of a suitcase for me with a grateful smile.

"I'm going to take a shower, then possibly nap myself," she murmurs, gesturing to her room.

I nod, then pick up my daughter and carry her into my room. I've already set up the cot for Peyton, so it takes no time at all before I've got her tucked in, blanket in one hand, and Snowberry the stuffed bear in the other.

"Snooze for a bit, then we'll go swimming, okay?" I whisper, smoothing the hair back from her forehead. Peyton's eyes are already drooping as she nods.

I stay there, watching my beautiful little girl drift off into an easy sleep. My heart is full, so fucking full of love for this girl. She's the reason for everything I do, every decision I make has her in mind.

Except for Hawaii. That's the first time since she was born that I did something solely for myself. The world didn't fall apart, I didn't fuck everything up, even if I was on the other side of the continent when she got hurt. It turned out to just be a sprain, not a fracture, and by the time I got home, they were back from the hospital with her little arm in a splint. Did I battle some parental guilt the entire twelve plus hours it took to get home? Of fucking course I did. But Peyton's fine, everything's fine, and now she's at last here with me.

As much as I hate it, Willow's right that nothing can happen between us now. I have to focus on what's important: baseball and my family.

"What do you think, Rocket?" I grin as I tug the Tridents jersey over Peyton's head. When we showed up at the stadium half an hour ago, I was stunned by the welcome my daughter and Mom got from the team. They're both now decked out head to toe in turquoise and gold, Tridents colours. Everyone has been amazing, greeting them both like they're family.

Which is exactly what I hoped for. Don't get me wrong, the two teams I've played for since Peyton was born were fine. They didn't give me too much trouble being a single dad, but especially in the early days, it was hard leaving my baby girl.

So far the Tridents' management has shown me childcare facilities that some of their staff use that Peyton can access if Mom is ever unavailable, and introduced us to the mascot, not to mention all of the gifts.

"I like the colours." Peyton tugs on my hand. "But can we see the field now?"

I chuckle. My girl loves the bright green grass and dirt path of a baseball diamond almost as much as I do. "You bet."

I pick her up, and with one last nod of thanks to the HR guy who was on hand to welcome us this morning, we head toward the elevators that lead from the office level down to the field level. Peyton is busy chattering in my ear about something when the elevator doors open, and Willow looks up from her phone.

Fuck, she's stunning. Wide-legged black pants hug her hips, and a blue body suit skims her upper body. Her lips are painted a bright red, and I want to kiss it off her.

Nope. No, I don't. Okay, that's a lie. I do, but I won't. I can't. Jesus fucking Christ. Did I say she's hard to resist? More like impossible. Being this close to her and not touching her? It's torture.

"Ronan," she says softly, then her eyes widen as she takes in my company. But Willow being Willow, she recovers instantly, a professional smile — big, but lacking in the genuine warmth I know she has inside of her — spreading across her face. "This must be your family." She puts her hand out and shakes Mom's hand. "I'm Willow, from the media relations team."

"Pam Sinclair. Lovely to meet you." Mom gives Willow an appraising look. She doesn't miss a damn thing. And Willow's first reaction at seeing us was more telling than she probably wanted it to be.

"And this must be Peyton." Willow beams at my daughter, but there's a hidden wistfulness that surprises me. "You look pretty great in your dad's jersey."

Peyton responds with a toothy grin. "Thanks. We're gonna go see the field now. I'm gonna hit some balls. Wanna come?"

Willow laughs lightly. "That sounds awesome, but I have to go to a meeting. I hope you have a great time."

Willow's eyes dart up to mine before bouncing back to my family. "Nice to meet you both. Ronan."

I give her a nod, and she brushes past in a cloud of sweet citrus. I have to exercise a lot of restraint to not turn and watch her walk away, but I can feel my mom's eyes boring into me.

"Okay, let's go to the field!" I say with way more enthusiasm than is probably necessary. We pile into the elevator and I let Peyton push the button, all the while keeping my gaze averted from Mom.

When we reach field level, I take them on a quick tour of the player facilities. Outside the gym, we run into Monty and Lark, the trainer the guys told me about, standing close together, having what seems to be a pretty intense conversation. Judging by the way they leap apart when I greet them, I'm starting to think Rhett's comment about Monty's feelings for Lark has some truth behind it.

"Hey guys, this my mom Pam and my daughter Peyton. We're just doing a little tour before checking out the field."

"Yo, Sin!" Monty gives me a fist pump and greets my family with a big smile, and it just reinforces again that moving here was a good idea.

"Hey Peyton, do you like Skittles?" Lark asks, her gaze darting up to mine to check if it's okay. I nod.

"I love them!" Peyton cheers, because what kid doesn't love candy.

Lark takes her hand and we follow her down the hall to what I assume is her treatment room, where she opens a drawer and lifts out a small treat-sized package of candy.

"Woah, you're letting her have some of Willow's secret stash?" Monty teases, leaning against the doorframe. My head whips around of its own accord at her name, but thankfully, no one seems to notice.

"Shh. She won't miss one package." Lark winks at Peyton.

My curious daughter tilts her head to the side and frowns. "Why do you have someone else's Skittles?"

Lark laughs, shaking her head. "They're her favourite candy, and if she has them in her office, she can't stop eating them. She says she would *look* like a Skittle from eating so many if I didn't keep them for her."

My daughter giggles, and I inwardly file that random fact away. There's so much I don't know about the captivating woman, and every time I learn something, I find myself wanting to know more. A serious problem when the lady in question is someone I really need to stay away from.

We say goodbye to Lark and Monty, and I lead Mom and Peyton through the locker room, then the dugout, and finally out onto the field. It still fills me with immense pride to walk out onto a major league field, even after six years.

I was lucky enough to be drafted into the minors right out of university and moved to the majors two years later. I spent a season down in Texas before moving to Toronto, which is also where I met Peyton's mom. When she told me she didn't want to keep the baby we conceived, thanks to a busted condom, it almost derailed my entire career. If my mom hadn't stepped in and insisted she would help me do this single parent thing, I don't know where I'd be. Because my daughter comes first, no matter what.

Watching her take off, running the bases with pure joy, just reinforces that. Her happiness is all that matters, and if I had to, I'd give up baseball in a second for her. Thank fuck I haven't had to make that decision yet. Her happy giggle floats back to us. Just like her dad, my kid has always been happiest out on the diamond.

"So, that Willow was quite beautiful."

"Don't start, Mom," I warn, unable to outright deny her statement.

Out of the corner of my eye, I see Mom lift her hands. "Simply making an observation."

"Yeah, well, keep it to yourself. I'm here to play ball. That's all." I fold my arms across my chest, but then drop them less than a minute later when Peyton rounds third and comes racing toward us. I crouch down, arms stretched wide, and she barrels into me. I let her push me back to the dirt, both of us laughing.

This. This is what matters.

Not stunning women with cherry red lips.

Chapter Fifteen

Willow

The stadium is quiet with the entire team, along with coaching and training staff, down in Arizona for spring training. Anyone left behind is busy in the admin offices, including myself and the media team. We're prepping media packages, brainstorming events and social media campaigns.

The offices are relaxed, humming with a positive but low-key energy, even with Lydia coming out periodically to demand something that's already been done. I don't know how she's not seeing the eye rolls that are coming more and more often as our staff grow increasingly annoyed with her antics.

Hopefully soon enough, we won't have to put up with catering to her any longer. And yes, I feel like a terrible person saying that as the one who wants her job, but there's no denying it's the truth. We're all just waiting for her to decide her official end date and announce her replacement.

"These look great, Sheena." I smile down at the junior staff who just shared a new concept for one of our social media accounts. "Let's run it for a week and see how it lands."

I'm walking back to my office when my phone starts to go crazy with incoming notifications, and my stomach plummets. Especially when I hear other members of the team also receiving notifications. That can only mean one thing: a big headline, and probably not a good one.

"Tridents' second baseman Maverick King has been identified in a now-viral video showing an altercation between two men outside a well-known Phoenix sports bar."

"Shit. Fucking shit, goddamn it, Maverick." I curse under my breath as I pivot on my heel and hurry down the short hall to Lydia's office. She's on the phone when I knock but beckons me inside. Just as she hangs up the phone, her door opens again and Uncle Mike walks in. Giving my shoulder a brief squeeze, we both sit down.

"Alright ladies, how are we gonna spin this one?" Uncle Mike asks grimly. He's looking at Lydia, and she's looking at me.

Okay, guess I'm up.

"Do we have any details on what sparked the fight?" I ask slowly, my attention still also focused on scrolling through media sites, trying to get a handle on things. "Have we heard anything from the crew down there?"

Uncle Mike is still looking at my boss, and she might not recognize it, but I can see his growing impatience. "Lydia?"

The woman in question shoots me a glare, as if this is all my fault. "Not to my knowledge. I'm waiting for my team to bring me more information before I can formulate a plan."

If my eyebrows went any higher, I think they'd shoot off my head. Waiting for her team? When we all just received the same notifications? What exactly is stopping *her* from getting on the phone to Arizona and figuring out what's going on?

I have to take several deep breaths. At the end of the day, she's still my boss, and still holds the key to my promotion.

"I'll call Rudy. He went down to catch some B-roll of practices, that kind of thing. Maybe he knows more of what happened." I'm already scrolling to his phone number on my phone.

Uncle Mike just nods. "I expect a response to be crafted and on my desk for approval within the hour." He stands up and looks at me. "Willow, are we still on for lunch?"

Um, what? I didn't know we had lunch plans, but I nod in agreement, nonetheless. I look to Lydia, but she's typing furiously on her phone, hopefully to someone in Arizona, but I doubt it. She's likely waiting for me to do that.

Sure enough, as I turn to leave with Uncle Mike, she calls out after me. "Willow, come back after speaking with Rudy and I'll let you know how to proceed."

"Okay." I bite back the response I really want to make. How did I ever let myself think Lydia was someone to admire? Maybe at one time she was, and maybe I've inadvertently enabled her to be like this, but I swear to God, the woman has made a mastery out of having someone else do her job for her.

She'll tell me how to proceed. Right. More like, I'll subtly suggest what I think should be done, she'll agree, then pawn the idea off to Uncle Mike as if it was all her swooping in to fix everything.

I've never had the guts to ask him why no one has said anything or done anything about her work ethic. It just seemed easier to carry the extra weight and make sure no matter what, our department ran smoothly and effectively. If Lydia got the acknowledgment for work that I actually did, oh well. We were a team. Or so I used to think. Besides, the last thing I needed was to be seen as the narc who went running to her uncle any time something didn't go her way.

But it's getting harder to stay quiet and respectful around her lazy sense of entitlement. For me and everyone else on our media team.

Half an hour later, a quick chat with Rudy in Arizona has given me enough information to come up with a draft press release, and I've eked out a promise from the assistant coach to get Maverick and his agent on a video call with us this afternoon to discuss how he needs to respond to any questions from the press.

I make my way back to Lydia's office, press release in hand, as well as waiting in her inbox. "Lydia, I've got a call with Maverick in an hour and the press release right here for your approval," I say by way of greeting.

Her eyes flicker up from her phone. "Fine. Send it on to Mike."

"You don't want to look it over?" I ask, purely out of professional courtesy.

"Do I need to? Or did you do your job?" she fires back. My fingers clench at my side, but I manage a tight smile.

"It's all done and proofed. We've got multiple witnesses confirming that Mav was —"

"I don't care what he was doing. I care that we keep our name clean," Lydia interrupts with a wave of her hand. "Send it to

Mike and make sure the articles for next month's Tridents blog are ready."

The blog articles that have been ready for a week? I'm starting to wonder if she ever checks her emails.

"Will do," I reply curtly. Then I march back to my office, sit down in my chair, and let out a massive, silent scream of frustration.

I thought last season was tough, what with our pitcher Rafe's surprise kid showing up, which led to his retirement and proposal to his now-wife after the final game of the season with no warning. All that, combined with my best friend moving to Vancouver Island, meant the spring and summer of last year were pretty freaking stressful.

But this year, with Ronan in town and Lydia being Lydia, might be even worse.

When I wake up the next morning, I'm exhausted and oh so grateful it's Saturday. So, when a video call from Tori comes in, I actually debate not answering for a second to preserve the silence and warm, cozy feelings.

When I do, it's clear she's not at home. "Are you on a ferry?" I ask, excitement washing away my exhaustion.

She nods, then pans the phone to the side so I can see Cooper holding his puppy Chloe, and Tori's boyfriend Sawyer, all grinning and waving. "Surprise! Got any room for some last-minute visitors?"

I scramble up to sit straighter on my couch. "Oh my God, of course, I do! Wait, why are you coming? Why didn't I know this?"

Tori says something to Sawyer off-screen before turning back to me with a wide smile. "Coop's going to visit his grandparents, and instead of them coming to the island to get him, we decided to come to the mainland. Sawyer's got a weekend off, and it was just a spur-of-the-moment decision." Her face grows serious. "Are you sure you have time, though? I know preseason isn't too busy normally, but I saw that video with Maverick."

I groan. "You did, huh? Yeah, he needs to learn better ways to handle things that don't involve fighting. But it's fine, we issued a press release and he's now on lockdown in Arizona."

"So it's good timing for us to show up uninvited?"

A big smile breaks free on my face. "T, it's always a good time for you to show up. I miss you guys so much."

"Awesome." She grins back. "We'll be at your place in an hour and a half. Coop wants to see you before we take him to his grandparents."

"Perfect."

We hang up and I leap into action, setting up the guest bedroom for Tori and Sawyer, and change out of my pajamas into some real clothes.

By the time Tori and her family get to my apartment, I'm so ready to see them. As soon as I buzz them in, I open my apartment door and wait, staring at the elevator, willing it to move faster. The doors open and I yank Tori into a huge hug.

"Oh my God, you're crushing me, woman." She laughs, but her arms are squeezing me just as tightly. For so long, it was the two of us and Cooper against the world. I've missed them so much, even though moving to Dogwood Cove was perfect for them.

Eventually, I let her go, only to open my arms wide and wait to see if Coop will still hug me. With him turning nine this year, I'm wise enough to let him decide. But he throws himself into my arms as well, and my heart bursts with love for my pseudo-nephew. I hold him equally tight.

"Where's my love?" Sawyer Donnelly's deep voice teases. We first met Sawyer and some of his friends at the BC firefighter's fundraiser gala last year. I pegged the three of them as outrageous flirts, but Sawyer saw something in Tori, and she saw the same in him, I guess. A one-night stand was supposed to be all there was to it until Tori moved to Dogwood Cove and discovered her hunky firefighter lived there.

It's not all that different to mine and Ronan's situation, come to think of it, except Tori was free to continue having a fling and a bunch of hot sex with Sawyer, and I'm most definitely not with Ronan.

"C'mere, you," I say, hugging Sawyer. "I'm glad you guys are here."

We enter my apartment, and Sawyer heads down the hall to the guest room with his and Tori's bags.

"We're meeting Coop's grandma in half an hour, then Sawyer is going out with his firefighting buddies for lunch. Meet me for sushi at Mizu in an hour?" Tori asks as Cooper and his dog Chloe roll around on my living room floor.

"Sounds perfect," I say, and it really does. Certainly beats the laundry and frozen pizza I had planned for the day. They all head out shortly after arriving, and Cooper gives me yet another hug.

"I kinda wish I was staying here," he mumbles into my shoulder and I squeeze him a little tighter.

"Maybe you can come over, just you, for a weekend when the season starts and we'll do a Cooper and Aunt Willow weekend," I whisper back. His enthusiastic nod is everything. I love that kid so damn much.

Just over an hour later, I slide into a booth opposite Tori in our favourite little sushi joint.

"I already ordered gyoza and sunomono."

I grin. "You're too good to me."

Tori picks up her green tea and takes a sip. "So. How's the Ronan situation?"

I grimace and sip my own tea, trying to decide how to respond. "Fine? Frustrating? Nonexistent? Hell if I know."

Tori sets down her tea and leans forward, her eyes filled with curiosity. "I want to know more about the frustrating part."

"Of course, you do." I chuckle. Tori has used my dating escapades as inspiration for her romance novels more than once, so it's no surprise this whole thing with Ronan is like catnip to her. "I don't know where to start. I mean, after the house hunting chaos, I haven't seen him much. That one time, he brought his family to the stadium but then they all left for spring training." I sip my tea. "Honestly, it's not easy. I always feel like I'm walking on eggshells, wondering if I'll see him at work. Do I want to see him? Do I not? I have no clue."

"Sounds to me like there's some unresolved feelings," Tori says quietly.

I lean back as the server sets down some food and takes the rest of our order. Once again, I'm trying to decide how to answer. "I mean, yes. Even though I know nothing can ever, and I do mean *ever* happen, there's a part of me that can't stop wondering what if. What if he hadn't left Hawaii early? Would we have spent the rest of the trip together? Would that make it easier or harder to be around him now?"

I shake my head, as if that could clear up the mess in my brain. "But it doesn't matter. The season will start, and I'll hopefully hear about the promotion soon so I can start transitioning into Lydia's position if I get it. And Ronan has to be just another player. Nothing more."

"Nothing more," Tori echoes thoughtfully. "Except he already is something more, isn't he?"

Yeah...he is.

Chapter Sixteen

Ronan

"There it is, Sin, good eye. Way to lay off the junk pitches," Coach Stirling says as he comes up to the plate. "Let's see that again tomorrow at the game against the Rose City Roasters, but watch for their ace pitcher. He's got a curveball that comes out of nowhere." He claps me on the shoulder as I walk off the field and knock fists with Rhett, who's heading up to hit next.

In the dugout, I drop to the bench and gratefully accept the bottle of sports drink one of the trainers hands to me. *I really need to work on learning all their names.* The Arizona heat feels intense for the second week of March. It's one month into preseason with another two weeks to go.

I try to remember the last time I had a good night's sleep, and honestly? It was Hawaii. The night before the one I spent with Willow.

Since then, it's been one thing after another, from going home to deal with Peyton's arm to finding out my team was putting me up for a trade. Then Christmas came with still no news on where I was going, only for it to be Vancouver, home of the woman I can't stop thinking about. Of course, I didn't know that at the time, all I knew was I had to scramble to get things ready for the big move. And even after I came out west and discovered Willow's connection to my new team, the stress didn't let up. It's been nonstop, with moving into the house, getting Rocket and my mom moved in and settled as best I could, not to mention trying to find my place on the team.

Spring training is meant to help with that. Help with all of us finding our groove and connection as a team. But part of me is still back in Vancouver.

Coach calls all players out on the field, then splits us off into groups to run through some fielding drills. I'm partnered with Maverick this time, a guy I can't quite figure out. He's quiet and keeps to himself, but I've heard from the others that he's a decent guy. Any time he's landed in a fight, it always seemed to me that he was arguing in defense of someone else, and never about himself. The black eye he's sporting is even more evidence of that, no matter how the media spins it.

I was there last night, and I saw that he only punched the guy because the asswipe wasn't taking no for an answer from some random girl at the bar. I gotta have some respect for him standing up for her, even if it is shit luck it ended up on social media. Would it have gone viral if it was anyone but Mav? Like a player who hasn't already got a bad rap in the press?

"That looks like it hurts," I comment as we make our way to an open spot on the field.

He just grunts. I've heard from Monty and Rhett that Mav's a solid player, but nobody knows much about him. Except that he seems to have a chip on his shoulder the size of Vancouver

Island and makes shit decisions in his personal life that bleed into his professional one.

Reaching my spot, I toss the ball at him. He powers it back at me full strength, taking me by surprise. "Guess we're not warming up?" I call out, whipping it back to him.

"Thought you could handle the heat."

"I can if you can."

We start throwing harder than we should be for spring training. Mav has one hell of an arm. And accurate as hell. I can already imagine being on the receiving end as we turn double plays this season. Whatever issues he's got, the others were right. The guy is one hell of a player.

After some infield drills, Coach calls us in for a debrief, and then we're free for the evening. The locker room is full of noise. Guys talking about training and the upcoming season.

"Hey Ronan, you're coming out for dinner, right?" Monty comes up beside me, a white towel wrapped around his waist, another in his hands as he rubs his hair dry.

"Is that wise given last night's events?" I ask in a low voice.

Monty shrugs. "Mav's not coming. He's on hotel arrest according to Coach. But Taco Tuesday can't be missed, my friend."

Tacos do sound good. My stomach rumbles in agreement. "Yeah, sure. Count me in."

I make my way to the showers, finish up quickly, and hop on the bus with the guys heading back to the hotel. Once there, I sit down on the small couch in my room and call Mom and Peyton, as usual.

Her face fills the screen seconds later and her expression instantly makes me worried. "Hey Mom, how are things?"

I see her glance to the side, and then she moves into the kitchen of the house I closed on just two days before leaving for Arizona. Boxes are still everywhere, but I paid a crew to do a rush job setting up Peyton's purple bedroom and the guest house for Mom, although with me away, she's using one of the spare bedrooms instead.

"Peyton's having a rough time," she says quietly. "I think it's just the timing with the move happening right before you had to go south. I've tried taking her to drop-in classes and the park, but she just isn't interested in anything."

"Shit," I mutter, raking my hands through my hair. "I'm stuck here for two more weeks. Maybe you can fly back down here for another short trip? At least then I could see her after practice."

Mom and Peyton came down to see me for a long weekend early on in training. Thank fuck the Tridents are so supportive of players with families.

"No, she'll be okay. She misses you, and it's been a lot of change in a short period. But she's a resilient kiddo. Coming down there again might sound like a good idea, but I don't think it's wise. She's used to you being gone, and another travel disruption won't help her adjust any faster. Besides, you've got to focus on the team."

"Peyton's more important than the team," I immediately protest, even though, deep down, I know she's right.

Mom nods. "I know you believe that, and that's what makes you such a wonderful father. But think with your head, not your heart right now. Peyton's safe; she might be unhappy at the moment, but she will be fine. I only told you about her sadness because I promised to always be honest with you about her."

"And I appreciate that, Mom, I do. But what the fuck am I meant to do?" I exhale sharply. This is when it's the hardest. When I know my baby girl needs me, and I can't do a fucking thing about it.

"You're meant to keep doing exactly what you always do. Focus on your job when you're on the field and focus on your daughter when you're not."

My eyes close as I take in a deep breath. "Okay. You're right."

"Of course I am, I'm your mother."

A small smile breaks free and I open my eyes to see Mom smiling, too. "Thanks, Mom. I love you."

"I love you, honey. Now let me go and get your little girl."

After a long chat with Peyton, where her somber little eyes almost broke my damn heart, I see a message from Monty confirming dinner plans. Dragging my ass off the couch, I force myself to shift out of guilty dad mode and into team player mode. Some days the transition is easier than others. Today, it's really fucking hard.

Down in the lobby, I join the group of guys walking down the street to the Mexican restaurant Kai said has the best tacos in Phoenix. If any of them notice that I'm holding myself back, they don't comment, and hopefully just chalk it up to being the new guy.

We sit around a large table, and a waitress immediately sets down pitchers of water and a large basket of chips, along with a trio of different salsas.

"Watch out for the red one, Sin." Rhett leans over to tell me. "It'll burn your fuckin' tongue off."

"Darling's just a wimp when it comes to spice," Kai calls out from across the table. He takes a chip, scoops a generous amount of red salsa onto it, and pops it in his mouth. Rhett visibly shudders, taking a chip and dipping it in a green salsa, taking only a small amount.

"I'd just rather keep my taste buds intact."

"Aren't you from the south?" I can't resist teasing, and the guys around the table all laugh. Rhett grins, and shrugs.

"Sure am. But I'm more a sweet tea and hush puppies kinda southern boy. Only place I want spice is in the bedroom." He winks and the table erupts again.

After some goading from Kai, I decide to suck it up and try the red salsa, which really is fucking spicy. Banter and laughter floats around me as the guys all settle in. Slowly, I feel myself relaxing and even enjoying myself. Peyton is forefront in my mind, but I'm skilled in compartmentalizing by now, so I just remind myself of what Mom said. She'll be fine, even if right now she's struggling.

"Alright, who's ready for the fishbowl?" Monty stands, lifting a bag he carried here onto the table. Out of it, he lifts a large glass fishbowl. The guys around the table cheer as I look on in confusion.

Monty starts passing out pieces of paper and pens that he also pulls out of the bag, and all the guys immediately start writing.

Looking over at me, Monty grins. "Tradition for the Tridents is every year at spring training, we come here for Taco Tuesday and fill this fishbowl with our goals and predictions for the upcoming season. Then, after the season ends, we get together for a barbecue and pull them all out to see what came true."

My eyebrows lift in surprise. "Really?"

Monty just nods sagely. "The tradition started about five or six years ago when we had a trainer on staff that was really into the new age woo-woo stuff. They were big on manifesting your destiny," he says with finger quotes. "But that year over half of our goals and predictions came true. So we keep doing it."

I take the paper and pen he hands me, and stare at it for a minute. Goal setting isn't exactly a new concept, but I can honestly say I've never done it at a taco joint with my teammates all around me, and I've certainly never put my goals into a giant fishbowl with a sticker of the team logo on the side.

But I play along. Only, instead of the obvious goals — win the championships or bat a three hundred average — I open my mind to something more specific. There's a brief moment of hesitation when I think about the team reading my goals out loud at the end of the year, but fuck it. If I'm going to be on this team for the rest of my career, might as well bare my soul and put it in a fishbowl.

Putting pen to paper, I write.

Make a home in Vancouver for my family. Lock in this team as MY team and take it all the way.

Chapter Seventeen

Willow

"Rudy, set up over by the entrance so we can see fans' expressions when the players do their parade. Sheena, you're live streaming the meet and greet, show me those portable chargers." I nod when she lifts up two. "Great. I'll be moving around, but I've got my radio on if you need me." Clapping my hands, I move to the doorway of the conference room we took over at the hotel in Abbotsford to use as HQ for this stop on our media caravan. "Let's go make some Tridents fans happy!"

With the season officially opening in four days, this is the busiest time of year for me and the entire media department. We want every seat to be occupied at every game. We want rabid fans on social media and at the stadium, wearing the merch, cheering on the players, and we want the Tridents name and logo everywhere.

And all that comes down to this. Three days of us bussing a handful of players around to smaller cities and towns in British Columbia, hosting meet and greets, press conferences, even a couple of charity outreach events, all designed to generate buzz and excitement for the upcoming season. The boys only just returned from spring training the day before we started the tour, and it's clear they're ready to play.

I've managed to successfully steer clear of Ronan thus far. It hasn't been easy, since I'm basically running the entire event with Lydia opting to stay in Vancouver for the first few stops on the tour. But she's here today, which means my stress notches up a few levels. Although, where she is right now when the event is about to start, I have no idea.

Making my way from HQ to the main room that houses the local press that came out to interview our guys, I check in with a few reporters I've come to know over the years. "Hey, Kate," I say, approaching an online sports blogger who never misses a Tridents event. "Got everything you need?"

She turns to me, eyes wide with excitement. "Absolutely. Thanks, Willow, you always host a great event. You know I appreciate being included like this."

I give her a professional smile, but pride warms me. "Of course. Your write-ups are always fantastic. Honest, factual, yet somehow funny. How do you do it?"

Kate just shrugs. "Pure, unbridled talent, I guess."

We both laugh quietly. But she's not wrong. In the male dominated field of sports media reporting, Kate stands out. Someday, she's going to jump from blogger to reporter, I just know it.

"I promise to only ask this one gossipy question," Kate starts, leaning in closer. "Is Ronan Sinclair as dreamy in person as he seems in interviews?"

My stomach clenches. *Yeah, he is, possibly even more than she's imagining.* I manage to school my expression before I answer. "He's a great addition to the team." Giving her one more professional smile, I make my escape. Answering that kind of question about Ronan is not on my agenda for today, or ever. "Excuse me, Kate, I need to make sure the players are ready."

The press conference goes off without a hitch, and an hour later, we're moving on to the next event of the day, the fan meet and greet. This is more casual, with fifty lucky fans who entered an online contest from our newsletter lined up outside, waiting to come and meet their favourite Tridents. I circulate around the room, checking the water tables staffed by hotel workers, giving them a nod of appreciation. There are pens everywhere, Trident branded, of course, so the guys can sign whatever items the fans might have with them. A merch station is set up in the corner for anyone who wants to purchase things, and every fan has been given a Tridents game ball on the way in.

The door opens, and the players walk in: Kai Yamiko, Dan Montgomery, Luis Ortega, Rhett Darlington, and Ronan Sinclair. Five tall, handsome men, decked out in their Tridents jerseys, wide grins on their faces. After all this time, I'm immune to the physical attractiveness of the players. All, that is, except one.

God, he's beautiful. He shaved this morning, his strong jaw smooth and soft looking. His hair is neatly styled, and he's got an easy grin on his face. One thing is clear, Ronan is officially a Trident through and through. He talks and laughs with the other players as if he's been on the team for years, not a matter of weeks. Deep down, I'm happy for him.

"Hello, boys," I say, walking over once I've mastered some control over my initial reaction. Reminded myself of two simple things.

Look, but don't touch. And don't let anyone catch you looking.

"You've all got a couple of pens, but if you run out, there are more throughout the room. I'll be here the entire time and Sheena is live streaming, so best behaviour," I mockingly admonish, knowing these players don't need the reminder. They're all good guys. "The fans are pumped up for this, but please don't spend too long with any one person. Remember, there's only five of you and fifty of them."

"Treat it like speed dating, gentlemen. Two minutes and move on to the next," Kai jokes, earning a laugh from the others and a head shake from me.

"Whatever works, Yami." My gaze darts over to Ronan, just in time to catch him staring at me. He looks away quickly, but it's too late. Just that flash of attention has me burning up inside.

God, this is so much harder than I want it to be. Being close to him, but not being able to touch him or even trust myself to talk to him without other people around. The day we went house hunting was the last time I was alone with him, and a part of me physically aches to be near him. Which, of course, leads to increasing levels of frustration at myself for not having better willpower. I'm stronger than this, for fuck's sake. I'm Willow goddamn Lawson. I don't let men ruin me. Not even sinfully hot ones like Ronan Sinclair.

The doors open and fans come streaming in, thankfully stealing my attention away from my self-flagellation. For the next two hours, I stay locked-in on my job, making sure everything is running smoothly and everyone is happy. This is the last stop on our tour. After this, we get a couple of days off before it's family day at the field for all players and staff, then the season opener right after that.

After the last fan leaves, I start cleaning up while the guys chat among themselves, giving the fans time to clear out before they head to the bus. I'm busy collecting pens from a table in one corner of the room when I sense someone walk up behind me.

"You did great, Willow. This whole thing has been run incredibly well, and I know it's because of you."

Good. Fucking. God. Ronan's deep, rumbly voice complimenting me on my job? Knees. Weak.

"Thanks," I whisper, not daring to turn and face him. My heart is racing, my mouth suddenly dry just from having him near. "You guys did a great job as well. It's easy to run a good media tour when the players behave."

Ronan chuckles. "That explains Maverick's absence."

Against my better judgment, I laugh along with him. I turn around, only to find him right there, leaning against the wall, his hands in the pockets of his jeans. He's so effortlessly sexy, it's impossible not to be drawn to him. "Seems you figured him out quickly," I say, then quickly finish. "He's a good guy, I can tell, but he makes stupid decisions, like in Phoenix."

"He was defending a woman who was being bothered by some drunk idiot. That's never a stupid idea."

My eyes widen at his emphatic response even as my gut clenches at my own painful memories. "No, it's not. But when you're a public figure, you need to handle things differently."

He shifts forward slightly, still leaning against the wall but somehow closer to me. "Trust me, Cherry, if someone was disrespecting you, there's not a chance in hell I'd hold back. I'd do whatever necessary to protect you."

I gulp. What am I meant to say to that? The sound of Lydia's voice from close by has me stepping backward so fast, I knock into a tall table, probably bruising my hip. "Ow."

Ronan moves forward, concern on his face, but I move out of his reach just as Lydia approaches. "There you are. What's taking so long? The hotel staff will do the clean up, Willow, we need to get moving if we want to get back to the city on schedule." The reprimand is clear in her voice, and with a start, I realize the room has emptied of everyone except me and Ronan.

"Sorry. I just need to grab my bag from the conference room." Without a backward glance, I hurry from the room, mentally cursing myself the whole way. Did Lydia see us? It's not like we touched, but we were so close to each other, it had to look suspicious.

Sure enough, she finds me in the conference room.

"What's going on with you and Ronan, Willow?" Lydia stands in the doorway, her arms folded across her chest. "If you really think you're ready to take over for me, then you had better think twice before leading one of the players on. That's not appropriate behaviour for the person in charge of media relations."

I bite my tongue at her chastisement. I didn't lead anyone on, and I already *am* in charge of the department, in every way except title. But she's not done verbally taking me down yet.

"I don't know if you think you're above the rules or just naive. Mike might have a soft spot for you, but his players will always come first. The team always comes first. And if you mess around with one of them, you'll be the one who will suffer the consequences."

My fists clench as I watch her leave. She has no right to come in here and accuse me of being naive. She couldn't be more wrong about that. But she's right about the other thing.

The team comes first.

Which means any feelings I might have about Ronan Sinclair have to stay stuffed in a little box and pushed to the back of my mind, never to be thought of again.

Chapter Eighteen

Ronan

Peyton's hand is clutching mine as we walk out onto the field where the entire team and their families, plus office staff and their families, are all milling around. The air is cold and damp, as is to be expected in the middle of March on the West Coast. It's a different feel to Toronto where there was every chance we might still have snow on the ground even this late in the spring. The stadium has one of those retractable roofs, but it's not raining today, so it's open, letting in the light from the rare late March sunshine.

When Monty told me about the kick off barbecue the team hosts every year, it just solidified my belief that this move was the right one. A team that cares this much about family is where I want to be.

"Daddy, where's Monty?"

I grin as she tugs on my hand. Peyton's already decided the friendly catcher is her favourite player. "He's here somewhere, Rocket. You gonna challenge him to a base race?"

Peyton giggles. "Yeah!"

“You’ll leave him in the dust.” I know the second Peyton spies Monty because she goes to drop my hand, but I don’t let her. “Hang on, kiddo, I’ll come with you.” We head toward him together. It’s not that I don’t trust that Peyton will be fine, but most of these people are strangers to her. I wouldn’t be doing my job if I didn’t keep close. Even if sometimes my little girl is too independent for my old dad heart to handle.

Monty spies us coming and drops down into a crouch, holding his fist out for Peyton. “Hey, kid.”

“Hi, Monty! Imma beat you in a base race,” Peyton announces with all the confidence of a four-year-old who’s been raised around ball players.

“You better make sure I’ve got someone there to record it.” Willow’s voice dances across the field at us. “Assuming Dad is okay with it?” She looks to me briefly, then smiles back down at Peyton.

“That’s fine,” I answer gruffly, feeling off-kilter having her here. She’s wearing a Tridents shirt. No name on the back, though, and a part of me really fucking wants to see her wear my name someday.

Peyton tilts her head up at Willow. “Got any Skittles?” she asks innocently, and now Monty and I are both fighting back a laugh.

“Wh-what?” Willow asks, stifling her own smile. “How do you know about my Skittles?”

“The trainer lady gave me some,” Peyton answers, but she doesn’t stop there. “She said you’d eat ’em all if they’re in your office, so she keeps them. And I got some. That’s okay, right? Ms. Kerry at preschool said sharing is caring.”

Willow's smiling down at my daughter so widely it makes my heart physically ache to see her so enchanted by Peyton. "Of course, it's okay. You're welcome to my Skittles anytime. And as a matter of fact —" she reaches into her back pocket and pulls out two packets "— I always have some with me." Handing one to Peyton, she opens the other and looks inside before picking out the yellow ones and holds them out to Monty. He takes them and tosses them back without a word, but Peyton looks at her like she's crazy.

"Whaddya do that for?" she asks.

Willow shrugs. "I don't like lemon-flavoured candy, so I always give the yellow ones away. Sharing." She winks.

"And we're always happy to take them off her hands," Monty interjects. Just then, Lark walks up with some preppy-looking guy with a bored expression on his face behind her, staring at his phone. If I wasn't looking at him, I might have missed it, but Monty's face grimaces when he sees the guy.

"Hey!" Lark says, giving Willow a hug, then lifts a hand for a high five with Peyton. "Good to see you again. Looks like you found yourself another Skittles fan, Wills."

Peyton looks sagely at Lark. "She doesn't eat the yellow ones."

Lark nods. "Yeah, lucky for us, she gives them away. Let me guess, did he take them?" She thumbs at Monty, and Peyton nods. "He'll eat anything."

"Hey, I have a discerning palate," Monty teases, and Lark shoves him lightly. "What? I do!"

"Cheese pizza and hot dogs is not discerning."

Preppy dude chooses that moment to cut in, tugging on Lark's arm like an impatient toddler. "Babe, I need to take a call. Where can I go for some privacy?" We all turn at the interruption, but he makes no move to introduce himself to anyone or even acknowledge our presence. Wow, the guy's a serious douche.

"Oh, you can use my room." Lark fishes out a key and hands it to him. "But don't take too long, okay?"

He gives her a backward wave, but that's it. When she turns back to us, she's twisting her hands together, an embarrassed flush on her cheeks.

"So, Peyton, is *Moana* your favourite movie?" Willow asks in an obvious move to get the attention off Lark. She flips the brim of Peyton's hat lightly.

"Uh-huh. Maui is the best."

"He sure is." Willow agrees with a nod. "That song? What can I say except you're welcome," she sings lightly. "That song is awesome."

"It's my dad's walk-up song," Peyton shares proudly, and now I'm the one about to blush. Not that it bothers me. I let Peyton choose my song as soon as I knew the trade was happening, and nothing would make her budge from her decision.

I shrug as I take in Lark, Monty, and Willow all trying not to laugh.

Monty takes that moment to clap his hands together. "Now that I've got that song in my head, Peyton, you wanna do that base race?"

"Wait!" Willow waves at a camera guy who's nearby. "Rudy, go stand at second and catch them rounding the bases."

Monty and Peyton jog over to the field, grabbing a couple of extra players and kids along the way. I stay put, happy to watch my kid in her element.

"She's adorable."

Turning slightly, I grin at Willow's quiet observation. "Yeah, she's pretty awesome. I hit the kid jackpot with her. Just don't come near her with a hairbrush unless you've got something to bribe her with."

Willow laughs under her breath as we watch the race unfold. Monty plays it up, pretending to trip a couple of times, doing a cartwheel, while Peyton runs as fast as her little legs can go, easily beating him. The next runners go, but it's obvious the kids are going to win. A loud cheer goes up at the end and Monty's lifting Peyton onto his shoulders. I don't even notice Willow's moved until I see her holding her phone up, capturing some more footage, a warm smile on her face.

She returns to my side and holds up the recording for me to see. "You're good with me posting it on socials?"

I nod. "Yeah, Peyton loves seeing herself on the team pages. Thanks for checking first."

Monty jogs up and deposits Peyton on the ground, both of them giggling. "Good race, kid. I'll beat you next time." With one last fist bump, Monty leaves, Willow moving as if she's also going somewhere else.

"Willow, could we trouble you to take a photo of us?" I ask suddenly, not ready for her to leave yet. She pauses, and I see her visibly swallow.

"Sure," she says with a bright tone. I unlock my phone and hand it over to her, and she stares at my screen for several long seconds. There's nothing to see, just a photo of Peyton as a baby, asleep on my chest. But she tugs her lower lip between her teeth before looking back up and smiling. "Okay. Let's do a nice one, then a silly one. Ready?"

I lift Peyton into my arms, and we both smile at Willow. An easy thing to do, to be honest. All I want to do is smile at her. And see her smile in return. Jesus, that sounds sappy. But I'm learning she's got a lot of different smiles. The coy, flirty one I got on the airplane. The frustrated-but-not-really one in Hawaii every time I'd ask her to dinner and she'd turn me down. The grateful one when I offered my suite. The sexy one when I made her come the first time. The professional one, the only one I don't like seeing pointed my way, and now I've got another to add to the collection. The soft, warm one she gives my daughter.

That one might just be my second favourite. After the sexy orgasm one, of course.

"Alright, you two, go and get some food before it's all gone. I need to check in on some things." Willow hands me my phone, but before she can leave, Peyton flings her arms around her legs. Willow looks to me in surprise before gently wrapping her arms around Peyton as best she can with their height difference.

"Thanks for the Skittles," Peyton says before breaking away and taking my hand. "C'mon, Dad, I'm hungry."

I let her tug me away to where long tables hold platters of food, chancing one glance back over my shoulder, only to see Willow still standing there, eyes on us, and something I really want to believe is longing written all over her face. But the second she sees me looking at her, it's gone and she's whirling around, walking in the opposite direction.

Oh, Cherry. You don't want to admit that you still want me, but I can tell you do...

Chapter Nineteen

Ronan

I'm not normally an emotional guy, but something feels different this year. Like this opening game is the start of something bigger than just another season. Even the national anthem has me choked up a little as I head over to my position at first base.

The lights in the stadium are on with the roof closed to protect the field from the rain. The bright green of the turf settles me. Feels like home, in a way.

The rest of my teammates take their places, and as much as I should be focused on the game, I can't help but wonder where Willow is watching the game. Will I see her today? Do I even want to? Fuck knows, the woman is a distraction. Then again, maybe she's a motivation. Because the thought of her watching when I'm on the field has my muscles burning with anticipation.

Monty settles into position behind home plate as Kai takes the mound. His first pitch is a fastball, right down the center of the plate, and the other team's first batter doesn't take a swing. Dumbass, that was a perfect pitch. The ump calls strike one. My eyes are glued to Kai's arm. He leans back and throws another fastball, but the player's learned his lesson and swings, the bat connecting with a loud crack. I follow the arc of the ball straight out to left field where Darling's waiting to pluck the fly out of the air.

The next player steps up to bat, and Kai knocks him out with just three pitches. My pulse is pounding with excitement. This is the way I love to start a game, making it clear to our opponents that we're not here to mess around.

The rest of the inning is a lot tighter than the start. Kai's on fire, but so are our opponents. The inning closes with them scoring two runs, meaning the pressure is on.

Before I know it, I'm walking up to the plate. There's one out, and Mav's on second base. Exhaling slowly, I shut out all the noise of the crowd, narrowing my focus on to the man standing sixty feet and six inches in front of me. He lifts his arm, and I load my swing. He lets the ball fly and muscle memory, instinct, and over twenty years of practice kicks in, letting me judge the pitch and make a call. I swing.

CRACK.

The ball flies into left field and I'm off and running. I can only hope I hit it far enough for Mav to score; all my focus is on getting to the bag. When I'm safe at first, I look to home, where Mav's walking off with my first RBI of the season.

Coach comes up to take my batting gloves and shin guard. "Nice hit, Sin. Solid start. Keep your eyes forward, be ready to hit the dirt. See if you can follow that RBI up with a run of your own."

I nod to show I heard him. Taking a small lead off, I'm laser focused on the pitcher. As soon as the ball hits the ground, I'm off to second base.

Minutes later, I'm racing for home after Darling smacks the ball to the outfield. The crowd is a roar, and my grin couldn't be any wider. Nothing to complain about, getting an RBI and a run in my first game with my new team.

There's no better feeling. Glancing up to the seats where Mom and Peyton are watching, I raise my hand in a wave as I head to the dugout. The guys slap my back, I take the sports drink offered to me, and pull off my helmet.

Did Willow see that? God, I sound like a fucking kid, wondering if my crush watched me hit the damn ball. Giving my head a shake, I finish the drink and toss the cup in the garbage.

"Fucking 'eh, what a start!" Monty walks over and sits beside me, half his gear on, ready for the next inning.

"Damn right," I agree as my breathing slows to normal. The crowd is in an uproar again as Darling rounds home, but the outfielder throws a rocket to the catcher, and it's gonna be close. We're all holding our breath, waiting for the call.

"Safe!"

"Fuck, yeah!" We explode. Three runs in one inning is a fantastic start, and we're not out yet.

When the game ends, the board is lit up with a more than respectable 8-5 win for the Tridents. Now, that's how to start a season.

The locker room is loud with boisterous energy. I'm quick through the shower, eager to find Mom and Peyton. Game nights are late ones for my girl, and normally Mom would take her straight home, but with tonight being the opener, I wanted to head home with them so I could be there to tuck her in.

"Heads-up, boys, I'm coming in." Willow's voice rings out above the noise and my hands freeze on the knot of the towel wrapped around my hips. The towel I was about to drop so I could get dressed.

I find her instantly, as if there's a homing beacon attached to her that has a direct line back to me. A sharp black blazer covers her Tridents shirt, her hair is twisted up in a ponytail, and she looks fierce. In charge and so damn proud as she smiles at all of us. It's clear it's not her first time in a locker room, seeing as she doesn't flinch at the various states of undress, and a weird wave of jealousy washes over me at that realization.

"Okay, we've got a handful of local reporters waiting to come in, so hide your bits, no flashing the public." Willow winks as she continues to talk. God, she's beautiful, a vibrant energy flowing from her. Her passion for the team and for her work is evident all over her face and in her words. "Give them a few sound bites and you're free to go."

Willow turns, I assume to leave, and as much as I wish I could speak to her, I get why that's not a good idea.

"Good game, Ronan."

I glance up, boxers in hand, and she's standing right in front of me. Gaze darting everywhere except at me. *Look at me Willow, just once.*

"Thanks," I say quietly as her eyes finally land on me. And quickly travel down to my bare chest. My lips quirk up in a grin that I immediately wipe off when she glances back to my face.

Her tongue peeks out to moisten her lips and *fuck*, keeping my hands off her is hard when I'm riding the adrenaline high of a win. And it's not the only thing that's hard. As soon as I feel things happening under my towel, my jaw clenches and I start reciting stats in my head. As if she's got some sort of radar tuned in to my dick, Willow's gaze drops to where my towel is starting to tent. Her eyes bounce back up to meet my smirk, and the pink on her cheeks is really fucking cute.

"S-sorry. I better go," she stutters, and if I were a betting man, I'd wager her panties are damp. That thought has things under the towel threatening to become a hell of a lot more obvious, which isn't what I need in front of the team.

"Sure," I say casually, turning around to face my locker, giving her my back as I speak. "I gotta go find Peyton and my mom anyway."

I wait a beat to see if she'll reply, but she doesn't. When I glance back over my shoulder, she's gone. And I feel her absence like an ache in my goddamn chest.

I dress quickly, and when I leave the locker room, Mom is standing in the hallway, a sleepy Peyton in her arms. I take my little girl and we start to walk toward the door that leads to the section of parking reserved for players and their families.

"Hey, Rocket," I say softly when Peyton lifts her head. "Did you have a good night?"

"Mm-hmm," is her quiet mumble of a reply. "I ate a hotdog."

My chest vibrates with my chuckle. "Did you see me waving?"

"Yup."

A wide yawn overtakes her little face as her arms tighten around my neck. We reach my SUV, Mom opens the back door, and I swiftly buckle Peyton in before grabbing the blanket and stuffed duck that lay beside her car seat, tucking them around her. I kiss her forehead, then gently close her door.

"You were wonderful tonight, honey," Mom says, and I finally pull her in for a grateful hug. She never missed a game when I was a kid, always my loudest cheerleader.

"Thanks," I reply gruffly, suddenly choked with emotion. It's been the two of us for so long, with Dad leaving when I was a teenager. She's the one person I've always been able to count on. Forever on my side, reminding me I can do it, even when it feels impossible. Whether it was playing ball, or raising a daughter on my own, Mom is my inspiration and my motivation. If I'm half the parent she is, I'll be happy.

But her prioritizing me and my demanding sports schedule is what broke up their marriage. By choosing to support me once it became apparent my talent on the field could actually amount to a career, Mom doomed her marriage to fail.

At least, that's what I overheard Dad say the night he left. He didn't understand why my future was more important to her than he was.

I resented him for so long. Filled with anger at the man who should have been there with Mom, who should have been playing catch with me in the backyard and taking me to buy a new glove when I outgrew mine. But time, and life, gave me a different perspective.

Mom made a choice. She chose me. And as I look in the rearview mirror at Peyton slumbering peacefully in the backseat, I know without a doubt that I would make the same damn choice every time.

I will always choose my daughter over a woman who can't understand and accept the pressures of my life, even if it means I'm alone forever.

But knowing that to be true, deep down in my soul, it still doesn't shut up the little voice in the back of my head that keeps whispering one thing.

Willow would understand...

Chapter Twenty

Willow

Bringing the team to the Vancouver Children's Hospital to visit with the kids is always a highlight event. Seeing the faces of all those children absolutely light up when the players and our mascot come walking into the room is the most soul-filling thing ever. We always plan one for right after the season begins, so the players are full of energy and excitement.

And the guys love it. It might be surprising to some, but baseball players really are just overgrown kids, playing their favourite backyard game from childhood on a much bigger scale. Which makes them the perfect candidates to get down on the floor and play with actual children.

Today is no exception. Kai, Monty, Darling, Ronan, and a few others are scattered throughout the giant, colourful playroom, the one we take over for this event each year, with a group of kids clustered around them. The energy is high, with lots of laughter in the air, and more than a few parents stand on the outskirts with happy tears in their eyes.

"Another successful day?" I turn to face Sadie LeDuc, the head of fundraising for the hospital's foundation. We connected a couple of years ago when she approached the Tridents for silent auction donations, and now she makes a point of stopping by any time the team visits. We've gone for drinks a few times, and even though she's a lot quieter and more conservative than I am, I like her.

"You know it," I reply, my gaze roaming over the room. Sadie shifts next to me, her gold-rimmed glasses falling down her nose slightly. Her red hair is pulled back tightly in a bun, and her black turtleneck sweater is tucked into high-waisted pants that look like she actually ironed the crease into the front of them.

"Want to grab a drink tonight?" I ask. I'd planned on inviting Lark out as well, since I'm craving some girl time. And with Tori not living locally anymore, I'm trying to do better at strengthening the other friendships I have in the city.

Sadie nods and gives me a quick smile. "That would be lovely, I'll check that Dirk and I don't have any plans. Can I text you?"

God, that boyfriend of hers. The couple of times I've met him, I've instantly wanted to shower afterward. He's just one of those guys that is equal parts smarmy and stick-in-the-mud. For all that Sadie's got this whole good girl thing going on, she deserves better than a boring, buttoned-up guy like him.

Then again, who am I to comment or make judgments on other people's relationships when I'm busy spending all of my time avoiding the only man to ever make me want something more.

"Sounds good." I touch her hand briefly. "I better get back to work. We'll catch up tonight."

After Sadie leaves, I make my rounds with the parents, making sure we have media releases signed where necessary, ensuring they know they can step out and get some refreshments from the table we have set up next door, and they've got their swag packs that include open-ended ticket offers for the current season. Other than those tasks, I get to spend my time chatting with anyone who seems like they could use some adult conversation that doesn't revolve around their child's hospitalization.

But throughout it all, my attention keeps wandering over to one tall, handsome man currently sitting on a small sofa with a video game controller in his hands. Kids are pressed in on either side of him, cheering on both him and the little girl who's racing him in Mario Kart. Ronan's got a wide grin on his face and is so relaxed among the kids. Makes sense, seeing as he has one of his own, but I had wondered if it would be hard for him, seeing sick kids and maybe imagining Peyton in their place.

The very thought makes me shudder involuntarily. Picturing that sweet girl in a hospital bed with tubes attached the way some of these little warriors have makes my heart hurt. I can't imagine the strength it takes for these parents — let alone the kids — to face this day in and day out.

As if he knows I'm thinking about him, Ronan lifts his head, his eyes finding me instantly. A small smile tugs at his lips and I feel my own turning up in return.

"He's a handsome one," the mom standing next to me remarks quietly. We'd just been talking about her teenage son who recently underwent a leg amputation because of an aggressive form of cancer. I should have been paying attention to her, not smiling at Ronan.

"Sorry?" I say, trying to pretend I don't know exactly who she's talking about.

But her shoulder softly nudges mine as she gives me a look that is a little too observant. "The new player that's sitting over on the couch. The one who can't stop looking at you. Lucky lady." Her smile is nothing but kind and friendly, but I suddenly feel a little too warm.

"Oh, that's not... He's not... I mean..."

Shit. Why am I so flustered, and in front of a stranger, no less? This is bad. I give myself a mental shake before turning slightly so I'm no longer facing Ronan. "There's nothing to see there. Can I get you a refill on that coffee?" I gesture to the mug in her hands.

She just shakes her head, still with that knowing look. "I'm good, thank you. And thanks again for organizing this. It means so much to the kids, and I know Bobby is looking forward to coming to a game once he's out of here. He loved playing baseball before..." Her voice trails off as her eyes start to brim with tears.

Her pain is palpable, and I hate that I can't do more to take it away. Fucking cancer. Hearing someone call my name from the hallway, I give her a small smile, pull out my business card, and covertly pass it to her. "Give me a call when you pick your date, and we'll arrange for Bobby to throw out the first pitch. Baseball doesn't have to be gone from his life forever."

She throws her arms around me for a quick hug, and when we break apart, her eyes are still shining wet, but there's gratitude in among the grief.

"Thank you."

Giving her a quick nod, I hurry out into the hall. The instant I'm not in the same room as Ronan, I can breathe a little easier.

But the issue in the hall proves to be inconsequential, Sheena simply needing me to figure out a network setup so she can post to our social media. Which means, minutes later, I'm back in the room. Ronan's no longer on the couch; now he's leaning over an air hockey table with his back to me. Meaning that ass, covered in denim, is pointing straight at me.

I have to bite my lip to hold back a whimper. Good freaking God, this is getting ridiculous. Why can't I move on? Why can't I just accept that while he might very well be the hottest man on the entire planet, he's not someone I can ever be with.

My eyes close for just a second as I lean against the wall, fighting to hold on to my control, my rules, my self-preservation. I haven't made it this far in my life and in my career to throw it all away simply because I fell for a handsome man.

Except, even as I think that to myself, guilt swirls inside of me. Because I know Ronan is so much more than just a pretty face. If he wasn't, I wouldn't be so twisted up inside with wanting to be with him.

"Did that wall do something to hurt you, or is your scowl directed at someone else?"

My eyes fly open at the sound of his voice coming from much closer to me than I thought he was. "I'm not scowling."

His bemused smirk tells me otherwise.

"You shouldn't be here talking to me," I hiss under my breath, folding my arms over my chest. "You're meant to be socializing with the kids."

"I have been," he says, far too calmly for my liking. "And I was just on my way to grab a cup of water when I saw you looking like Eeyore, and I wanted to make sure you're okay."

I can already feel my resolve softening. *Nope. Can't.* Straightening up, I push away from the wall. "I'm fine." As I move to walk away, his hand catches the inside of my elbow in a light hold.

"Are you? Because I'm not."

I glance down at his hand, and as soon as he drops it from my arm, I look up at him, with what I hope is cool detachment and not the desperate yearning I actually feel.

"You need to figure that out for yourself, Sinclair. Because these little moments you keep trying to have with me have to stop."

His jaw clenches for a second, then relaxes. I hate the flash of sadness I see cross his face, hating even more that I'm the cause of it. But the resolve in his voice when he speaks belies any sorrow.

"Eventually, you're going to have to face the reality that whatever this is between us isn't going to just disappear because you want to ignore it. You can push me away, but that doesn't erase anything. It's still here. I'm still here."

I turn my face up to him, ready to deny what he's saying even though it would be a bald-faced lie, but before I can get a word out, someone calls his name from across the room. He looks over and lifts his hand in a wave of acknowledgment before looking back at me. And before he walks away, he leaves with a parting shot straight to my heart.

"I'm here, Cherry. And my feelings aren't going anywhere."

Chapter Twenty-One

Willow

Trying not to obsess about Ronan Sinclair has me exhausted.

Why does the man have to be so freaking perfect in almost every single way? He's respectful, kind, humble, talented, and so goddamn sexy it makes me shiver every time I see him. My uncle adores him. He's the kind of dad every little girl deserves. He loves baseball, possibly even more than I do.

But I can't date a player.

The number of times I've had to remind myself of that fact has grown exponentially over the last few months. It's like having your favourite, most delicious food laid out in front of you and then being told you can't touch it, can't have even one single taste. The longer you sit there, staring at the perfect feast, the more desperate you become to have it. The more willing you are to risk everything.

Ever since the hospital charity event, I've felt my defenses starting to crumble. The temptation to give in to what I know he wants is growing. He wants me. *And godfuckingdamn it, I want him, too.* But I won't be another woman whose accomplishments are ignored just because of her relationship status. I have always refused to ever be known as Willow Lawson, so-and-so's girlfriend, just like I have always refused to be known as Willow Lawson, the owner's niece.

But Ronan is proving to be harder to resist than anyone else in my life ever has been. He's under my skin, in my head, and he's cracking the walls around my heart.

However, it seems that freaking annoying thing called fate that Ronan insisted was at play in Hawaii is up to something, yet again. The team is playing a home game later tonight, so who do I run into at a park halfway between Ronan's house and my apartment when I'm out for a jog?

The Tridents' new first baseman himself. And his adorable daughter.

I come to a stop, placing my hands on my hips as I try to slow my breathing down to normal. The air is cold as I suck in a breath, and now that I'm not moving, I take the windbreaker off from around my waist and put it back on, zipping it up for some added protection.

Ronan is pushing Peyton on the swings, and I can hear her high-pitched laughter even from the other side of the grassy area. There's no one else here, just a gorgeous man and his gorgeous daughter...and me. The weirdo who can't stop thinking about him.

Peyton spies me first, and I see her twist to say something to her dad before pointing at me. Ronan grabs the swing and pulls it to a stop so she can jump off, and the next thing I know, a miniature version of Ronan only with darker hair is running toward me.

"Finish line!" she yells, her arms open wide, and I look at Ronan in confusion. He crouches down and opens his arms, and I instantly mimic the position. Just in time, thank God, as Peyton barrels into me, wrapping her arms around me, almost knocking me over.

"Hi, Willow, got any Skittles?" she asks as she bounces back out of the impromptu hug as Ronan comes jogging up.

"Pey, it's nine in the morning, you don't need Skittles."

I bite my lips together to keep from laughing at the fond, yet exasperated, tone in his voice. He looks to me with an apologetic expression.

"She's been up since six," he says with a grimace that Peyton misses, thanks to our height differences. "Figured some morning park time would be a good idea, so maybe there's a *n-a-p* later."

"I know what that spells, Daddy." Peyton pokes him in the thigh, and this time, I don't succeed in fully concealing my snort of laughter.

"Oh, yeah? If you're so smart, then you're smart enough to know that a tired dad is not a fun dad. That nap isn't just for you, missy." The teasing growl to his voice is adorable, but also an uncomfortable reminder of how that growly voice sounds in bed.

Awkward.

"Can we play Maui and Moana now? Willow could be Heihei!"

"Willow's not a chicken." Ronan chuckles as he lifts his cap off his head and spins it around backward.

Goddamn it, why is that seriously the hottest thing a guy can do? Well, top ten, at least.

His gaze darts over to me. "And I don't think she wants to play —"

"Excuse me, but that chicken is the best character in the entire movie," I interject, my hands on my hips. Peyton gives me a toothy grin, and I know that my Disney movie expertise has just won me some points in her mind. "The comedic sidekick is crucial to any good story. How do we play?"

Peyton's eyes light up. As she starts to babble on about how to play her make-believe game, I chance a quick look over at Ronan. To my surprise, he's not watching his daughter, he's watching me, and there's an indescribable expression on his face. A mix of awe, gratitude, and desire. With something else that I can't put my finger on.

Thankfully, Peyton's game seems like a mix of tag and pretend, making it easy to play along, even though I didn't pay close attention to her instructions. For the next short while, we run around the field and playground, my pride taking a beating as I *bawk* like a chicken and flap my arms. However, Peyton's laughter makes it all worth it.

But when my watch vibrates with a text from Uncle Mike, it sobers me instantly. "Hey, sorry, P, but I gotta get going," I call out, slightly breathless from running around. Four-year-olds should be personal trainers with how high their energy is. Who needs sprints when you can just chase a kid up, down, and all over a playground.

Peyton dashes over and hugs my legs. "Thanks for playin' with us." She looks at Ronan, who's come up beside us. "Can I go on the slides?"

He just nods, and she's off without a backward glance. Fearless and confident in her father's love. As she rushes off to the play structure, Ronan's eyes don't leave her until she's climbing up the steps to the slide. All of a sudden, I feel him shift closer to me, his warm, spicy aroma floating over to tantalize my senses. And then I can't help but suck in a gasp when his fingers brush against mine, one latching onto my pinkie. My pulse races at the unexpected contact. So small, yet, I feel it throughout my entire body.

"Thank you for playing with her like that. The move hasn't been easy; she's missing her friends and her old preschool teachers." The quiet pain in his words makes my heart ache for the man who's clearly desperate to do right by his daughter.

"She'll be okay," I say lamely. Even though I can't know that for sure. I don't remember what it's like to be uprooted from everything you know, having been less than two years old when my mom abandoned me. I was lucky enough to be adopted quickly, and my mind has simply wiped most of those two years from my memory completely. All I remember is love and stability, courtesy of my adopted dad.

He never dated, there was never a parade of men in and out of the house. I knew about his sexuality as soon as I was old enough to understand. For a while, I fantasized about him and Uncle Mike being in love and me having two dads, but it didn't take long to realize that while their preferences swung the same way, all that was between them was a deep-seated friendship. Deeper and stronger than love or blood.

I never got the chance to ask Dad why he didn't date, I guess I was too scared to hear the answer. The last thing I ever would have wanted would be for him to stay alone for my sake. But that's the kind of dad he was, always putting me first.

It's the kind of dad Ronan is, too. And the thought of him being alone until Peyton's an adult makes my heart twist even further in my chest. He's a man with a lot to give, and he deserves to be happy. Even if I don't think I can be the one to give him that.

His finger gently slides up and down mine in a soft caress that draws me back to this moment, this slight physical connection with a man who means far more to me than he should.

"It's really fucking hard to keep my distance from you," he whispers, still looking straight ahead at his daughter, who's now squealing as she goes down the spiral slide. "You've got your walls up, and I really want to know why. But if you can't tell me, then can you at least tell me I'm not the only one suffering? Tell me it's hard for you on the other side of that wall, too." The desperation in his voice is paired with so much wistfulness, so much longing. It takes everything I have not to turn and throw myself into his arms and go back to the blissful few hours when the only thing that mattered was each other.

But I manage to take the smallest of steps to the side, losing the link between our pinkie fingers.

"I can't do that, Ronan." I force the words out past my lips, even though they feel like a lie, despite being the cold, hard truth. “Those walls you talk about are there for a reason, and I can’t just take them down.”

“Can’t or don’t want to?” he asks, and there’s no accusation in his tone, no anger, just a sad acceptance that somehow hurts even more.

“Does it matter?”

“Yes. To me, it does.”

I turn to face him. “It wouldn’t change anything. I still can’t be with you.” Taking a step back and then another, I put space between us. Even though I really wish I didn’t have to. “Say goodbye to Peyton for me. And good luck at the game tonight.”

Then I turn and run.

Chapter Twenty-Two

Ronan

Games that are easy wins are nice and all, a good boost to the ego and team morale, but there's something to be said for a hard-fought battle. One that comes down to the last inning, bases loaded, score tied, and it all rests on one more hit.

Those are the games I love. Those are the wins that fill me with more pride and determination to come back stronger every time.

Today was one of those games. It's fucking cold and damp out here, even with the roof protecting us from the worst of the rain that is so typical for a West Coast spring. Kai pitched the first half, and for a while, it looked like we'd maintain a lead. Then the other team came from behind with two out of the park home runs and some solid double and triple plays. The second half, we were neck and neck, each team coming out to the plate strong and every player in the field on top of the ball.

But the Tridents came out on top, eking out a one-point win.

Coach calls me over as we head off the field. "You're on media duty, Sin." He points to the side, where a reporter and cameraman from a local news station are already busy talking to Rhett.

I look around for Willow but don't see her at first. Then some guy in a suit steps to the side and there she is, talking with one of our cameramen — Rudy, I think is his name. She's gesturing to the dugout, and he takes off at a jog. I should be focused on getting to my own interview, but I can't drag my eyes away from her. In grey wide-legged pants and a Tridents teal blouse with her hair in a high ponytail, she's effortlessly beautiful. Put together, in charge, and all professional.

Her head turns, and our gazes meet. But there's nothing. Not even a flash of recognition or any emotion whatsoever. Just the same as it was at the game on Saturday after we saw each other at the park.

I don't know what I was expecting, but it wasn't this. There are professional boundaries, and then there's cold shoulders. And right now? I feel chilly. And not just from the weather.

"Careful with Maxine, she's a shark. Loves to get deep into your personal life, even if she only has a few seconds for a sound bite." Rhett leans in close as he walks past me, coming from the very reporter I'm on my way over to.

"Thanks, man," I mutter as I make my way over to them. I watch the woman with the microphone in hand plaster on a news-worthy smile as I approach and the camera light turns on.

"Ronan Sinclair, thanks for coming over. Maxine Parker, City News. You're new to Vancouver, new to the Tridents. How do you think things are going so far for you?"

Okay, that's an easier question than I was expecting, given Darling's warning.

"Just great, Maxine, thanks. Vancouver has been very welcoming, and the team is strong. I'm very happy to be here."

She gives a brusque nod before tilting the microphone back toward herself. "And your family? Have they been happy with the relocation?"

What the hell that has to do with the game we just played, I don't know, but I guess Rhett warned me. I've always been circumspect with how much I reveal about my family, and I'm not about to cave under pressure from one reporter.

"They're settling in just fine. Proud to wear Tridents colours."

Maxine nods, and it's as if I can see the wheels turning in her head as she tries to pivot. Jesus, is she a sports reporter or a tabloid reporter?

"It must be tough to have such a demanding career, as well as being a single dad. How do you balance it all and still find time for yourself? For love, perhaps? The women of Vancouver are very excited to have a hot new bachelor in town, I'm sure."

Oh, for fuck's sake. My jaw grinds together as I try to remember every bit of media training Gage has forced down my throat ever since Peyton was born. It's not the first time my dating life has come up in an interview, but not normally on the field when most self-respecting reporters want to talk about the game.

"It's not easy for any parent to juggle a career and their family, but I've got a good support system."

Maxine opens her mouth, probably ready to spew more garbage questions, but I'm saved by an angel.

"Maxine, our players need to get ready for the postgame debrief. I trust you got the sound bites you wanted?" Willow's voice is brittle as she comes to stand beside me, arms folded across her chest, her eyes full of annoyed fire, all directed at the reporter.

"Yes, thanks, Willow. We're done here," Maxine simpers, shooting daggers right back at Willow, making it clear there's no love lost between the two. She and her cameraman turn and walk away to the gate that lets them out of the field.

"Sorry. I should have warned you about her."

I turn to face Willow, but she's not looking at me. Her body position screams *back off*, with her arms still folded across her chest. "It's okay, Darling let me know she tries to dig up personal stuff. I was ready."

Finally, she looks up at me, but her expression is still guarded. "I guess it's not the first time you've been asked about your personal life."

I shrug. "Nope, but it's not as bad as when the news first broke about Peyton. I keep her out of it as much as possible. Control when and where she ends up in the public eye."

"Well, I'll be sure to follow up with Maxine's boss about off-limits questions. She's a pain in our asses, always trying to be more salacious than sports. Thankfully, City News doesn't send her out often. Their other sports guy is far more professional. I think Maxine thinks she's in lifestyle, not sports."

I chuckle because that's exactly what I was thinking. "Does she even like baseball?"

Willow is fighting back a smile, and I fucking love it. The *back off* vibes are lessening, and she even drops her arms. Granted, only to hold her phone in front of her, but it's a step in the right direction. She might not want to admit there's something between us, but there is. And subconsciously, she can't deny it forever.

"I wanted to thank you again for Saturday," I say, keeping my voice low so no one else around us hears. "Peyton had a lot of fun with you. And I'm sorry if I crossed a line."

Her eyes flutter closed for a second, and when they open again, she's looking at me with a vulnerable expression. "You didn't. I'm sorry I took off so fast. I had fun, too. But..." she trails off.

I give her a quick nod. "I know. But I want you to know this conversation isn't over. This isn't the right time or place, but I do want to finish what we were talking about the other day." My heart is pounding. Am I pushing too hard again?

Fuck, I don't care. I need her to know I'm not giving up so easily.

"Soon, Cherry. Soon, we're gonna talk. And I swear to you, I'll listen. But only if you do, too. Because this —" I subtly gesture between the two of us "— isn't something you just ignore."

Her eyes flare wide with something I really want to believe is desire, or at the very least, agreement. Just then someone calls her name, and the moment is broken.

"I...I have to go," she says quietly but firmly. "We'll talk later."

She walks away, but with those three words, I feel something surge to life inside of me.

Hope.

A couple of hours after the game and that goddamn interview, Peyton's in bed, fast asleep, and I'm on the couch with a beer. The TV is on in the background, sports highlights playing, but I'm not paying attention to it. Instead, I can't stop thinking about Willow.

I've never been so mixed up about a woman. What we had that night in Hawaii was fucking fantastic. Best sex of my goddamn life. She can be so easy to be around, natural, like breathing. But then she throws up those walls so fucking high, I can't see a way over them.

But I want to. She could be it for me, I know it, even as it feels crazy to admit to myself. What other woman would understand the pressures of my life, love the game that means so much to me, and be so amazing with my daughter?

She says we can't do this, but I need to know why. Because for the life of me, I can't stop thinking that we could. And we should.

Standing up, I walk out to my backyard and knock on the door of the guest house. Mom's got lights on, so I know she's home and awake.

"Hi honey, everything okay?" she asks when she opens the door, concern written on her face. I get it, normally I wouldn't bother her when I'm home unless it was an emergency.

"Yeah, everything's fine, but would you mind coming to the main house for a few hours? I just got a text that some of the guys are getting together at one of their houses to watch some game footage. I figure it would be good to keep building relationships with them." The lie rolls off my tongue far too easily, and I inwardly wince. But I've got to do this. I can't keep going, wondering if I'm crazy, imagining the want in Willow's eyes, the longing that matches my own.

"No problem, I'll be right over." Mom's smile and easy answer doesn't ease my guilt. She's never hesitated to help anytime I've asked. Granted, this is the first time I've asked her to babysit so I could go see a woman. Normally, I'd keep these sorts of things to away games, one night with a random woman I don't have to see again. And even that was infrequent.

But twenty minutes later, I'm cruising down the street to Willow's apartment building. It's started to rain outside, but even the rhythmic sound of my windshield wipers can't dull my anticipation or my nerves. When I pull into a visitor parking stall, I open my text messages and my thumb hovers as I try to figure out what to say. How to get her to agree to see me.

In the end, I opt for being direct. Getting out of my car, I walk up to the front door and send her a text.

RONAN: I'm outside. Will you let me in so we can talk?

The text bubbles pop up immediately, which I hope is a good sign. But it takes forever before a reply shows up.

WILLOW: Buzzer 4052, Unit 414

Moments later, the elevator opens and I find her apartment. My hand raps on the door, three firm knocks, and when it opens, she's there.

Wearing sleep shorts and a tank top, her hair is cascading over her shoulders. Her face is clear of makeup, but her expression is back to being guarded, and it physically hurts not to reach out and cup her face, to smooth away the worry with my thumb and my lips.

"Thanks for letting me up," I murmur, earning the briefest of nods, yet she doesn't move to let me in. The hallway is deserted, but this isn't exactly where I want to be having this conversation. I'm not about to be picky. I know I've already pushed her out of her comfort zone just by coming over and insisting we talk. If things go well, she might invite me in. If they don't, then I guess I'll be riding that elevator back down to my car a lot sooner than I want to. I study her for a minute, because even though I thought about what to say the entire drive here, I can't decide how to start.

But as soon as I open my mouth, it just comes pouring out.

"You keep saying you can't date me. That we can't be together. And I hear you; I've respected that as best I can, even though it's fucking torture being near you and not having you. Here's the thing, Cherry. I want, no I need, to know if it's a *can't* or a *don't want to*." I chance a step closer, but still keep enough distance so she doesn't feel crowded. "When I asked you that at the park, I told you it mattered, and here's why. I think you've been told you *can't* date someone like me. I think something or someone convinced you that being with a baseball player is somehow the worst possible idea. And I want to figure out who or what did that, so then I can figure out how to convince you that you're wrong. But only if you say it's a *can't*, and not a *don't want to*."

She visibly swallows as her luminous eyes lift to meet mine. Taking one more step, I slowly raise my hand to rest it on her hip, waiting to see if she'll pull back. She doesn't; if anything, she leans into my touch. Following the cues of her body, I lower my head and run my nose up the column of her neck. When I feel her shiver underneath my hand, my lips crease into a small smile. She might not be able to find the words to say she wants this, but her responses tell me clear enough.

"If it's truly a *don't want to*, then I'll walk away right now and you'll never have to feel my hands on you again." Taking a risk, I drop a kiss to her soft skin, relishing the gasp I hear from her. "You'll never have to feel my kiss again."

Her pulse jumps under my lips, and I kiss her a second time. Then, even though it pains me to do so, I lift my head and step back, the only contact remaining between us being my hand on her hip.

Your move, Cherry.

Her eyes flutter open, and the heat in them is obvious. But so is the hesitation. I drop my hand and take another step back.

"Wait —" She reaches for my hand, chewing on her lower lip.

"I don't want to force you into anything you're not ready for," I say, my voice gravelly. "You know where I stand. When you're ready to tell me what's in that beautiful head of yours, I'll be here."

"It's not that I don't want you," she whispers, tugging me closer. "If anything, it's because I want you *too much.* It scares me how much I want you."

Thank fuck. I can work with that. Placing my hands back on her hips, I step in close. "Don't be scared. We're in this together. You jump, I jump."

A short burst of laughter escapes her, and I know the cheesy line was exactly what was needed.

"Did you just quote *Titanic*?"

I smirk. "Did it work?"

Her answering smile is blinding as she loops her arms around my neck, nodding.

Then, finally, after months of agony from being close to her, and even longer since I last kissed her, I feel her lips on mine again.

Chapter Twenty-Three

Willow

We fall into my apartment, a whirlwind of clothes flying everywhere. Ronan has me spun around and pushed up against my door that he somehow managed to close, my leg around his waist before I regain some of my senses.

"Stop," I gasp, pushing at his chest. He immediately complies, still holding me, his chest heaving, but giving me space to breathe. That restraint, thin as it may be, given how I can sense him vibrating with need, is really freaking sexy. "What does this mean?"

"It means we're finally admitting how much we want each other and that staying away was fucking awful."

Tension lines Ronan's body, and I know he's waiting for me to move. All I can do is sag back into his arms. Thank God that's enough. He kisses me again, and I meet him, frantic stroke for frantic stroke. If I'm going to risk everything, I'm damn well going to make it worth it.

But part of me still can't fully let go. Even when his lips wrap around my breast, sucking hard, I can only feel the heat building, but from a distance. Like I'm an observer, not a participant.

An observer who's still thinking about what the outcome of our choices tonight might be.

I try to give my head a mental shake. Stop worrying about the what-ifs and focus on the very hot, very determined man in front of me. Maybe a location change will help. Running my fingers through his hair, I move away from the wall and lead him to my bedroom.

But I apparently underestimated his ability to read me.

Ronan tugs me to a stop just inside my bedroom. "What's going on in that beautiful head of yours, Cherry? Do you want to stop?"

"No." I shake my head emphatically. "Of course not. I'm sorry, I'm just... Whatever. Nope, we're good. Continue." I wave my hand in the air with what I hope is my game face.

Yeah, that didn't work.

"Willow."

"Ronan." I fold my arms across my chest, the movement feeling kind of stupid since we're both almost naked.

His hands run up and down my upper arms before pausing on my shoulders. "Talk to me."

The very fact that he can ignore the monster erection tenting his boxers, all to talk me through my overthinking freak-out, is the biggest green flag of all time. Yet, I still can't get out of my head. Knowing he might decide I'm not worth the trouble, I decide to let him into the jumbled mess of my brain right now.

"I don't know what's wrong. I'm sorry," I whisper, and it's no lie. Do I want to fuck him? Hell yes, I do. But can I relax and enjoy it? For some reason, no. Not right now. This isn't like me, not at all. I'm not indecisive about sex, I don't hold back. Then again, I quite honestly can't think of a time when there's been anything more than sex on the table. And with Ronan, there's no way I can deny the possibility of both of us wanting *more*.

"I don't want to be seen as the girl who's fucking a player on her team. That never ends well, especially not for women who work in professional sports. This could change everything for me, and not in a good way."

To my surprise, Ronan leads me to the bed, sits down on the edge, and pulls me into his lap. I'm seated sideways as he tucks me against his shoulder, his chin on my head, his hands comfortingly stroking my bare skin. There's nothing sexual about his actions, other than the hard cock I can feel underneath me. But it's clear, he's focused on comfort, not arousal.

"I won't pretend to know where you're coming from because I can't possibly imagine what that feels like. But I swear to you, I will do everything I can to never put your job in danger due to us being together. I respect you. Hell, everyone on the Tridents respects you. And if you're worried that would change somehow, then I understand."

He's putting me fully in control of what happens. Whether that's everything or nothing at all.

"Can we keep it just between us for now? Not tell anyone, I mean?"

His beautiful blue eyes study me for a second before he nods. "Yeah. If that's what you need to feel safe, then that's what we do."

It's as if he instinctively knows that control is what I need to settle my thoughts. And that realization alone is enough to snap me out my overthinking spiral of doom. I seize that control and take full advantage. Maneuvering myself so I'm straddling his thick thighs, I rake my fingers through his hair and cup the back of his head.

"You're going to be one hell of a catch for some lucky woman one day." Something flashes over his face, too fast for me to register. "But right now, I want to be the one getting lucky."

It takes a second, one that feels like it stretches on too long, but then finally his handsome face breaks into a wicked grin. "There's my good girl."

Oof. Nope, not going to think about how my thighs want to clench hearing him say that.

"You like that? Being called a good girl?"

God, am I that obvious? Biting my lip, I nod. His grin grows wider. "Noted." Suddenly, I'm airborne as Ronan stands up, spinning us around before lowering me down to the bed on my back. "Now. Back to the whole naked plan."

My bra is unfastened and thrown over his shoulder one second, my panties pulled down my legs the next. When I take in the look of pure wonder on his face as he runs his hands up my bare legs, my breath catches. He's looking at me like I'm the most beautiful thing he's ever seen. Like I'm the sole focus of his attention, the only thing that matters in this moment.

Being the recipient of that intensity is a heady experience.

His lips pepper kisses along my inner thigh as he pushes my legs apart, settling on his stomach with his head hovering right above my damp sex. The warm air from his exhale has my hips undulating when it lands on my already sensitive skin. "Mmm. This pussy is mine tonight."

"Yours," I breathe, nodding rapidly. "Just hurry the fuck up."

I can feel his deep chuckle as he latches his lips on to my clit and sucks, drawing out a breathless exclamation. *"Ronan!"* My hands find purchase in his wavy hair, gripping the soft strands tightly, holding him right where I'm desperate to have him. His tongue laps and swirls, a loud moan escaping me when I feel the rough pad of his finger brush over the short, damp curls. He slides it through the moisture pooling there, slippery and warm.

"Holy fuck, Ronan." My head starts to thrash back and forth. Then, with no more warning, he plunges his finger into my pussy, curling it over to graze over the spot begging for his attention. Just when I think he's out to torment me, his lips close over my clit at the same second he pushes a second finger in, unerringly finding my G-spot and pressing down. My legs start to shake, squeezing his broad shoulders as my orgasm hurtles through me, unexpected, and yet, a welcome relief from the tension that was threatening to overwhelm me.

"God, yes!" I cry out as my back arches off the bed and I convulse through the spasms of pleasure. Ronan licks me throughout, slowing his motions as he senses me coming down from the release.

He rolls away, and I can't help the whimper that escapes when he's no longer between my legs. But he's back seconds later, tearing open a condom packet. "Wait," I cover his hand with mine. "I want to taste you first."

His eyes widen with anticipation. He lets me push him so that he's the one lying down, and I come to the side of his hips, my hand eagerly wrapping around his cock that's already leaking precum. My thumb swipes through the liquid, and bringing it up to my mouth, I suck it off.

"Fucking hell, Cherry. Put those lips where they belong."

His gruff command sends a wave of mini clenches between my legs. Bending down, I shuffle backward until my head is hovering right above his length. Turning my head to look at him with a saucy wink, I say, "Is this where they belong?"

His only answer is to wrap his hand in my hair and gently guide my head down. Not forcing but making it perfectly clear what he wants. Ronan's perfect balance of command and respect is like nothing I've ever experienced with a man. He's yet again letting me be in control, but also leaving no doubt as to what he wants and expects from me. And the weird part is, in this moment, I want to give him everything.

All of me.

My lips close over the weeping head of his cock, and I suck lightly, my tongue swirling around the tip before I feel his hand pushing lightly. Taking his cue, I swallow him down as far as I can, relishing in the moan it draws from him. Bobbing my head up and down, I use my hands and my mouth to drive him wild, loving how his grip alternates from letting go to stroke my head, murmuring praise, then gathers my hair in a fist as he lets out a deep moan.

"Fuck, I'm close. I'm gonna come down that perfect throat if you don't stop."

His warning does nothing but spur me on as I suck him down faster, my hand squeezing his base as the other reaches between my own legs to try and ease the ache that's building for me.

"Hell no, Cherry." A slap lands on my ass, then fingers dig into the flesh. "That pussy's mine, remember? You don't come unless I make you."

I pop off his dick with a gasp as he somehow levers his upper body to grab my hips and lift me over his face. "Shit!" I squeak as his mouth lands back on my pussy.

"Suck."

One word, mumbled against my throbbing clit. I dive back down, sucking him off as fiercely as I can while he destroys me with his tongue.

My whimpers of pleasure are drowned by his dick, and I feel him start to swell in my mouth as his hips start to rock up into me. He grunts out a warning, and I double down, desperate to feel him let go. Seconds later, warm liquid shoots into my mouth. I swallow every drop as I feel his teeth graze my clit, making a second orgasm rock through me.

Letting his cock slip from my mouth, I suck in a trembling breath, resting my head on his thigh. I could be smothering him for all I know, but he's a big boy. He'll manage.

"Damn," he groans, the word vibrating against my sensitized clit. He kisses my sex once more, then his hands squeeze my ass gently, caressing where he spanked me earlier.

It takes way too much effort to move off him, my limbs feeling heavy with that satisfied, tired feeling that comes from really good orgasms. Once I manage to ungracefully flop onto my back, my feet land somewhere by his head, but I'll be damned if I can make myself move. With my eyes closed, I can't see, but I can sense him move until I feel his body pressed against my side, his hand landing on my chin, tipping it over to the side. Soft lips kiss my own, and I can taste my release on him.

"You with me?" he asks, and I can feel his lips curved up in a smile. "Or is it death by orgasm?"

That makes me giggle, and I blink my eyes open to see his blue ones twinkling back at me. "I'm not done with you yet, mister."

His arms gather me into his embrace, kisses peppering my bare skin. "Good answer." Ronan rolls us so that I'm back on top of him, and I can feel his semihard dick between us. But there's no urgency, no rush, just a contentedness between us as we swap languid, deep, sensual kisses.

When was the last time I just kissed a man? With no agenda to move on to the next thing as quickly as possible, just enjoyed kissing him.

Oh. Seven months ago, in a hotel room overlooking the beach.

Chapter Twenty-Four

Ronan

I could kiss this woman for hours and never get enough of her. But eventually, things start to heat up of their own accord. My dick is ready for more, and judging by the way Willow starts to writhe on top of me, she's ready, too.

Pulling away, I look in her eyes, heavy with desire. "Next time you come, it's gonna be on my cock, Cherry."

Her eager nod is both adorable and fucking hot. She reaches to the side for a condom, bringing one of her nipples directly over my head. I mean, I have to suck it. It's like, a rule. Nipple in my face that belongs to the gorgeous woman I'm in bed with? I'm gonna suck on it.

"Ronan," she moans, but she doesn't move. "Your cock. In me. Now."

Well, okay, that's some instruction I can follow. Releasing her breast with a pop, I let her settle back over my hips and roll the condom down my already leaking dick.

"He's eager." She giggles, and my cock jumps in her hands.

"He likes you." I grin. "But he likes being inside you even more."

Her impish smirk as she lines up her hips and sinks down slowly is pure perfection. "I happen to like him inside me, too." Leaning down, her lips graze across mine. "And I like *you*."

I don't get to respond before she kisses me harder and starts to bounce her hips up and down. I grab her ass, digging my fingers in as I help her rock along my length. Her lips break away from mine, her forehead landing on mine as she starts to pant.

"Fuck, yes."

She pushes up, her hands coming to my chest as she arches her back and undulates forward and back, the change in motion obviously stroking something inside of her, judging by the cries and whimpers escaping from her mouth.

"How. The heck. Do you. Do this. To me," she pants, her head tossed back. She's a fucking goddess above me, working me up into a frenzy. Recovery time? What the hell is that? I can feel myself ready to blow, and start reciting All-Star stats to try and push away my orgasm.

"Oh my God, Ronan." She's close, but somehow, I can sense that wall from earlier, the one that wouldn't let her relax, starting to creep back in. She's getting caught up in her head again.

Not on my watch.

With her upright, I can access her clit easily, and I pinch it, rolling it between my thumb and fingers as I start to lift my hips up to meet her movements. "You're gonna come for me, Cherry. Squeeze my fucking cock and explode all over me. You can do it."

Her nails dig into my chest as her moans grow deeper.

"That's my good girl."

I feel the clench of her pussy around me, and then she's pulsating, every wave pushing me further over the edge into my own orgasm. I stop trying to hold back and let it come over me with a roar as she screams my name, collapsing onto my chest.

We stay like that for a moment before she rolls off me. "That was amazing," she murmurs, a soft smile on her face. I take advantage of her closed eyes and just drink her in. Her skin is flushed with a sheen of sweat, her lips swollen. God, she's stunning.

I move to get up, figuring I should deal with the condom, find my clothes, and get going, even though it physically hurts to think about leaving right now. But we still haven't talked about what we're doing or what happens next, and I don't want to push Willow too far, too fast.

There's also the not-so-small matter of my kid at home, and the fact that I didn't tell my mother I'd be gone all night.

"Where are you going?" Her soft voice hits me, still husky with pleasure but now with a thread of confusion and hope that I don't want to read into too much.

Glancing over my shoulder at her, I try to ignore the part of me that really doesn't want to leave.

"Home?" I phrase that one word as a question, partly because I don't know what's the best course of action here, and partly because I know just how easily I could give in and stay just a little while longer without a second thought to the repercussions.

Her lower lip is tugged between her teeth, and my hand automatically reaches out to free it.

"You could stay."

Her whisper is so quiet, I would have missed it if I wasn't so tuned in to everything Willow says and does.

"I could," I reply softly, moving back to lie down on the bed. "But only for a little while."

She shifts over, into my open arms, laying her head on my chest. "I know, Peyton needs you." She lifts her head so we're eye to eye, her hand resting on my skin right above my heart. "I would never want to come between you and your daughter; I know she comes first."

I tuck a piece of hair behind her ear, rising up just enough to meet her lips in a gentle kiss. "And that's exactly why I'm still here."

Awareness comes to me slowly. The tickle of soft hair under my chin, the rise and fall of someone else's chest against mine. For a second, I'm back in Hawaii, waking up with the ocean shores right outside our hotel room, the warm tropical breeze waiting for us, nothing to worry about, no one to interfere. Just me and Willow.

But we're not in the islands anymore.

Real life is waiting for us just outside this apartment. It's pitch-black outside, and I panic, realizing I fell asleep with Willow in my arms.

I carefully reach over, not wanting to disturb sleeping beauty, grab my phone, and see a text from my mom.

MOM: Not sure how late your team thing is going, I'll sleep in the guest room. No rush.

Guilt swamps me. It's well after midnight, and I glance back down at Willow, who's somehow still asleep. Briefly, I consider sneaking out and not waking her, but she deserves better than that.

"Cherry," I whisper softly, stroking her hair. "I gotta go home."

"Mmph." The adorable noise she makes as she nuzzles in even closer has me smiling, despite the turmoil of guilt mixed with absolute contentedness. Fuck, how I wish I didn't have to go, a sentiment extremely familiar to how it felt leaving her in Hawaii.

That time I didn't wake her up and regretted it ever since.

"C'mon, beautiful, I need you to wake up." I pepper little kisses over her forehead and down her cheek until I feel her turn and meet my kiss with her own.

"I'm awake," she says sleepily. "What time is it?"

"Just after one in the morning. I have to go home." Regret laces my tone as Willow pushes up to sit, the sheet pooling around her waist, baring those perfect tits that moments ago were pressed up against me.

"God, you're so fucking beautiful." I lean in to steal another, deeper kiss. "I wish I could stay here and worship your body for hours."

"Ronan," she moans as I suck her neck, her fingers tangling in my hair.

"Tell me I can see you again," I murmur against her soft skin, breathing in the aroma of sex and Willow. "And I don't mean from a distance at a game or some damn event. I mean like this."

"Seeing me naked might be a challenge," she says, but there's humour — and desire — in her voice.

"Challenge accepted."

Pressing one final kiss to her neck, I lift my head and cup hers in my hand. "I want to take you out on a date, Willow Lawson. A real one, where I pick you up, take you out, and at the end of it, bring you back here to show you exactly why dating me is a really good idea."

A seductive smirk crosses her face. "So you're saying that sex is the only reason I should date you?"

"You mean really fucking good sex? Not the only reason, but one of many."

Willow's smile falls slightly as she sobers. "Ronan, I meant it when I said we have to keep this a secret for now. I've never dated a baseball player. And now I'm dating one who plays for the team I work for? I just...I need us to move slowly."

I nod, keeping my eyes locked on hers so she knows I hear her. "I understand. And we'll go at whatever pace you need. I'm just grateful you're giving me a chance to show you this could work if we're just open to it and honest about the fact that something exists between us."

Her hand lifts to cover mine that is still cupping her cheek. "You and your belief in fate, huh?"

I shake my head as she turns to kiss my palm. "Not just fate. There's so much more between us than just that. I want you like I've never wanted any other woman. I've never encountered anyone that makes me want to believe I can have it all. Not until you."

A part of me is panicking that I'm moving too fast. That I'm being too honest, too vulnerable, by coming clean about everything I feel — have felt since meeting Willow. But when I look at her, I don't see panic, I don't see a woman ready to run in the opposite direction.

I see a woman ready to say yes.

"Can I take you out on a date?"

Her smile is blindingly brilliant. "Yes."

Chapter Twenty-Five

Ronan

"I really wish you'd tell me where we're going," Willow says for the third time as I drive us to our date location. Just like the first two times, I just smile.

"Where's the fun in that?" I squeeze her thigh lightly with my hand that's been resting there since we left her apartment. The scorching-hot blue dress she's wearing skims her body like it was made just for her, with a plunging V-neckline that shows off her breasts in a way that instantly had me hard. "You look stunning, Cherry."

"You said that already," she teases, lifting my hand from her leg to kiss my fingers before placing it back, only slightly higher this time.

"The truth is always worth repeating."

Her light laughter fills the space between us, and it's a carefree, happy sound reminiscent of our time in Hawaii. This is the Willow I've missed for months.

We turn off the highway and start to climb up the side of Burnaby Mountain. Willow turns in her seat to face me as soon as we do. "Are you taking me to The Lookout?" Her excitement is clear, and I flash her a grin as an answer. "Oh my God, Ronan! Did you know this is my favourite restaurant? But it's so hard to get into, how did you get a reservation so quickly?"

I pause for a second before answering. I've never been the type to flash my celebrity status or use it to get things, but I sure as shit did to make tonight happen. The question is, how will she feel about that? Willow's never seemed blinded by my status, never shown any interest or care whatsoever about the ridiculous salary I get paid to play a game, even though I'm certain she's aware.

"I made a call. I don't want you to think I do that a lot because I don't. But I heard you telling one of the trainers about this place when he was looking for somewhere to propose to his girlfriend, and you said it was your favourite restaurant. I wanted tonight to be special," I finish lamely, gripping the steering wheel tightly with my one hand.

"Ronan," she starts softly, taking my other hand in hers again. "That was almost two months ago that I told Henry about The Lookout."

All I can do is nod.

"You remembered that? All this time?"

"I remember everything about you. Everything you've said, all the things that have made you happy or sad."

Out of the corner of my eye, I see her rest her head back on the seat. And she's still holding my hand.

"You're kind of amazing, Ronan Sinclair."

Thank fuck, we've reached the parking lot. I quickly pull into a spot, turn off the car, and turn to face her fully. "You deserve amazing, Willow. I just want to be the lucky fucker who helps you believe that."

The play of emotions across her face is something to watch.

"You're something else, you know that?"

My mouth quirks a grin at her enigmatic statement, said with wonder in her voice. "A good something, I hope."

In response, she leans over and kisses me softly. "It would seem that way."

As much as I want to stay here and kiss her for hours, this isn't the romantic setting I've got planned. We're still in my SUV with Peyton's car seat in the back, along with various toys and an unmentionable amount of goldfish cracker crumbs. I tell her as much, earning a light giggle and a caress of my cheek with her soft hand.

"Your dedication to your daughter is not something to be embarrassed of. Not with me."

I stare at her, completely transfixed by the incredible woman in front of me. "How do you know just what to say, every time?"

Willow just shakes her head slowly. "I don't, trust me. I just know how I feel. How you make me feel. And I'm done trying to fight that."

This time, my smile is big. Huge. "And there you go, you just did it again." Leaning in, I press one more kiss to her luscious red lips before getting out of the car and going around to open her door. She takes my outstretched hand as she climbs out and lets me pull her straight into my embrace. "Tonight is for you, Cherry."

She looks up at me with pure happiness etched across her face. "For us."

I can't resist kissing her after that, even though we're now several minutes late for our reservation. Then again, I rented the entire rooftop patio, so they can fucking well wait.

When the maître d' himself escorts us to the table set at the edge of the patio, overlooking the twinkling lights of Vancouver and the neighbouring towns, Willow's gasp is audible.

"Ronan," she murmurs, squeezing my arm tightly. "This is incredible."

I reluctantly drop her arm to pull out her chair, and when she sits down, I bend over to kiss her bare skin. Thanks to strategically placed heat lamps, there's not even a hint of a chill in the springtime air. The weather gods are cooperating, with this, thankfully, dry May evening. Plan B was a private room inside, but I knew Willow would enjoy this more. Thanks again to fate, I suppose, for all of my plans working out this time around.

"Told you, you deserve incredible." I sit down across from her, and she reaches for my hand, lacing our fingers together on top of the white tablecloth.

"Thank you."

Two simple words spoken with so much genuine emotion, I get a little choked up. I can see a future with Willow, a future that's becoming clearer and clearer with every passing moment I spend with her. A future that includes fancy dates like this to spoil her, and casual ones that are more my speed. Days with Peyton at the park, nights spent in bed. It's crazy to be feeling all of this so fast, but then again, it's been months of watching Willow, wanting her from afar, falling for her with every smile, every gesture.

A waiter materializes out of nowhere with a tray carrying two drinks and a little glass dish. When he sets the items down on the table, delighted laughter bursts out of Willow.

"Is that..." She gestures to the two cocktails and the dish of extra maraschino cherries.

"The drink from our dinner in Hawaii? Yes. I called the hotel bar and begged for the recipe so they could recreate it for us tonight."

Willow's shaking her head, but she's smiling. "Wow. No one has ever done this kind of stuff for me." Her eyes widen like she can't believe she just admitted that and I squeeze her hand to show her I understand.

"Good. I like knowing I'm the first man to give you what you deserve." My voice is husky with the unsaid second part of that statement — that I want to be the only man to give her what she deserves. *First, last, only.*

But even I know it's too soon to put voice to that. It's been too many months of wanting this woman from a distance, and now that I have her, there's a lot we have to work out. Her fears about how our relationship might be perceived, and of course, I've got Peyton to think about in all this. Even though, I'm pretty confident my daughter is as taken with Willow as I am.

I lift my glass and Willow does the same, clinking them together. "To our first date in the real world."

We take a sip, our gazes locked. Then Willow lifts the cherry from her glass and pops it in her mouth. I watch, amused and more than a little turned on, as her tongue moves around in her mouth. Then she opens up to show her tongue holding the tied stem. She lifts it off and holds it up. Her lips curve up. "To first dates."

Dinner is perfect. I can tell Willow is enchanted by everything I planned. All the time I spent listening, observing, and casual questions asked of those who know her better than I do has made it possible for me to orchestrate an evening full of her favourite things. From the wine — courtesy of a winery on Vancouver Island near where her best friend now lives that she told one of the HR guys about — to the meal — a lobster ravioli I overheard her raving about to Lark. That's the thing with my woman. She wants everyone to be happy and enjoy life. She doesn't hold back from sharing the things that make her happy, and it's all in an effort to make everyone else happy, too.

She gives and gives to everyone around her without ever expecting anything in return. She gives away her yellow Skittles because she doesn't like lemon, but I've noticed how she also sneaks in a couple other colours. Purple for Lark, red for Monty. I asked him about it, and he just shrugged and said red was his favourite flavour.

Willow doesn't hesitate to give if she thinks it will bring joy.

And all I want to do is give that to her.

After our dessert plates are cleared, I push back from the table and stand, extending my hand to Willow. "Come with me?"

She takes my hand and stands wordlessly, letting me lead her over to a secluded corner of the patio, where there's a bush with small white flowers bursting all over, letting off an intoxicating scent.

"Jasmine," Willow whispers, fingering the small white flowers. "Reminds me of Hawaii."

I can't answer, can't formulate words as I just look at her, the moonlight behind her and the warm light from the restaurant making her glow.

"Thank you. This whole evening has been spectacular." She rests her hands on my shoulders and I bend down to kiss her upturned lips. But then she pulls back, and something shifts.

"Ronan, I..." she starts, then stops, looking off to the side at the city laid out in lights below us. "I'm sorry we can't just be together like a normal couple. Maybe someday, once I have the promotion. You're such an incredible man, and I just hope you don't feel like I'm ungrateful by not wanting us to be public."

I gather her into my arms. "Willow, babe, no. Not at all. I know you've worked hard to get where you are, and I would never want to jeopardize that. Do I wish we could be together in public? Of course, I do. But I swear, I respect your need to keep things secret for now."

I'm saying the words, and I mean them. I really do. Yet, as I pull her back in for another kiss, a voice inside of me is warning that secrets don't exactly mix well with relationships.

Which means it's a matter of time before something breaks. I just hope it isn't us.

Chapter Twenty-Six

Willow

RONAN: Peyton wants to know if you would like to join us for movie night…

RONAN: There's popcorn. And skittles courtesy of my daughter's new obsession. I blame a certain woman for that by the way. It's a good thing she's pretty, and I can't stop thinking about her, or I might have to be upset at her for getting my kid hooked on candy.

A giggle escapes me and I clap my hand over my mouth, hoping no one heard me. The media room is half empty, with most of my coworkers already gone home for the day. But Lydia's still in her office, and a few others are out in their cubicles finishing up. When no one asks me what was so funny, I relax and re-read Ronan's messages with a big smile on my face.

WILLOW: Oh, Peyton wants to know does she?

RONAN: Yup. Hey she can be very persistent when she wants something.

WILLOW: Hmmmm I wonder where she got that trait from.

RONAN: What are you insinuating, Cherry?

RONAN: That I'm the kind of man to go for what he wants? No lie detected there, I kind of have to be that way. How else would I be playing for the top Canadian baseball team?

I'm shaking my head as my thumbs fly over my phone, typing out a reply. His cheekiness is adorably endearing, and as risky as it may be to start something with him, I can't deny the happiness I've felt ever since dinner the other night. Ronan didn't stay after dropping me off but made me weak in the knees with a goodnight kiss at my door that went on and on until we both lost track of time. If my neighbour hadn't been headed home from their own night out and interrupted us, who knows how long we would have stood in my doorway, making out like teenagers.

WILLOW: I said nothing...

RONAN: You didn't have to. I know what you're thinking.

WILLOW: Really? What am I thinking right now?

RONAN: Let's see... You're thinking about what kind of pizza you want me to order for dinner tonight. Pey and I are partial to ham and pineapple, but will eat pepperoni if we have to.

WILLOW: Good thing I love ham and pineapple.

RONAN: So you're coming? Peyton will be thrilled. See you later, beautiful.

I drop my phone down on my desk, and after quickly looking around to make sure no one can see me, do a little wiggle of excitement. Something about this man makes me giddy like a girl whose crush has finally asked her to prom.

There's not a chance of me being productive any longer. I shut down my computer, grab my purse out of my desk drawer, and head for the elevator.

"Willow, can you come here?"

It's a good thing no one can see me cringe at Lydia's shrill call. Turning around slowly, I compose my features. "Actually, I'm just heading home for the day."

From her office doorway, she glances up from her phone. "Well, I need to discuss the content plan for Coaches Corner on the blog. I'm not so sure these questions will interest our fans." She looks at me expectantly, and I realize just how much I've enabled her behaviour from years of simply giving in and doing her bidding with little to no boundaries. It might be too little, too late, but goddamn it, I don't want to stay here and deal with her when I've got a wonderful man and his adorable little girl waiting for me.

"Sorry, Lydia, that will have to wait. I have an appointment." The white lie falls off my tongue, and I'm not immune to the fact that with Ronan and I finally giving in to our feelings for each other, more lies are in my future.

Her sound of discontent almost has me wavering in my decision. After all, I still need to stay on her good side until they announce her replacement — which, hopefully, is me.

Her response comes as a surprise. In a gruff voice, her gaze once again on her phone, she says, "Understood. But I expect to see you in my office first thing tomorrow, Willow."

I muster up a smile and a nod of acknowledgment. "Got it. But for what it's worth, the questions were all generated from a poll of our existing fans via email marketing. This is what they've said they want to know."

With that final word, I turn and press the elevator call button, praying it comes quickly. The doors open almost instantly and

I step inside, breathing a sigh of relief when Lydia doesn't try to hold me up any longer.

Less than an hour after leaving the stadium, I'm standing on Ronan's front step, wringing my hands together. My earlier excitement has faded into nerves. It's one thing to go out on a private, luxurious date with the man, it's another to visit his home and spend the evening with him and his daughter. This feels big. Monumental. Bigger than us spending an entire night together, even, something we still have yet to do.

I'm raising my hand to press the doorbell when the door swings open, and Ronan leans against the doorframe, lips curved up in a knowing smile. I can't help it, my eyes drop to his bare feet, sweep up the grey joggers that hug his muscular legs to the T-shirt that looks so soft and comfy, and finally land on his relaxed, happy face. This is Ronan in his element, possibly as much so as when he's on the baseball diamond.

"Were you planning on coming inside or just spending the evening on my front step?"

I let out a little huff. "I was about to ring the bell."

He steps forward, swiftly kissing me on the lips. "Good. Because Peyton would be really disappointed if you didn't come inside."

Vulnerability bleeds through as I look up at him. "Only Peyton?"

Ronan grabs my hand and lifts it to his lips, pressing a kiss to my knuckles. "She'd be disappointed. I'd be devastated."

Why I needed that last little piece of confirmation he wants me here, I don't know. I've never been the insecure type, but maybe it's because I recognize just how big of a deal this is — him inviting me into his home to spend time with him and his daughter. Maybe it's because, deep down, I know this relationship is already different from any other I've been in.

Keeping my hand in his, Ronan takes a single step back into his house. He doesn't pull me with him, instead letting the space between us grow, giving me the power. I can follow or not.

I step inside.

"Willow! You're here!"

Peyton's excited shriek hits me the second Ronan closes the door behind me. His hand trails over my lower back, and I feel the whisper of his lips on the back of my head as he walks past, into the kitchen, just in time for Peyton to come running toward me from the same direction. This time, I'm ready for her, dropping into a crouch.

"Finish line!" she yells as she flings herself into my arms, and there's no hiding my massive smile. This girl is pure joy and sunshine wrapped up in an adorable package. Her energy and excitement is infectious, especially when it's all directed at me.

"Hey, kiddo, thanks for inviting me tonight."

"I told Daddy we had to watch *Moana* because Heihei is your favourite." She breaks free of my hug and grabs my hand. "C'mon. We can start it now that you're here."

We walk through the kitchen, where Ronan looks up from plating pizza and cut up veggies to give me a happy smile, and into the large space that overlooks the backyard. When we saw the house months ago, this space was staged as a formal sitting area. Now, it's been transformed into the ultimate family room. A large comfortable-looking sectional is covered in a pink fuzzy blanket and stuffed animals are lined up in a row. A play kitchen is off to one side, kids' books are stacked on the coffee table, and the mantle is covered with photos, all of Ronan, Peyton, and Ronan's mom. I wander over and look through them, each one only making my heart melt even further for this family. The love between them is evident in every single photo and every single inch of this house.

"Okay, who's hungry?"

I turn to see Ronan setting down plates on the coffee table. Moving closer, I ask, "Can I help with anything?"

He glances up with a smile. "Go and help yourself to a drink. There's wine or beer in the fridge, and if you wouldn't mind grabbing Peyton's water on the counter, that would be great."

I walk to the kitchen, absorbing all of the cozy family vibes as I hear Ronan tell Peyton to go and wash her hands. Footsteps scamper off and then warm arms wrap around my waist.

"You look amazing, Cherry." His lips land on my neck, and I tilt my head to the side to give him more access. "Keeping my hands off you until Rocket goes to bed isn't going to be easy."

"Why do you call her Rocket?" I ask as I turn in his arms, looping mine around his neck. I'm guessing we don't have long before Peyton returns, but I'll take this stolen moment with him.

I'll take any moment I can have with him.

Love for his daughter is etched all over his face as he replies, "Because she's fast as a rocket. Always has been. As soon as she started to walk, she started to run, and she hasn't stopped ever since."

"Daddy, can I start eating?"

We spring apart at Peyton's voice, but she's not in the kitchen, she's already on the couch, rearranging her stuffed animals. Part of me worries she might have seen Ronan and I embracing, but he doesn't seem concerned, so I guess I can let it go.

"Sure thing, baby girl," he calls out. Then, squeezing my hip with one hand, he reaches into the fridge and pulls out a beer, tilting it toward me. I shake my head and go for the bottle of wine instead, my hand stilling when I see a jar with bright red cherries inside.

Glancing back at Ronan, I smirk and raise my eyebrows. His gaze travels to what caught my attention before he leans in close.

"Can't help it. You've got me addicted to cherries."

Chapter Twenty-Seven

Willow

"What can I say, except, you're welcome!" Ronan and Peyton are swaying back and forth, singing along with the movie loudly and very much off-key while I watch in amusement from the opposite end of the couch. They're two peas in a very adorable pod, Peyton clutching a bear while Ronan has his arm around her shoulder.

The song finishes, and I clap and cheer. "Bravo! Wonderful, that was a masterpiece."

They both laugh, and Peyton moves across the couch to snuggle into my side. "It's okay, Willow. Daddy knows he can't sing very well," she stage whispers, earning another snort of laughter from her father.

"Ouch, thanks, kiddo. And here I was about to go and get the movie snacks."

Peyton pops up, narrowly missing my chin with her head. "Snacks?"

I move to stand, but Ronan lifts his hand to stop me. "You two stay and watch the movie, I'll be right back."

A few minutes later, he returns, dropping down to the couch beside us. He sets down three bowls of different sizes and winks.

"You separated the Skittles?" I murmur, looking over the top of Peyton's head at him. But he shakes his head in denial.

"Peyton did."

I look down at the little girl staring at the TV, oblivious to the emotions she's stirring up inside of me simply from separating out the yellow Skittles. She reaches to the table, bypassing the bowls of Skittles and picking something out of the largest bowl instead.

"Caramel popcorn, too? Wow, I'm a lucky girl tonight."

Peyton turns to look up at me with a mouth full of buttery sweet popcorn. "Ith ma favwite."

"Peyton, manners," Ronan says sharply but with a loving smile on his face. His little girl gives him a guilty grin, then swallows her mouthful.

"Caramel popcorn is my favourite," she says again.

"Guess what?" I whisper. "It's my favourite, too."

Peyton's eyes grow wide with amazement. "Really? Daddy likes the salty stuff, but I like this one. Maybe now you're here he won't try to make me eat the salty popcorn anymore."

I fight back a laugh at her obvious distaste for Ronan's choice of movie snack. He chooses that moment to stretch his arm along the back of the couch, and his hand comes to play with the hair at the nape of my neck, sending shivers down my spine. I chance a quick glance over at him to see his eyes locked on me, something indescribable etched across his features. My lips curve up in a smile that he reflects back at me, and something settles inside.

This is good.

At some point, Ronan leaves, but Peyton and I are engrossed in the movie. Then a big pile of fabric lands in my lap.

"You look cold," he says gruffly.

I slip the sweatshirt over my head, and a wave of Ronan's scent covers me. Closing my eyes, I subtly lift the collar up to my face and inhale. Peyton's thankfully unaware, but I sense Ronan shifting on the couch and feel his hand settle down again on the back of my neck, stroking back and forth over the top of his sweater.

By the time the credits roll on the television, Peyton is slumped against me, asleep.

"Let me take her," Ronan whispers, shifting to stand. I watch this perfect, wonderful, handsome man lift his daughter into his arms with such loving care it makes my heart ache. Both with missing my own father and longing for a family of my own. I'm starting to realize just how much I miss Tori and Cooper. How connected we were and how they were basically my stand-in family. We had many movie nights just like this, sharing snacks and laughter, Coop cuddled into my side when he was younger.

And then they moved. Leaving me here alone.

Standing from the couch, I gather up the bowls and plates from our snacks and carry them into the kitchen. I'm so lost in my own thoughts that I don't notice Ronan's return until his strangled whisper has me turning around. And the intensity on his face floors me.

"Damn it, Willow." He closes the distance between us and cups my face in his large hands. He does that a lot, and I never thought I would love such a possessive, protective gesture as much as I do. But it's what he says next that shoots straight to my heart. "You're making me want things I never thought I could have. You, in my sweater, cuddled up with my daughter. Fuck, Cherry. It feels so damn right."

His voice is rough, laden with emotion, desire at the forefront. His sweatshirt is so big on me, the sleeves drape well past my hands. But they fall back as I wrap my arms around his neck and thread my fingers into his hair so I can guide his head down to meet mine.

I can't find the words to reply to him, so I let my kiss do the talking. Hoping that it somehow conveys what is in my heart, even though my head hasn't quite caught up. We lose ourselves in the moment, lips fused together, tongues dancing. His air becomes mine, our hands desperately roaming each other's bodies, seeking connection anywhere and everywhere we can.

"I need you," he growls, spinning us around and lifting me up to sit on the counter. "You have to be quiet. Can you do that for me, Cherry? Can you stay silent while I devour you?"

I don't get a chance to answer before he's tugging down the hem of my leggings. Lifting me so he can strip me bare, I gasp at the cold marble under my ass. But then Ronan's pulling me to the edge, one hand pushing my legs wide so he can drop down between them, and the other tangling with mine on the counter.

"Fuck. This pussy is heaven. Absolutely perfect. You're perfect." His mouth covers my sex and he sucks my clit hard without any further warning, making me bite back a garbled moan.

"Shh," he murmurs against my skin, dipping his tongue to stroke up my slit. "Not a sound or I stop."

A small whimper escapes me when his teeth graze my sensitized skin and he freezes, looking up at me with a devious smirk.

"Sorry," I whisper, letting him see my smile. "I'll be quiet."

He just raises his eyebrows, keeping our gaze connected as he lowers his head back down. This time, when he flattens his tongue and swipes it up to swirl around my clit, I bite my lip to stop from making any noise. I know the risk, Peyton could catch us, but I trust him to know his daughter and know if this is okay or not.

Besides, there's not a chance in hell I would turn down sex from this man ever again. He's just as I thought that day at the airport. A veritable god among men. The best lover I've ever had. A fact he proves again as he slides two fingers inside my aching pussy, twisting and fluttering them inside of me, driving me wild in an instant. The necessity of silence somehow makes everything even hotter, that tiny hint of danger making my heart race.

"Come on my face, Cherry. Let me feast on this beautiful pussy."

That's all it takes. I clap my hand over my mouth to hold back my muffled cries as my body spasms and clenches around his fingers. My hips are writhing around on the cold, hard counter, and Ronan has to hold me in place with one hand as he wrings every last drop of my release from me. When I finally stop shaking with the most intense orgasm I've ever had from oral sex, I feel limp and oh, so satisfied.

To my surprise, Ronan picks up my panties and my leggings, and methodically helps me get dressed again, lifting me off the counter. He sneaks in a squeeze of my ass but doesn't make any move to take things further.

I reach out and cup his very obvious erection pressing against the front of his sweatpants. "Don't you want to..."

His hand covers mine. "If I fuck you, I won't want you to leave." His tone is a mixture of rough arousal and regret. And I know, without a doubt, he's fighting an internal battle between Ronan, the father and Ronan, the man.

I try to convey how much I understand with my smile, even as I'm dropping to my knees. "Okay. No sex. But that doesn't mean I can't help you with this situation." I look up at him as I take the hem of his joggers in hand. His breathing is ragged, his eyes hooded with desire, but he doesn't stop me as I pull them down over his cock. The second it springs free, he groans softly.

Time for a taste of his own medicine.

Tilting my head to the side, I give him a warning shake of my head. "Uh-uh, you've got to be silent, or I stop."

His answering chuckle is cut off abruptly with a sharp nod when I squeeze the base of his cock gently, but the glint in his eyes is all I need to see.

Dipping my head down, I lick a circle around the tip of his cock, lapping up the salty precum that's already started to leak. Ronan's hands tangle in my hair as he holds me in place. I wrap my hand around his length, my other hand reaching between his legs to cup his balls. His fingers tighten, the tug on my hair slightly painful, but also making me wet between my own legs.

Opening wide, I envelop him in my mouth and slide down as far as I can go, letting my hands cover what I can't. Up and down I move, closing my eyes and losing myself to the subtle sounds he can't hold back, the feel of his hands in my hair, and the taste of him in my mouth.

"Willow, I'm gonna come." His growled warning comes just a few minutes later, and instead of backing off, I intensify my movements, squeezing tighter, rocking up and down faster, until I feel his body tense and jets of cum hit my throat. I swallow him down, every single drop, until he curls over me, kissing my head, his hands coming under my arms to lift me up and into his embrace.

"Fuck. Cherry. That was..." he gasps into my ear in between kisses.

"I know," I murmur back.

Eventually, we're both dressed and he's leading me to the front door where we lose another several minutes kissing each other. I know I have to go, but I really, *really* don't want to, and the only thing making it okay is knowing a part of him wishes I didn't have to, either.

"Someday soon, we're gonna have an entire night together," he growls into the top of my head after crushing me into his arms.

I nod against his chest, then force myself to step back. I move to lift his hoodie off, but he stops me.

"Keep it. It looks better on you, anyway," he says roughly.

I go up on my tiptoes for one more kiss, keeping it brief this time. "Thank you. For tonight, for sharing your home and your daughter." I finger the hoodie. "And your sweatshirt."

He chuckles at that and kisses me once more. "Okay. You need to go before I change my mind and carry you to my bedroom to have my way with you."

"Don't tempt me with a good time," I say with a grin, even though I know that can't happen. Not yet, at least.

But as I drive away, I let myself imagine a future where that could happen. Where I'm not leaving late at night, but instead falling asleep in his arms. Waking up to Peyton climbing in between us.

And I like that idea. I like it a lot more than I should, perhaps. Because that future will only be possible if I face the biggest risk of all.

Telling my uncle about our relationship.

Chapter Twenty-Eight

Ronan

Good thing I caught the fucking ball.

That's honestly the only thing going through my head as I limp off the field, trying to hide the grimace of pain. In all my years of playing, never once have I landed wrong after leaping up to catch a pop fly. Until today. I knew the instant my foot rolled underneath me that it wasn't good. I'm just hoping it's not that bad, either. It's only the fourth inning, and even though I'm smart enough to know I'm not likely to play anymore today, I'm holding out hope our team can beat these fuckers.

Lark is already waiting for me in her treatment room.

"Get me a cryotherapy boot." Her barked command has one of the assistant trainers hustling out of the room as I haul myself up onto her table. "Geez, Ronan, you went down hard. How does it feel?"

"Like I came down on it wrong with all two hundred and ten pounds of body weight." I wince as she removes my cleat and sock. There's no bruising yet, which has me sighing in relief. A sentiment Lark soon echoes.

"Well, there's no bruising and the immediate swelling is mild. I think you got away with just a —"

"Ronan? Are you okay?" Willow bursts through the door of Lark's room with the assistant trainer fast on her heels with the cryo machine. She comes up short just before reaching for me, but I'm guessing it would be obvious to anyone looking there's more to her reaction than simple professional concern.

"He's fine," Lark cuts back in, hip checking Willow away from my side with a pointed stare at her that tells me she at least suspects somethings going on. Willow steps back, and Lark starts to wrap my foot in the cryotherapy boot. "As I was just telling him, I think it's a mild sprain. There's no major bruising or swelling, so some good old rest and ice therapy for a couple of days will, hopefully, settle it down. But we'll reassess tomorrow."

She steps back after setting up the cold therapy and folds her arms across her chest, looking from Willow to me. Yeah, she knows something's up, that's very apparent, given the smirk she's fighting back.

"I'm going to step out and deal with the injury reports. Willow, I'm guessing you need to talk to Ronan to prepare his statement?" She's speaking loudly, and I quickly clue in it's for the benefit of the coach and other people milling around in the main trainer room. "Take a few minutes here to do that while I update everyone."

The second the door closes behind her, Willow rushes over and flings her arms around me. "Oh my God, I was so worried when I saw you limping."

"I'm fine, Cherry," I say gruffly, kissing the top of her head. "But if you wanted to keep this relationship a secret for longer than the past six weeks, you probably shouldn't look at me like you want to kiss my boo-boo and make it all better." I push her away slightly so she can see my smirk. "Unless you want to kiss Monty's and Maverick's boo-boos, too? I bet Kai's shoulder is sore..."

Exactly as I'd hoped she would, Willow laughs and smacks my arm. "Point taken. I will be a cold, unfeeling robot around you."

I tug her back into my arms. "Don't you dare." I kiss her softly, loving the feel of her relaxing against me. But voices from outside Lark's room remind me this isn't the time or place. Willow steps back and lifts her hands to her hair, smoothing it down, even though it's already perfect.

She's already perfect.

Even though my ankle sprain is mild, it still means I'm out for the rest of the game. Lark does let me go back to the dugout to watch, but I almost wish she hadn't. Our opponents are assholes, playing dirty. Unfortunately, they're also talented. They manage to get a lead on us, one we can't make up, and we lose.

After the game, I head back to the trainer's area to find Lark, who wants to give me some sort of compression sleeve to wear. By the time we're done, the stadium feels empty. It's always this way after a loss. No one wants to hang around, the energy is low, and we all just want to get home.

Willow had texted, saying she'd meet me in the parking lot. It's risky, there's still a chance of someone seeing us, so I can't help but hope her wanting to meet is a sign she's coming around to the idea of going public. Telling her uncle and everyone else about us.

I slowly walk down the hall that will converge with the one coming from the visiting team's locker room before opening into the player and staff parking lot. I'm hoping the other team has also cleared out, since the last thing I need when I'm not at my best is to run into any of those assholes. But no such luck. When I round the corner to where the corridors meet, there's at least half a dozen players and staff milling around talking. I scan the group, and when I find Willow, what I see has my blood boiling.

Some asshole from the other team is standing way too fucking close to her, and it's clear from her body language she's uncomfortable. She's leaning away, but her back is to the wall, so there's nowhere to go. Her arms are crossed tightly over the Tridents shirt she's wearing, and if I were him, I'd be withering away from the glare she's shooting this fucker.

Every fiber of my being wants to go over there and push the guy away. To protect my girl. It's physically painful to hold myself back, but causing a scene is the last thing she'd want.

Instead, I slowly move closer. Because if this piece of shit makes one wrong move, I won't hold back. I'm not a violent guy, but no way will I let anything happen to Willow when I'm around to stop it.

"Hey, Sin, how's the ankle?"

I ignore Monty, intent on reaching Willow's side. Then I see the asshole lift one hand up and place it on the wall next to her head, his other moving toward her arm. *No fucking way is he going to touch my girl.*

I reach them in an instant, grabbing his arm and shoving him away from her, inserting myself between them. "What the fuck do you think you're doing? Get your fucking hands away from her."

He lifts his hands, but then the asshole snickers. "Sorry, bro. Didn't know she was taken."

"Ronan, stop. I can handle this."

Willow's voice from behind me sounds angry, and I know she's probably worried about what anyone else might have seen or heard, but right now, all I care about is that she's okay. I start to turn around when the fuckhead decides he's not done pissing me off.

"It's too bad, though. I like 'em tall. Perfect height to bend over the couch, y'know what I'm sayin'?"

I'm spinning around, stepping forward, my fist plowing into his face before I can even stop to think about my actions. My punch lands with a crunch, his head snapping back. And now my right hand hurts almost as much as my ankle. *Fuck.*

"Holy shit!"

"Ronan, no!"

"Someone get security."

Voices hit me all at once as the other guy staggers back, clutching his jaw, shooting daggers my way. People rush up around us, and in the back of my mind, I wonder where the fuck they were earlier when he was harassing Willow. But my attention is solely focused on the woman still with her back against the wall, her expression guarded, arms wrapped around her middle.

I stalk back to her and without asking permission or saying a damn thing, I pull her into my arms, pressing my lips to the top of her head as I try to calm the rage inside of me. But she's stiff against me, making no move to hug me back.

I step back, my eyes searching her face for some sort of reaction, anything to tell me I haven't fucked everything up. But her expression is blank. And there's no chance to talk before I'm being led away.

"Come on, Sinclair, let's get that hand checked out and leave this piece of shit for someone else to deal with." Coach sounds angry, and that's when it all comes crashing down on me.

It's not just that I punched another player. It's that I have a sinking suspicion I just outed mine and Willow's relationship to the entire fucking team.

Chapter Twenty-Nine

Willow

There's a fog around me, muffling voices and trapping me in a whirlwind of my own emotions. Shock at the aggressive approach of the other player and the lack of respect for my discomfort. Relief at Ronan coming to my rescue. Anger at Ronan for outing us to everyone present.

I don't know what to think or feel right now; all of those feelings are competing with each other in my head for dominance. And there's a thick layer of fear covering it all. Because it feels like everyone is looking at me with eyes that tell me they saw — and heard — everything.

I turn, unsure where I'm headed but certain I need to get away from everyone. I head back toward the offices, trying to get my brain to focus on work. We'll need to get ahead of the news, since it's guaranteed someone is going to leak something. And if I can just focus on that, maybe I can ignore the fact that so many of my colleagues, so many players, are probably reaching the same conclusion right now.

Willow Lawson is dating Ronan Sinclair, and he just punched a guy because of her.

But before I can reach my office, my phone vibrates with a text.

UNCLE MIKE: Come to my office.

Oh God. Someone told him. My body feels numb as I make my way down the hall. I can handle whatever's coming, as long as he isn't disappointed in me. That would break me.

Of all people, Lydia catches up to me as I near my uncle's office, grabbing my arm and yanking me to the side.

"What the hell happened? You're causing fights between players now?" she hisses under her breath, condemnation written all over her face. "That sort of drama can't happen, Willow. You don't lead players on or whatever the hell you did to cause Ronan to confront the other guy. And as for Ronan? Well, I *knew* something was happening. You just couldn't keep your hands to yourself. It's like you didn't listen to a word I said about not getting mixed up with players, and now look what's happened. This mess is your fault, Willow. And even your uncle can't save you from it now."

"You've got to be fucking kidding me."

Ronan's angry tone reaches us, and I stay frozen when he strides up beside us. Out of the corner of my eye, I see his red knuckles. His throwing hand is injured because of me. My stomach drops even further. I want so badly to lean into the security and comfort he's offering, but I just can't. Not when a part of me is still furious that he outed us. Why couldn't he have pushed the asshole away and left it at that?

But I know why. Because that's not who he is. Ronan gives his all to everything. And watching the woman he's dating be harassed from the sidelines isn't something he would tolerate. Truthfully, I love him for that, even though I'm now facing my worst nightmare because of it.

He puts his back to Lydia, and the worry and affection I see brimming in his eyes is almost my undoing. "Willow, are you okay? Don't listen to her, please. And I'm so sorry for what happened back there. I just couldn't —"

"Ronan, this is not a conversation you need to be involved in," Lydia clips back at him, and he turns on her, growling in frustration.

"Like hell I don't. You have no right to give Willow any grief for what just happened. None of it was her fault. Not a single bit. She didn't lead him on, and she didn't do anything wrong. *He's* at fault for harassing her. And I'm not going to stand by and let you tell the woman I love that she's somehow to blame."

My breath catches when he says he loves me. But it barely has time to register before another voice reaches us.

"Would someone like to explain to me what the hell is going on here?"

We all turn at Uncle Mike's loud voice. He's standing in the doorway of his office, looking straight at me, but I can't make myself meet his stare. He gestures to all of us. "Inside, *now*."

Lydia's hard glare follows me into the room. But I'm too drained, too overwhelmed to pay her any mind.

"Mike, we have this in hand," she starts, but he stops her with one hand in the air.

"No, you don't."

If it were any other situation, I'd find it entertaining how her mouth flaps open and shut like a fish, but this is not the time for amusement.

Uncle Mike sits down behind his desk and gestures at the chairs in front of it. I sit in one, Lydia in the other, Ronan hovering behind me like he's my bodyguard or something. I ignore the furtive glares Lydia keeps sending our way. I know she thinks I should stay quiet, not cause any trouble. But I'm done with following her bullshit.

"Alright. What happened. Because getting a call from my head coach telling me my new player just punched another guy isn't exactly how I saw this evening ending."

For a brief moment, no one speaks. And I realize it's because they're waiting on me. Dragging my eyes up, I look at my uncle. Thank God, all I see is worry and compassion.

"A player from the other team was being inappropriate. Ronan stepped in to help me. It escalated."

"Your personal life created a media disaster," Lydia says sharply. "It won't be long before it hits the headlines that one of our players hit another one over a woman. Good God, as if Maverick didn't cause enough trouble with his bar fight in Arizona."

"Lydia, enough!" Uncle Mike roars, slamming his fists down on his desk. "Don't you dare try to insinuate what happened is Willow's fault when I've already received multiple messages from eyewitnesses stating a player from the other team was borderline harassing my niece. I've heard from Coach Stirling and two others that they were seconds away from intervening when Ronan did. And for you to suggest she did anything to bring this situation upon us is violently abhorrent and inappropriate. You can leave, Lydia. I'll meet with you tomorrow morning."

His tone leaves no room for discussion. I watch, the blood roaring in my ears as Lydia stands and without a second glance at me, storms out of the office, closing the door behind her. Now it's just the three of us with the tension so thick, it weighs the air down. My body feels heavy with it.

Uncle Mike walks around his desk, pulls me up to stand, and gathers me in for a hug. And unlike with Ronan, when I was in shock and freaking out about everyone watching, I fold myself into his arms as if my life depends on it, hugging the man who is the closest thing to a father figure I have left. And maybe my life *does* depend on it. Because he holds my future in his hands. And I've never before felt so unsure about what he'll do with it.

"Alright, you two. Now. Is there anything else I need to know?"

Taking in a ragged breath, I prepare to have the conversation I've been dreading. But first, I turn to the man whose fists are clenched in front of him, and I know without a doubt, it's to stop himself from pulling me into his arms. Which makes what I'm about to say even harder to get out.

"You should go home, Ronan."

Ronan and Uncle Mike both stare at me after my quiet statement.

He takes a step forward, one hand already stretched out toward me. "What? No, Cherry, let me be here for you. We can talk to Mike together."

I'm already shaking my head. "I need to do this alone." With my arms wrapped around my middle, I look up at him, and the confusion and hurt I see there almost makes me relent and let him stay, let him lend me his strength. But I can't right now. I need to face this on my own.

"Willow, I —"

"No." I put my hand up to stop him as he takes another step toward me. "Please. Just go home." My words ring out in the tense atmosphere.

Uncle Mike is silent throughout, but I feel the weight of his stare on me as Ronan and I face each other.

"Cherry," he whispers, pleadingly. But when I give a small shake of my head, I see his resigned acceptance.

He gives me a slow nod in return. "Will you text me when you get home so I know you're okay? Please?"

"Yes."

He moves to the door, pauses, and looks back at me for a second before leaving. And when the door closes behind him, I collapse back down into a chair, my head falling into my hands.

"Oh, Willow."

At Uncle Mike's soft voice, I feel myself break even further. He doesn't sound mad, just weary. Because of me. Then his hand lands on my shoulder, rubbing it comfortingly. I hear him sit down in the chair beside me and I make myself look at him.

"I'm so sorry, Uncle Mike."

To my surprise, he looks mildly offended. "Sorry for what, exactly? Because from what I just heard, you've done nothing wrong."

"Ronan and I..." I start to say, but he waves me off.

"Your relationship with Ronan is not my priority right now, your emotional well-being is."

“I’m okay, really,” I say quietly. “The other guy was just being an asshole. It was inappropriate, but there were plenty of people around. I knew he couldn’t do anything too bad.”

“It still should never have happened, and I’ll be on the phone to the commissioner later tonight. A player who thinks it’s okay to harass women has no place in this league.”

Part of me sags in relief, both that he’s taking it seriously, and hopefully, that player won’t have the opportunity to harass anyone else.

“Thank you.” I gulp and sit up straighter. “But we do need to talk about Ronan. I’m so sorry I’ve put you in this position. I swear, I never wanted to make things complicated for the team. You have to know, when we met in Hawaii last fall, I never expected to see him again. It’s the only reason we...” My face feels warm, and I’m sure I’m blushing. Uncle Mike clears his throat and gestures for me to continue. “But then he got traded to our team. I tried to stay away, I promise. I can only imagine how it must look, the owner’s niece dating the new player.”

Uncle Mike scoffs. “All it looks like to me is two consenting adults developing feelings for each other. There’s no rule against interoffice dating as long as it doesn’t impact performance. On or off the field.” He takes my hands in his and stares straight into my eyes. “And if that man was being honest just now, if he’s smart enough to fall in love with you, then I’d be a selfish fool to stand in the way.”

“I never wanted to put you in a position where you’d have to choose between a player and me.” My voice cracks, and Uncle Mike gathers me back into his arms.

"There wouldn't have been a choice to make. You always come first, Willow. Always. Before any player, any team, anything, and anyone. I promised your father I'd take care of you, and it breaks my heart you didn't realize that, my girl."

Fresh tears brim in my eyes and start to fall. Not just because of Uncle Mike's immediate approval of my relationship with Ronan, but with the realization that Ronan said he loved me. The timing could not have been worse, and part of me is reeling from how suddenly everything feels flipped upside down in my life. But he loves me. Everything he did today was to protect me.

But a decade of believing that being in a relationship with a player on the team would be the worst sin I could possibly commit doesn't just disappear in an instant. And today has been a lot. Too much. All I want to do is go home and crawl into my bed and try to make sense of everything.

Chapter Thirty

Ronan

"You keep staring at that phone like it's magically gonna sprout wings and fly away."

Of all the people I would've expected to drop down into the seat next to me on the bus carrying us to our hotel, Maverick wasn't even on the list. My frown deepens as I flip my phone upside down.

It's been three days since I last saw Willow in her uncle's office. Three days since I said I loved her and she didn't even acknowledge it. Three fucking days since she last communicated with me at all. A two-word text that simply said, *I'm home.*

I'm no idiot, I know she wants space right now, even though every fiber of my being wants to be with her, hold her, and tell her everything will be okay. Except I don't know that it will. Not until I can talk to her. In my caveman protect-at-all-costs-claim-her-as-mine moment, I revealed our secret and my feelings. And I haven't stopped berating myself ever since.

And of course, we had to leave on a six day away series the very next morning. I texted her before we left, an apology even

I know isn't nearly good enough, and a plea to talk as soon as she's willing. My hope was that she'd call, but I think I have to accept this isn't going to be fixed while I'm away.

But knowing whether or not she's alright would be a really good thing right now.

We're currently somewhere in the midwestern United States, but my head is back in Vancouver. A fact that hasn't gone unnoticed by the rest of my team. Thankfully, my ankle is fine, and I was declared fit to play by the team doctors and Lark before we left. If only I could blame my yips on an injury instead of the mess with Willow...

Yesterday, I struck out both times I was at the plate. I missed an easy pop fly in the third inning, and my throws have been wild. I'm playing like absolute shit, and I knew it was only a matter of time before someone came to talk to me about it. After all, the gossip about what went down the other evening has spread like wildfire. Everyone knows I punched a guy and why. Just like everyone saw me kiss Willow's head and has jumped to the logical conclusion.

Which brings me back to my initial surprise that Maverick, of all people, is the one to be here.

"Willow doing okay?" he asks, taking a small circular metal object out of his pocket, flipping it between his fingers.

I let out an aggravated huff. "If I knew, I wouldn't be checking my phone."

He just nods, staring straight ahead. Damn, this guy is hard to read.

"She's good people. If you were defending her, then that makes you good people, too."

With that statement, Maverick stands up and moves to the back of the bus. I crane my neck to follow him, somewhat baffled. That's all he came here to say? Good job for defending Willow? *What the fuck?*

I twist back around and like a putz, check my phone again. Still nothing. Letting my head fall back against the headrest, I close my eyes and try to stop worrying about what it means that she still hasn't responded to me.

We pull into the hotel we're staying at tonight and everyone files out of the bus. It's late; I just want to go to sleep and hope that tomorrow Willow ends the communication freeze before I have to go out on the field again.

But that's not in the cards for me. As we enter the hotel, someone calls out my name. I turn and see none other than the Tridents' owner exiting a dark SUV. He buttons his suit jacket and strides over to me. That's a surprise, seeing as he doesn't usually travel to away games. Which means he must be here for a reason other than baseball.

My stomach feels like it fills with lead.

"Have a drink with me, Sinclair."

There's no way I can decline, even if a drink with Willow's uncle, who may or may not approve of our relationship is the last fucking thing I want to do right now.

"Yes, sir."

I follow him into the building, veering left to the hotel bar instead of right to the concierge. Monty looks over with a concerned expression, but I pretend not to notice. Instead, I sit down next to Mike at the bar.

"Two bourbons. Neat." The bartender gives Mike a nod, and only then does he turn to me. "Hope that's okay?"

"Yeah, it's fine. Thanks." My voice is gruff, unease filling me. I don't know what to say right now, what questions he might ask and how I should answer. I fucked up once already, and I really don't want to do it again.

"Ronan, I'll cut to the chase. What you did for Willow might have caused a bit of a nightmare behind the scenes, but I'm grateful. You protected someone who I consider family." The bartender sets down our drinks, and Mike picks his up, tilting his head at me. "Thank you for defending our girl. I know she's processing a lot right now, and she likes to push people away when she's dealing with emotions. Trust me, I've been on the receiving end of a Willow Lawson freeze-out. But she'll come around."

I toy with my glass before answering. "I hope you're right, sir. But Willow has every right to be upset with me. She wanted to keep our relationship a secret because she was really concerned about it potentially causing issues with her position with the Tridents. And if I can be blunt, your reaction to it. If she has a lot to process right now, that's mostly my fault for not keeping our relationship private the other night."

"She had no reason to be concerned about my reaction, and I'll carry the guilt for somehow making her think she did." He takes a sip of his drink and fixes me with a cool, unwavering stare. "Did you mean it?"

I lower my glass and swallow the smooth liquor before asking, "Meant what, exactly?"

"When you said you loved her. Did you mean it? Because if you did, then you better understand that she deserves the world. More than that. She deserves everything a man can give her. That woman might seem strong and independent, but inside, she's lonely. Her parents didn't want her. Her adoptive dad, God rest his soul, loved her immensely but died far too soon. I've done my best, but it's not the same. She wants someone who loves her above anything else. Someone who will make a family with her. Someone who will cherish her and never let her feel alone again. Someone who will defend her, protect her, and stand at her side, just as you did. But I need to know if you're truly going to be that man for her, now and forever. Because if you're not, then walk away."

I try to catch up to everything he's said and everything it means. "You're not mad that we're dating?"

Mike scoffs, waving his hand as he picks up his drink. "Hell, no. And I said this to her the other night. You're two consenting adults. As long as you treat her right, with love and respect, and don't let it affect your performance on the field anymore, I have no problem with it. I recognize she's faced adversity being a woman in a man's world and fighting against those who believe I'd be stupid enough to hire her just because of our relationship. The last thing she wanted was to be seen as just a WAG, the same as she never wanted to be seen as a nepo hire. But neither one of those are true, and I know it just as well as you do. She needs someone to help her believe it, even when people challenge her on it. So if you love Willow and can make her happy, then that's all that matters."

"I don't plan on saying those particular words again until I'm certain she's ready to hear it directly from me and without an audience," I say solemnly. "But rest assured, what you just said is what I believe as well."

"Then there's no problem I can see except for how we're going to get your head back in the game. I need my star player back."

This time I raise my glass first, inclining my head toward the man who's just single-handedly told me I have a chance at having everything I've ever wanted.

"Thank you, sir. I promise you, I'll be ready for tomorrow."

The clink of our glasses has my lips quirking up. The struggle isn't over; I still have to convince Willow to give our relationship a chance to exist out in the open. But having Mike on my side should make that task a whole hell of a lot easier.

A short while later, I step out of the shower, wrapping a towel around my waist. Picking up my phone, I ignore the pang in my chest when there's still nothing from Willow. There is, however, a message from my mom, saying Peyton's heading to bed soon.

After I pull on some pajama pants, I sit back against the headboard of the bed and open up a video call with them. As soon as the screen fills with my little girl, I grin. "Hey, kiddo!"

"Hi Daddy! Can I see your room?"

I dutifully stand up and take her on a brief tour of my room, including pointing the phone out the window, despite the sky already being dark. When I'm done, I settle back on the bed. "So what did you get up to today?"

"Gran took me to the park at my new school, then we went for ice cream, and then I coloured a picture for Willow. Wanna see it?"

"Of course, I do." My stomach flip-flops. The one piece of the puzzle I haven't yet fully thought through is Peyton. If Willow can't move forward with our relationship, my little girl will be devastated. She's just as attached as I am. Peyton disappears from the screen for a couple of minutes before returning, brandishing a green piece of paper. She holds it up, and I see a drawing of four stick figures, and something I assume is an animal. There's a small circle above their heads, and their hands are up.

"Looks great, baby girl. Can you describe it to me?"

"It's you, me, Gran, and Willow playing baseball. Can't you tell?" Peyton sounds exasperated in a way only a four-year-old can. "See? There's the ball. You're gonna catch it. And that's the dog I wanna get."

"A dog, huh?" I force a smile, even as my throat feels thick with emotion. "I love it, Pey. You're a great artist."

"I wanna give it to Willow. When is she coming over again?" Peyton bounces up and down on the couch in the family room, the same couch where she was cuddled up against Willow watching a movie not that long ago.

As soon as she asks that oh-so-innocent question, that thick feeling in my throat intensifies. Because it's not one I can easily answer. "I'm not really sure. I'll talk to her when I get home, how about that?"

"'Kay. And will you give her my picture?" Peyton goes on, blissfully unaware of how her dear old dad is tied up in knots about the very woman she wants to give a drawing.

"You bet," I answer, raking my hand through my still-damp hair. "It's bedtime now, though. I'll be home in a couple of days, maybe you could draw me a picture as well? My locker at the stadium could use something new."

"I'll draw you one like Willow's. Then you guys can match."

"Sounds great." I muster up a smile. "Now, get your booty to bed."

"Love you, Daddy."

My smile automatically grows a lot bigger at those three words. "Love you, too, Rocket."

We hang up, but I don't put my phone down. Instead, I switch over to my text messages and hover over Willow's name. I want to respect her need for space, but I also need her to know I'm not giving up easily.

RONAN: Hey Cherry. Just want to say I miss you, and I hope I haven't screwed things up so badly that I never get a chance to tell you I'm sorry in person. Or to say the other words I shouldn't have said that day, even if they were – and still are – true. I'll give you as much space as you need, I swear. But I'm not giving up on us. And I'm not going to let you give up without a fight.

I stare at my screen after I hit send, overthinking every word I just typed. Until my phone starts to vibrate in my hand with an incoming video call.

My mouth goes instantly dry as I hit answer. "Hi."

Willow's beautiful face fills my screen, making my heart ache. Fuck, I wish I was there right now.

"Hey," she replies softly, and I see her settle into the corner of her couch. "I hope this is okay to just call?"

God, I hate that she sounds unsure. As if I would be upset that she called. "Cherry, this is more than okay. It's so good to see you. I've missed you."

"I'm sorry I wasn't ready to talk, it was just...so much happened that day. I needed a minute."

"Baby, don't apologize for needing some time. Please." I want to reach through the phone and pull her into my arms, to ease the stress written all over her face. "I hope you know just how sorry I am for how things went down that night. I'm not apologizing for defending you against that asshole, or with Lydia, but I am sorry for the outcome. For our relationship ending up public knowledge before you were really ready for that. And I never should have confessed my feelings in front of your uncle and Lydia. Not only because you wanted us to keep things a secret, but because that's not the way you deserve to hear me say I'm falling in love with you. You deserve to hear those words when it's just you and me, and when I can not only say them, but show you. But I'm not going to deny those feelings any longer, either. I can't."

I watch her brush away a tear from her cheek when I finally finish blurting out my apology and my hand clenches in the sheets beside me. I'm trying hard not to be frustrated that we're having this conversation over the phone, instead of when I'm home and can hold her. But I'll be damned if I'm not going to seize this opportunity to tell her how I feel.

"I love you, Willow Lawson. I never expected to, never thought I deserved to have a woman like you when I'm already blessed with a career like mine and an amazing daughter. I didn't think I could have it all, but now I realize I just never found a woman who was worth fighting for. A woman who would be worth the work of balancing a demanding career, my daughter, and a relationship. But you're worth it. Hell, you deserve even more than what I can give you, but I'm hoping you'll let me try to be the man you deserve."

"Ronan," she starts with a whisper, and my heart freezes. "I hear you. I hear those beautiful words, and I want to be ready to say them back. But you have to understand, everything I thought I knew, or believed to be true, has been flipped upside down. And I know it's a good thing. That Uncle Mike is fine with our relationship. But things have changed now that everyone knows about us, and I just need a minute to wrap my head around that new reality."

"Cherry, you take whatever time you need to adjust. Just know that I'm not going anywhere, and I'm not giving up on us. What we have is too good, too right. You need to see that it's safe to love me, that nothing bad will happen, and I swear, I'll be right here waiting to prove that to you whenever you're ready."

Chapter Thirty-One

Willow

Waiting three more days for Ronan to come home after our long emotional call has been torture. He loves me. He's not going to stop loving me just because I needed a bit more time. And he's made it very clear just how serious he is about winning me back. I can't wait until I see him in person to tell him he doesn't have to win me back. Because I'm already his.

Still, having a fresh cup of coffee fixed exactly the way I like it waiting on my desk each morning was a nice surprise. Although, I have no idea how he managed it from the road. And now, today, there's a giant glass jar full of Skittles sitting on my desk without a single yellow one.

My smile is wide as I open my text messages, snap a photo of the jar, and send Ronan a text. The team just got back into town early this morning, and I'm guessing he's spending the day with Peyton.

WILLOW: You realize I make Lark keep my skittles so that I don't eat them all at once, right? This is dangerous…

His answer shows up seconds later.

RONAN: You're the strongest woman I know, you can handle the temptation. Besides. When they're all gone, I'll just refill the jar.

WILLOW: So you'll still like me when I balloon in size from eating a million skittles a day?

RONAN: Cherry, I'd still love you no matter what you look like. You're beautiful, and you always will be to me.

His easy use of that L-word makes goosebumps appear along my arm, and my grin doesn't subside.

"Willow, can you come into my office for a meeting? We've got a situation." Uncle Mike's voice is grim from the doorway of my office, making my attention snap up to him from my phone.

He takes in the candy jar on my desk with raised eyebrows but doesn't say a thing. His face does, however, soften as he looks at me with a small knowing smile.

I stand up, grabbing my phone and a notepad before hurrying after him to his office. Once we're inside, he closes the door.

"What's going on?" I ask nervously. "Should I call Lydia?"

Uncle Mike shakes his head. "No." That cryptic one-word answer has my eyes widening, but he shoots me a look that silences me.

"The issue at hand is Maverick King." Steepling his fingers together, Uncle Mike takes a long breath in and out. "He's in the hospital."

I gasp, but he holds up his hand.

"That's not the real issue. I mean, it is, but there's more. There's a video all over social media that's going viral." Uncle Mike turns his phone around so I can see it. And it's not good.

Maverick is standing face-to-face with some other guy, a small group of people behind them. It's hard to see with the shaky video quality, but Mav looks angry. They're out on some country road I don't recognize. He climbs into a red sports car, the other guy into a black one, and the next thing I hear is the roar of engines and the squeal of tires as both cars take off at top speed.

This can't be good.

Off camera, I can hear someone talking about the cars, placing bets on who they think might win. Then there's a sickening sound, and the cameraman starts yelling before the video cuts off.

"What happened?" I demand.

"Maverick's car hit a telephone pole," Uncle Mike answers, and my heart plummets.

"Oh my God," I say in absolute shock, even as my brain starts spinning with what needs to be done on our end. "Is he okay? Was the other driver hurt?"

"Maverick is the only one who crashed. As for how he is, he'll be fine after surgery and rehab, apparently," Uncle Mike says grimly. "He's got a fractured collarbone and bruised ribs according to his agent, who's at the hospital right now. Our priority is figuring out our narrative for a response and trying to keep the press from finding out where he is. I'll be honest, I don't know how this is going to play out for Maverick. What he did was incredibly reckless, not to mention potentially illegal if it's confirmed to be a street race. He's looking at fines, if not worse. Also, who knows what his injuries will mean for his career."

Uncle Mike's face is sorrowful as we're both silent for a moment. A broken collarbone could be devastating for a baseball player depending on the severity of the fracture. I pick up my own phone and start scrolling through the headlines that are already popping up all over. The video of Maverick and the other guy right before they get into the cars is everywhere, but I can't find any other videos with different angles that show the crash, or details of why he was out there. And so far, there's nothing indicating where he was hospitalized. Nonetheless, managing this is going to be a circus.

"It's not looking good for Maverick or for the team the longer we go without issuing a statement. How do we do that — condemning Mav's actions without selling him out completely? That's what I need you to answer, Willow."

My head shoots up. "Wh-what?"

He nods. "I'm very aware that you've been carrying Lydia's weight for months. I would have stepped in sooner, but I know how you feel about things looking like nepotism." He shakes his head. "But after the other week, hearing her try to blame you for that man's actions? Well, I'm sorry, my girl, but nepotism be damned. This morning, I suggested to Lydia that she should take her remaining vacation time as early retirement. And she agreed. You're the woman who should be leading our media team, and everyone knows it. So step up and lead."

It's late before I manage to leave the office, and when I do, Uncle Mike is still in his office on the phone. The rest of the office is empty, but I know he won't leave until he feels like he's done all he can do.

He thinks of each and every player as one of his family, just like I do. But for him, it's different. I know he feels responsible for them all, and I know Maverick's antics get to him more than he lets on. Just as I know he's not going to throw Maverick under the bus, despite the challenges he presents.

But none of that helps right now. With Lydia apparently leaving the Tridents sooner than expected, I've been thrust into the official leadership position, just in time to manage a potential publicity shitstorm. Together we crafted a press release, which has been sent out already. I've put up a statement on our socials and our website, but there's nothing more to be done until we talk to Maverick and his agent.

Which is tomorrow's problem, not today's.

I stagger into my apartment, dropping my bag at the door as I kick off my heels. I move straight toward my bathroom, piling my hair on top of my head. Once I've got my tub filling with hot water, I go back to my kitchen, pour a large glass of wine, then return to my bedroom to strip and climb into a steaming hot bath.

Sinking into the water with a sigh, I close my eyes. The next few days are going to be absolutely insane. The team is scheduled to be in town for a set of games starting tomorrow, and Maverick's absence will be felt. I've already had several messages from staff asking about the videos circulating online, despite the memo Uncle Mike sent out to all players and staff giving a brief summary of the situation.

Everyone's worried about Mav, including myself. But I can't do anything more for him tonight.

What I really want is to see Ronan. I won't lie, I'm disappointed I haven't heard from him since our text exchange this morning. Just then, as if he's reading my mind, my phone rings with an incoming video call. Keeping my current nudity in mind, I angle the phone so all he can see is my head and press answer.

"Hey, beautiful, I just saw the email from Mike. What can I do to help?"

Maybe it's the fact that his first reaction is to offer me support; maybe it's just my exhaustion and how much I miss him. Whatever it is, my eyes instantly fill with tears.

"Cherry, are you crying? Shit, don't cry," he says, looking distressed, even through the phone. "Fuck, I knew I should have come over. But I was with Peyton all day, and then tonight, Mom had plans to go out. God, I'm sorry, baby."

I swipe away the tears and try to muster a weak smile. "I'm okay. I'm tired and worried about Mav. But I'm okay, I swear."

I hear a door open in the background, and Ronan's head turns to the side. Peyton's voice is sleepy and muffled. Ronan says something to her, then looks back at the phone.

"Willow, I have to go, Peyton needs me. I'll call you right back."

"No, it's fine. We can talk tomorrow."

He stares at me as if he wants to fight me on that, but then I hear Peyton's voice again.

"Go. She needs you. Goodnight." I give him a watery smile and hang up the call.

Setting my phone down, I pick up my wine, only for the damn thing to start ringing again. I debate ignoring it, but then I see it's Tori calling, so I answer, putting her on speaker.

"Don't tell me you saw the video as well?" I say by way of greeting.

"I did, and yikes. Is he okay? In jail? Want me to come over for a few days and keep you company so you don't go insane and forget to feed yourself?"

It's the second time in just a few minutes that I've been offered help by people who genuinely care about me, and something about that indisputable fact breaks through the walls around my heart completely. Tori might not live in the same city as me anymore, but she's still there for me. She's still my best friend, my family.

And Ronan's first concern wasn't his injured teammate's situation being splashed all over the media, but rather how I — the person handling the media outfall — was managing.

"Tori, I think I'm in love with Ronan Sinclair."

Silence meets my abrupt declaration. I stand up, let the water out of the tub, and climb out to wrap myself in a towel, clarity and peace settling over me. Then, finally, my best friend answers me.

"Um, that's not exactly what I was calling to discuss, but okay, let's switch subjects. Why do you think that?"

I frown. "Do you think that's a bad thing?"

"Hey now, that's not what I said," Tori protests. "Stop overanalyzing me. I've had a hunch this moment was coming for a while, I just want to hear you say it. What's so special about him? Why is he worth you breaking your rule and falling for a baseball player?"

My frown instantly softens into a smile. "Because he's so much more than just a baseball player. He's kind, and caring, and he's the most amazing dad to a wonderful little girl. He sees me, he gets me, and he respects me. He's humble and not afraid to admit when he's wrong. He wants to worship me, Tori, and I want to let him."

Letting out a low whistle, Tori replies, "You deserve a little worshipping, Wills. And he does seem like a good guy. Have you forgiven him for spilling the beans on your relationship in front of everyone?"

I nod, even though she can't see me. "Yeah, I think I did almost immediately. He was protecting me, T. That's all. Besides, it had to come out eventually if we were ever to stay together. Do I wish it hadn't happened that way? Yes. Of course. I wanted to talk to my uncle myself, not have it play out like a soap opera, with fistfights and public declarations. But he was trying to protect me, and I can't stay mad at the man I love for that."

"Have you told *Ronan* you love him?"

"Why do you ask the hard questions?" I grouse as a stab of guilt hits me.

"Because I love you, and I know you. And your inability to let people get close to you isn't new."

I let that sink in, nodding, even though she can't see me. "You're the best, T. Thanks for loving me even when I'm being an idiot."

"You're fine, Wills. But I'm not the only one who needs to hear that."

She's right, again. "I know."

We're both quiet for another minute but my exhaustion has faded. Forget sleep, I want to run through the streets straight to Ronan's house and tell him how I feel.

"Well, my romance author heart is happy," Tori finally says. "The sexy single dad and the badass boss babe find their happily ever after. Five stars, would recommend."

I laugh, flopping back on my bed with a stupid grin on my face that quickly fades when I remember the reality I have waiting for me at work. "Yeah, except with the Maverick situation, this isn't exactly the best time to tell Ronan how I feel. How long do I have to wait?"

Tori's giggle isn't especially comforting. "You'll survive, Wills."

"Easy for you to say," I grumble. "Your hottie firefighter lives with you. You've got twenty-four seven access to orgasms and cuddles."

"Yeah, right, except for the fact that he works insane shifts, and I've got my kid to contend with," Tori fires back with laughter in her voice. "You'll see. Having a relationship with a single parent, combined with a demanding job? You're gonna have to get creative at finding moments to be together. But when you do? Those moments are amazing."

"I want amazing moments," I whisper into the phone.

After a beat, Tori whispers back, "You'll get them. I promise."

And as I go to sleep that night, I rest easier than I expected.

Because she's right. Ronan and me? Our amazing moments are waiting for us. And I'm ready to experience each and every single one of them, with him and Peyton, together.

Chapter Thirty-Two

Ronan

You'd think after our recent conversations, Willow and I would be desperate to see each other. And I, for one, am. But that doesn't mean it's been simple trying to get a moment alone with my woman. Not with my responsibilities to the team and to my family, and her work obligations.

She's been working late every day as management figures out how to handle the mess Maverick ended up in. I had dinner sent up to her last night, but every time I tried to check on her today, she was on the phone or in a meeting. Now the team is set to leave for another set of away games tomorrow, and I'll be damned if I'm gonna go out of town without seeing her first.

Which is why, instead of heading home tonight after a quick conditioning practice, I texted Mom saying I'd be home late, then hung around under the pretense of needing extra time in the ice bath. I know I need to just tell her about Willow, especially since Peyton's already mentioned her a few times in front of Mom. So far, she hasn't questioned me, just given me a few raised eyebrows.

The stadium is cleared out except for the janitors, and when I make my way up to the executive floor, it's also empty. Except for one light — in Willow's office. When I get to her door, I stop and just watch her for a moment. The soft glow from the table lamp illuminates her, making the dark hair piled on top of her head glow. She looks tired, and I want nothing more than to take her home, feed her, put her in a hot bath, then curl up around her in bed for the night.

We've still never had an entire night together, and I long to feel the sensation of waking up in the morning with her in my arms.

"Ronan?" Her voice breaks through my fantasies, and I blink to see her looking at me, confused. "What are you doing here so late?"

I push off the door frame I was leaning against and walk into her office, coming around to her side of the desk. "I could ask you the same thing, Cherry. Everyone else has gone home, so why are you still here?"

Her shoulders slump with exhaustion. "It's this situation with Maverick." She waves her hands. "I shouldn't talk about it with you. Sorry."

I move in behind her and squeeze her tense shoulders. "Its okay. We all know what's going on anyway, so I'm here if you need to talk about it. If it helps, he's a good guy, Willow. He fucks up a lot, but he's a good guy in a shitty situation. And if there's anyone that can help him figure out a way through, it's you."

She twists in her chair to look up at me with such wonder, it confuses me for a minute. "How do you sound so confident, so sure, when I don't even feel that way about myself?"

Leaning down, I press a simple kiss to her forehead. "Because, Willow Lawson, you're a force to be reckoned with. You're strong, you're capable, and you're smart. You know what matters for the team and for the players. And nothing will get in your way of making sure everything works out. That's why you're here, doing this job, with everyone's respect and admiration."

She spins around fully, stands up, and leans into me, finally letting me hold her. And it's such a precious gift, this moment in time when I feel her walls come down, I want to savour it. Stay just like this and soak it in. I want to help her, protect her, but most of all, support her. Because she doesn't need me to fix anything, she just needs me to remind her she can do it. Whatever it is. She can, and she will.

Willow might have been the woman to show me I deserve to have it all as long as I put in the effort to balance everything, but I want to be the man to show her she doesn't have to be alone anymore. That there's someone out there who wants to see her succeed. Who believes in her ability to be anything and everything she wants to be. Who respects her drive and passion and doesn't try to stifle it with their own needs.

I take a small step away, still holding one of her hands in mine, and reach into my back pocket, withdrawing the picture Peyton drew when I was on that damn away game series. When I didn't know if Willow would ever give me another chance.

"Peyton wanted you to have this." I watch her face as she unfolds the paper. Her mouth turns up in a smile as her whole being softens with affection toward my daughter.

"This is amazing," she murmurs. When she looks up at me, her eyes are shining with emotion. "Ronan, please tell her I love it."

I stuff my hands in my pockets and try not to appear antsy. But God, I hope that someday, a picture from my daughter isn't the only thing she says she loves. "I will."

She moves around her desk, over to a whiteboard on the wall of her office. Picking a magnet off the board, she sets Peyton's drawing up in the top corner, securing it with the magnet before turning back to me with a smile. "It's perfect."

My gaze is glued to her as she walks over to me. Am I imagining things or is there a bit of a sway to her step, a seductiveness in her moves? When she doesn't stop, coming straight up to me so that just inches separate us, I get my answer. Lifting one hand to wrap around the back of my neck, Willow pulls my head down toward hers.

Her lips meet mine and I can't hold back my groan. The relief that washes over me at having her back in my arms is intense. All-consuming, just like her kiss. Everything that was in turmoil inside of me settles with just the press of her lips against mine.

"Fuck, I've missed you, Cherry."

Her arms squeeze me even tighter. "I missed you, too."

My hands find her ass and I lift her up and into my arms, setting her on the edge of her desk so I can press in close to her.

"Ronan," she murmurs against my mouth, and I feel the upward curve of her smile. "This isn't exactly appropriate workplace behaviour."

I pull away slightly as I laugh. "You started it, woman."

Her affronted look is in direct contrast to the laughter I see her holding back. "Listen. It's not my fault baseball players have great butts." Tugging me back in close, her hand roams down my back to squeeze my ass. "And they look even better in compression tights and shorts."

I smirk. "So, my decision to hang around after training was a good one. Is that what you're saying?"

"For more than one reason." Willow guides my head down to whisper in my ear. "There's no one here except the janitors. Close the door."

I move fast, shutting and locking her office door and returning to my place between her legs in seconds. Her giggle is throaty, sexy, and sends a jolt of lust straight to my dick. "I thought you were worried about appropriate workplace behaviour?" I rumble, capturing her earlobe in between my teeth. Her fingers rake through my hair as she tilts her head to the side, presenting the smooth column of her neck for me to kiss.

"Maybe that's not such a problem anymore."

I still, needing to hear the words from her, despite her obvious intentions. "Does that mean you're ready for this? For our relationship to be out in the open?"

Willow straightens, smiling softly at me. "That means you're mine and I'm yours. In private and in public. I don't want to hide anymore."

"Thank fuck," I growl immediately before taking her mouth again, giving everything I have to our kiss. Her ankles lock around my waist, her desk putting Willow's hot core at the perfect level. There's just too many layers of clothes between us.

My hand snakes down between us, popping the button open at the top of her pants and sliding down the zipper so I can slip my fingers inside. She's drenched. "Damn, Cherry. Is this all for me?"

Her answering moan as I play with her slick folds is all the answer I need. With a wicked grin, I drop to my knees. Willow helpfully lifts her hips so I can slide her pants down and all the way off as she kicks her shoes to the side. Then she's spreading those long, luscious legs, baring herself to me.

Her back arches as soon as my tongue hits her damp flesh. I swipe up and down her slit, lapping up every drop of her. I want to go slow, to make our reunion last for a long time, but all hope of that is lost when she grips my hair, moaning low and long with pleasure. I circle her clit a few times, flicking the tip with my tongue. I want to bury my entire face in her sweetness. Drown myself in it. As much as I want to watch her come undone, my eyes close as I press my face in closer, moving faster, plunging my tongue in as deep as I can until her thighs clamp around my head and she starts chanting my name. Just when I think I'll lose the ability to breathe, her body hits the precipice and topples over into her orgasm. And I slow my movements, licking and sucking gently until the tension leaves her body and her legs go limp.

When I move to stand, my knees ache a little, but the pain is worth it when I see the dreamy and dazed but completely satisfied expression on her face. After I wipe my wet mouth on my sleeve, I lean in and press a soft kiss to her upturned lips.

"Mmm," she hums, opening her eyes. She might not be ready to say it, but I can see her feelings for me written across her face. "That was...perfect."

She's perfect. And finally, I get to start proving that to her. One orgasm, one smile, one moment at a time. Nothing can ruin how happy I am right now. Everything I never knew I wanted is mine.

Chapter Thirty-Three

Willow

There are pretty strict rules during away games when it comes to hotel rooms. The guys all get their own room, but they're not meant to have guests. Like, not at all.

Which makes my decision to sneak into Ronan's room on this stretch very risky and very unusual for me, the girl who doesn't break the rules often.

But this man makes me want to throw my damn rule book out the window. I want him constantly. Even more so now that we've worked through the drama from the other week, and the world hasn't ended with everyone knowing about us. Which is why I jumped at the chance to fly out and join the team for the last few days of their away game series, even though my workload managing Maverick's situation is still heavy.

Three days out of town to watch the games and appreciate Ronan's talent openly without worrying about who's watching?

Yes, please.

Two nights of lying in my lonely hotel bed, knowing he's just one floor above me, also lying in a lonely hotel bed?

No, thanks.

Which brings me to the present, opening the door from the stairwell on Ronan's floor and peeking around the corner to see if anyone's out in the hall. It's late and the guys are tired after winning their game today. It's the last game of the series; tomorrow we'll hop on a plane and head home to Vancouver. And try as I might, I can't stay away from Ronan a minute longer. I need to feel his arms around me, his lips on mine, his cock inside of me.

I'm desperate for an orgasm only he can provide.

All it takes is one soft knock and his door whips open, a hand reaching out to pull me inside. I muffle my giggle as Ronan closes the door and flips over the security latch. "Did anyone see you?" he whispers in a low rumble.

I shake my head as I toe off my shoes, already turned on just from the sight of him, shirtless, wearing nothing but a pair of soft plaid pajama pants. "No one." I tear my sweater off over my head.

"Fuck, I've missed you," he groans softly as it falls to the floor. He stays at the door, watching me with a predatory gaze. "Having you so close these last few days but not being able to kiss you whenever I want, not holding you in my arms every spare second, not being able to *fuck you every night* has been torture."

My pants drop and I step out of them, clad only in my lace underwear and bra, and put my hands on my hips. "Who said you couldn't kiss me?"

He's breathing heavily, his arousal evident, given the bulge in his pants. His eyes are like molten fire, staring at me. "I was trying to be respectful."

Slowly, I advance, prowling toward him. "Word is out that we're together now; you can be respectful and still kiss me," I whisper as I reach him, placing one hand on his muscular chest, raking my nails lightly through the short hairs. "And there's no reason you can't fuck me now. In fact, I'd be very pleased if you would."

Ronan stoops down slightly, only to lift me up into his arms. My breathless giggle is swallowed by his kiss as he moves quickly into the bathroom. The only light comes from the bedside lamps, making the bathroom dark. It's intimate, the soft glow reflecting on the mirrors of the bathroom, the dim light making us rely so much more on touch.

And oh boy, do I want to touch. My hands roam across his chest and shoulders as we kiss. He's still holding me, my legs locked around his waist. Somehow, with one arm still tightly banded around me, he manages to use his other hand to turn on the shower. The room quickly fills with steam and only then does he set me down. He pulls a foil packet out of his pajama pocket, setting it on the shower ledge with a wink aimed my way. My hands hurry to unclasp my bra, and then I wiggle out of my panties as he pushes down his pants. He takes my hand and leads me into the large shower, turning so that the force of the water is on him and I get just a light spray of damp heat. Water droplets cling to him, tracing a path down his body that I want to follow with my tongue.

But Ronan tilts my chin up with his hand and kisses me swiftly. "Kai is in the room next door, Cherry. And these walls are thin. Which means you've got to be quiet. That's why we're here. So the water can hide the sound of you moaning my name when I make you come."

He tugs my lower lip between his teeth when he's done talking, biting gently before sweeping his tongue inside my mouth. We stay there, making out like sex-crazed maniacs for several minutes. The steam from the shower swirls around us, adding to the erotic energy. Stealing my idea, Ronan presses one more deep kiss to my lips before dropping to his knees, his tongue tracing the fall of water over my body.

"Mmm. I've missed you." He tilts his head up to look at me, and the look of pure wonder and happiness on his face almost brings me to my knees with its intensity. This mixture of sweet, romantic Ronan and the dirty words he speaks to me is the perfect blend of everything I've always wanted.

His lips graze my belly button, and then down farther, until he kisses the top of my mound. So close to where I want him, my hips move on their own, searching, seeking his touch.

"Ronan, please," I whisper, my head thrown back against the tile wall of the shower as he ghosts his lips around my sex. His hands dig into my hips, guiding me to widen my stance. And then, finally.

With the first swipe of his tongue, I have to clap a hand over my mouth to hide my moan of relief. The second swipe, I'm digging into the strands of his hair to hold him in place. The third, I'm lost. My hips writhe under his touch with every lick, suck, bite, and kiss.

After the last few days of *look but don't touch*, I'm ready to combust.

"More. Fuck. Yes. More. Ohmygod, Ronan. Right there!" My whispers become frantic, it's hard to stay quiet when he sucks my clit into his mouth, sliding one finger into my greedy sex. But just as my orgasm is within reach, he releases me, and there's no muffling my whine of discontent.

"Why are you torturing me?" I half growl, half whine as I slap his chest once he's standing up, towering over me again. I can feel his hard length between us and reach down to wrap my hands around it. But he stops me, his hand covering mine.

"Because I need to feel that pussy squeezing my dick. Holding me inside of you, where I belong."

"Then what are you waiting for?" I mumble against his lips, feeling his curve up in response.

"Are you aching and desperate for me like I am for you?" He leans back giving me an arrogant smirk.

My head bobs up and down.

"Good."

Fingers probe my entrance, sliding in and out easily as I gasp and let my head fall back, eyes closed. He teases me just for a minute or two more before withdrawing. My eyes fly open and I'm about to let him know just how I feel about this edging, but then I hear the telltale crinkle of the condom wrapper, and when I look down, he's rolling it onto his cock.

"Fucking finally."

Ronan just laughs at my impatience. With one hand, he lifts my leg, encouraging me to wrap it around his waist. He has to bend his knees slightly to line us up, and then he's thrusting into me, shallow at first, then deeper every time until our hips meet, flush against one another and he's fully inside of me.

"God, yes," I moan, and the sound echoes in the dim bathroom.

His mouth covers mine for a second, then without fully lifting his lips from mine, he whispers, "Shh."

Slowly, he starts to move. In and out. Our height difference makes his cock stroke my inner walls at just the right angle, the slight curve to his cock hitting me with every snap of his hips. The cool tile behind me contrasts with the intense heat of the water and of Ronan's body against mine.

With all his teasing earlier, it's all I can do to hold off my orgasm. I might want the release, but I don't want this to end.

"Fuck, Willow," he whispers against my skin as our foreheads press together under the spray of the shower. "I can't hold off, Cherry. I'm sorry. I have to —"

He's cut off by his own orgasm, and his low groan triggers my own as I gasp and writhe in his arms, my body clenching around his throbbing dick that I swear, I feel pulsing inside of me.

His head drops to my shoulder as he takes in a ragged breath before lifting his head to press the sweetest of kisses to my lips.

To my surprise, tears gather in my eyes. It hits me then, all the times I thought I saw something unreadable or undefinable on his face — it wasn't that I couldn't read him. I just wasn't ready for the truth of what was written so clearly.

He loves me. This man loves me.

And I love him, too. I just have to be brave enough to tell him.

A little while later, we're tangled together in his bed. I'm back in my bra and panties and Ronan's wearing his pajama pants to give us some hope of restraint. I can't stay the night, as much as I want to. The chance of getting caught sneaking out of his room goes up exponentially tomorrow morning. Which means I have to leave soon. But not right now.

Right now, I'm warm and comfortable, cuddled up against his side. His hand is drawing lazy circles across my bare skin, and his lips keep pressing soft kisses to the top of my head. There's an easy silence between us, and in that space, my mind starts to fill in the gaps, illuminating the parts of our relationship I tried to ignore.

The parts where I held back, afraid to tell him my deepest fears.

"In university, I had this professor. She was a former journalist. And she used to tell us stories of her time spent working the sports circuit. How women were treated as second-rate, about the rampant misogynism. It was horrible. She warned all of us girls that we'd have to work double hard for half the reward if we went into sports. That we'd constantly be fighting to prove we belonged in that space. That message never left me." I suck in a deep breath, letting the feel of his hand on me settle me. "When Uncle Mike offered me the internship, I almost said no. The Tridents were where I always wanted to work, but I wanted to earn my way. But in the end, Uncle Mike agreed he would never get involved in my career path, and he pointed out that using connections wasn't necessarily a bad thing." A small smile graces my face remembering that conversation. "Still, that fear of being seen as nothing more than a nepotism hire, the niece who couldn't get a job on her own, the woman who needed a man's help to get anywhere, it never really faded. Even after years of hard work, proving I belonged, and that I had value. It's never fully gone away. I struggle with it, even now. But anyway, about a year after I graduated and started my real job working for the team, the Vicki Daws story broke."

I see him frown in confusion. It's possible he never knew about this, but it's something I've never forgotten.

"She worked in HR for a team in Arizona. And she started to date one of the players. I'm sure it wasn't the first time something like that happened, but their breakup was especially ugly. She ended up losing her job and having to leave the state. It was a message to women working in sports everywhere. The players come first. I vowed then and there to never get mixed up with a player, especially not one from my team. My job, proving I deserved to be there, was too important to me to risk on something like a relationship."

Lifting myself up onto my elbow, I rest one hand on his chest and stare straight into his eyes.

"I've never once been tempted to break that rule for myself. Not until you. Somehow, you convinced me that what we had was worth the risk. Because you made me feel safe and like maybe I could somehow have it all. The player and the job. Turns out, I was right." I end with a soft smile, hoping he can see the words I'm not quite ready to say, even though my heart knows they're true.

Ronan lifts his head to kiss me. "I know what a gift that is, you trusting me and letting me in. I don't take it for granted, Cherry."

"I know you don't." I continue to stroke my hand over his chest. "That's why we're here right now. Because I do trust you. You're worth me letting you in — to my life and my heart." This time, I lower my head to kiss him. And when his hand comes up to tangle in my hair, holding me in place, I melt into him, into his kiss.

If I could, I'd stay here forever. But I can't, which is why, after making myself dizzy from his kiss for several minutes, I pull back. "I have to go," I say with more than a little reluctance as I climb out of bed.

Ronan's groan echoes how I feel. "Goddamn it. Mark my words, someday we won't be sneaking away from each other in the middle of the night. Someday, I'm going to fall asleep with you and wake up with you."

"I want that, too," I reply as I zip up my jeans. His gaze narrows in on the action and he frowns.

"I hate that you're getting dressed right now. Why did I think that once our relationship was public we'd have more time together?"

Crawling back across the bed in only my jeans and bra, I kiss his pouty face. "Because you forgot that you're still a famous baseball player who has to get some sleep so he can win all of his games."

"I'm not playing a game tomorrow," comes his grumpy reply. But when I move to back off the bed, he grabs me, pulling me down on top of him. "All I have to do tomorrow is sit on a plane and keep my hands off you. This whole 'no guests allowed in your hotel room' is bullshit."

A giggle of pure happiness escapes me. It's a heady feeling, being the focus of his attention like this. Knowing he wants me as much as I want him, if not more.

"Bullshit or not, we're going to be good," I chide gently as I once again disentangle myself from his arms. "Which means I'm going back to my room, and we're both going to get some sleep. And tomorrow, no one will be any wiser about what happened here tonight. Got it?" I arch my brow at him, but the effect is lost when paired with my big goofy smile.

Ronan's is much softer in return, once again brimming with what I now fully believe is his love for me.

"Got it. Make sure you save the seat next to you on the airplane."

I pick up my shirt and nod. "Definitely." I pick up the white teddy bear he travels with and toss it at him. "You'll have to make do with cuddling Snowberry tonight."

"A poor substitute for you, Cherry."

I blow him a kiss, then creep out the door, checking that no one is around to see me sneaking out.

Once I've made it back down the stairs and into my own room, I flop down on my own bed with a very satisfied sigh.

He really is worth breaking the rules.

Chapter Thirty-Four

Ronan

When I roll over the next morning to an empty pillow beside me, I stare at it in annoyance, wishing there was a head of silky brunette hair spread across it.

What's a guy gotta do to spend the night with his girlfriend, for fuck's sake?

I get up and grab my phone to text Willow a photo of me pouting next to an empty pillow in hopes of making her smile, only to see a text from my mom that makes my heart stop.

MOM: Hi honey, hope you're doing okay, you didn't call last night. Peyton's fine, she was a bit disappointed but went to bed no problem. Give us a call when you can.

"Shit," I curse, raking my hand through my hair as I grapple with waves of guilt and anger at myself. In the four years I've been doing these calls, I've never missed a single one. And when I do, it's because I'm too busy sneaking my girlfriend into my hotel room for some secret sex.

Fucking hell.

With the time change, it's late enough on the West Coast that I know Peyton should be up by now, but when I call my mom's phone, there's no answer. Switching over to my texts, I shoot her back an answer.

RONAN: I'm sorry. Got caught up with something last night. Is Peyton okay this morning? Are you guys out?

I stare at my phone, willing it to ring, but instead, a reply pops up.

MOM: She's fine honey, promise. She's completely forgotten about it by now. We're just at a morning playgroup and she's having a great time.

A picture follows of Peyton at the top of a slide, grinning. It brings me some relief to see my girl happy. Thinking about it rationally, I know I'm probably beating myself up more than I need to about missing one call. But I've always said Peyton comes first in my life, and last night that wasn't true. I put my selfish needs and pleasures above my duties as her father. And as I stare at the photo on my phone screen, I'm forced to remember why I've never tried to have a relationship before.

Because balancing my role as a single dad and that of a boyfriend is going to be really fucking hard. And the only reason I'm willing to try is because Willow is the only woman worth trying for.

After typing out a quick reply to Mom with a promise to text when we land back in Vancouver, I get in the shower to start readying to leave. Of course, being under the hot water brings back memories of last night, making me hard just remembering Willow in my arms, our bodies slippery and warm. She feels like heaven when her pussy is hugging my dick. My hand reaches down and wraps around my semi, but it's a poor substitute for her body. I give it a tug and close my eyes, imagining it's her hand and not mine. Pretending I can feel her lips on mine, that I can smell her sweet citrus scent, and hear her soft moans of pleasure.

Before long, I'm painting the walls of the shower with my orgasm, hanging my head low as the water beats down on me.

I thought my heart was owned by one little girl, and now, suddenly, it's split in two. And Willow holds the other half in her hands.

A couple of hours later, I'm on the plane, seated next to a window, waiting for Willow to get on and sit next to me. I haven't seen her yet this morning, what with getting caught up in a team meeting after breakfast to review the schedule for the coming week.

But instead of my girlfriend, I end up with my teammate. Monty plunks down in the seat next to me and looks at me with a grin.

"Kai was telling me he went to take a leak last night and heard some moaning from his neighbour." His eyebrows do some ridiculous dance as I frown at him, determined not to say a word. "Weren't *you* his next-door neighbour?"

Out of the corner of my eye, I see Willow finally board the plane, which spurs me into action. Fixing Monty with a glare that hopefully conveys my message of *shut the fuck up*, I hiss under my breath, "I don't know what you're getting at or what

Kai heard, but *if* there was any noise, I'd hope there's some sort of bro code on this team and everyone would know to keep their mouths shut."

A manicured hand lands on Monty's shoulder, and we both turn to look up at the most gorgeous woman in existence.

"Hello, boys. Monty, you don't mind if I steal this seat from you, do you?" She gives him a winning smile, one I'm sure could melt icebergs if she tried.

"Of course." Monty hops up and gestures with his arm toward the seat. "All yours." As she sits down, he catches my eye, mimes a zipper across his mouth, and gives me a wink.

Internally, I sigh in relief. I hoped I could trust the guys to be cool with me and Willow, even in the face of an illegal hotel hookup, and it's good to know that trust isn't misplaced.

"Hey, you," Willow murmurs, leaning in to brush her lips against my cheek.

Grabbing her chin, I turn her head, deciding to say hell with it and really put everyone's acceptance of our relationship to the test. I kiss her properly. Long and deep. When we part, her eyes are glazed, her lips glossy and plump.

"Hey, yourself."

"What was that for?" she asks with a quirk of her lips. I just shrug, leaning my head back against the seat, looking at her.

"Do I need a reason to kiss my girl?"

Her head moves from side to side. "No, but..."

I lean in and peck her lips again, briefly this time. "There is no *but*, Cherry. I wanted to kiss you hello. Weren't you saying last night since word has spread that we're together, we don't need to hide?"

Her soft smile is full of affection. "Fair enough." She lets me pick up her hand and place it on my leg, our fingers twisted together. Lowering her voice, she tucks in close to me to whisper, "Did I really hear Monty saying Kai heard us?"

She sounds worried, so I give her hand a reassuring squeeze. "It's fine, Cherry. If anyone wanted to give us shit, it would've happened by now," I say under my breath. "Besides, even if they had caught us, it was worth it to finally feel you come apart around me again."

Her inhale is audible, and there's no missing the way her legs squeeze together. It makes me grin with a primal sort of pride. She's my woman, and I can turn her on with just a few words. Fuck. Yeah.

The rest of the flight is uneventful. A few of the guys come up to chat, and no one says a word about Willow and I holding hands. It's as if we've always been together. It's normal, totally accepted. And I hope that's enough to ease her worries about our relationship impacting the team in any way.

At the airport, we walk together to the small parking lot that's reserved for the private jets. I escort Willow to her car, helping her load her bags in the back before gathering her in my arms.

"I'll see you tomorrow?" I ask, kissing the top of her head. She nods against my chest, her arms tightening. "Peyton wants you to come over again soon, too. Maybe another movie night."

Her head tilts up. "I'd like that."

I kiss her upturned mouth, softly at first, then taking it deeper because there's no way I can stop myself from feasting on her lips. Sweet, plump, perfect. The vibration of my phone in my pocket makes me growl in frustration as I lift my head from hers.

"Goddamn it."

Willow laughs and reaches into my pocket to pull out my phone. "It's probably your mom."

Glancing down, I see she's right. It is Mom, asking what I want her to prepare for dinner. Sometimes I feel like I don't deserve her. She does so much. "I'm gonna tell my mom about us soon."

"She doesn't know?" Willow raises her eyebrows, and I cringe.

"Um, not exactly. I didn't know what precisely we were, so didn't say anything. But now that everything's good, I want her to know. I want you to get to know each other."

Willow's face softens into a grin. "Are you a mama's boy, Ronan Sinclair?"

I grin right back. "Damn straight. Listen, that woman raised me almost single-handedly. She's the reason I'm the ballplayer I am, and the reason I'm the parent I am. She's amazing."

Willow's arms pull me in tight again. "I love that. And I'd love to get to know her better."

We kiss once more before reluctantly separating. "Drive safe, okay, Cherry? Text me later?"

"Deal."

I open Willow's door, watch her get in, and close it behind her. She drives off, and only then do I make my way over to my own vehicle. My entire drive home, I shift gears from ballplayer and boyfriend, to dad and son.

It's easier than I thought it would be to go between the different parts of who I am. Which gives me hope that finding the balance I know I need won't be so hard after all. And when I get home and open my front door to a whirlwind of four-year-old girl throwing herself at me, I know. Missing one phone call doesn't matter as much as I think it does.

Being here and being the best dad I can also means being the best man I can.

And Willow makes me that man.

Chapter Thirty-Five

Willow

When Ronan opens the front door, his shirt is unbuttoned, his feet are bare, and his hair is sticking up in all kinds of wild directions. I smother my laugh, reaching up to smooth down one particularly wayward lock.

"You don't look like you're ready to schmooze your way through an endorsement dinner," I remark as I walk inside.

"That's because I'm not." His voice sounds strained as he kisses my forehead. "Thanks for coming over. I'm sorry to do this to you. Mom woke up this morning not feeling great and her fever started an hour ago." He grimaces as my fingers start to button up his shirt.

His hand covers mine, and when I look up, he's staring down at me with so much love and affection it floors me.

"You're saving my ass, Willow."

The emotions are overwhelming me, so I opt for humour. "Well, I wouldn't want the executives thinking their new star player was slacking on his promotional duties."

His throaty chuckle sends tingles down my spine. "Good thing I've got at least one of the bigwigs on my side." This time, his kiss lands softly on my lips. But we're interrupted by an excited young voice.

"Willow's here? Daddy, why didn't you tell me?"

We pull apart quickly, but Ronan doesn't look upset that Peyton caught us kissing. In fact, to my surprise, he wraps his arm around my shoulder after I give the little girl a quick hug.

"Okay, Rocket. You're gonna be good for Willow, right? Go to bed on time, eat your dinner?"

Peyton nods. "Yup. And only one treat after supper." She turns to me and says, "Daddy bought more caramel popcorn!"

I grin down at her excited face. "Excellent, we'll have to choose a movie. And maybe make a blanket fort?"

Her audible gasp of delight warms my heart, even as Ronan pretends to groan. "Oh man, I'm missing a blanket fort? Dang it!"

Peyton takes my hand, dragging me away from Ronan. "C'mon, let's go start finding blankets!"

I look back over my shoulder at Ronan, still with a partially-buttoned shirt, standing at the base of his staircase. That look is back on his face, the one that tells me he wants me to stay here in this happy home. To make it mine.

It's tempting, there's no denying that.

Peyton and I gather up armfuls of blankets and pillows from her bedroom and playroom, dumping them in the family room and then continuing to find more. She leads me to the upper floor, and into a room I have never set foot in. Ronan's room.

"Daddy?" Peyton calls. "Can we take your blankets, too?"

He comes out of the en suite with an indulgent expression. "Not all of them, kiddo. I need somewhere to sleep."

"You can sleep with me in the fort," she replies matter-of-factly, and Ronan just shakes his head with a rueful grin.

"Okay, Rocket. Go for it." He walks over to us, fidgeting with his tie. "Can you help me out, Cherry?" I reach up and straighten it, smoothing my hands down the front of his shirt when I'm done, feeling the muscles bunch and tense.

"You look great," I say softly.

He leans down to kiss me, but I lean back, glancing around for Peyton, but the room's empty.

"She's not here. And I want to kiss you properly," he growls before capturing my lips. We fuse together for several minutes, and I itch to reach up and mess his now-styled hair. When we part, I can see his pulse fluttering in his neck, and I drift my hand over it.

"Just curious, what does Peyton think our relationship is?"

Ronan tucks a piece of hair behind my ear, letting his fingers trail down my neck. "She's four, her understanding of romantic relationships is limited. She's also never seen me with a woman." He pauses, looking thoughtful. "I told her you and I are really good friends, that I liked you a lot, and I would be holding your hand, hugging you, and kissing you sometimes. She asked if it would be like when I hold her hand." He chuckles. "Trust me, trying to decide how to explain the difference wasn't easy. So for now, I sort of glossed over it. I hope that's okay?"

He sounds earnest in his checking in with my feelings, which touches me. It's his daughter, but he's making it clear that I matter, as well.

"Of course it is," I reply easily. "I'll go along with whatever you think is best."

He tilts his head down, his lips finding my forehead again. "We're a team in this, Willow. She's my daughter, but you're my girl. Your opinion matters."

"And that means the world to me." I lift up on my toes to kiss him properly, just in time for Peyton to return.

"Daddy, I'm hungry."

Giving my man a smile, I wink. "I've got this, you need to get going." Grabbing Peyton's hand, I lead her out of his room. "C'mon, Pey, you can help me make dinner."

A few minutes later, Ronan hugs both of us goodbye, and then he's gone, leaving me with his precious little girl. The level of trust that shows he has in me isn't something I'm taking for granted.

Together we make macaroni and cheese with some veggies I cut into funny shapes, a trick I used to try with Cooper when we were struggling to get him to eat vegetables. Star-shaped cucumber slices were his favourite, and to my relief, Peyton loves them, too. After we eat and I put the dishes into the dishwasher, I turn to the little girl with my hands on my hips.

"Alright. What are we going to play now?"

"Baseball!" Peyton chirps excitedly, running off to her playroom. I follow her down the hall and find her struggling to set up a small plastic tee, holding a foam ball and bat in her hands.

I hurry over to her side, taking the bat and ball out of her hands. "Hold on, one step at a time. Are you allowed to do this inside?" I ask somewhat skeptically. But she nods so emphatically, I guess I'll believe her.

"Yup. Only with the foam ball. If I wanna use a hard one, we hafta be outside and Daddy wears his glove. He says I hit real hard," she states with a proud smile.

"I bet you do," I say in return. "Alright, let's see it, slugger."

"Wait, we need the net."

Marching over to the closet, Peyton pulls out a small net that she stands at one end of the room. There's no denying she's a baseball player's kid with this setup. I help her line up the tee, then step back.

"Watch this, Willow." She swings wildly, missing the ball and whirling around with a giggle. "Oops."

"Plant your feet," I say encouragingly. Her little tongue pokes out the side of her mouth as she takes another swing, this time connecting, sending the little foam ball into the net.

"Excellent! Home run," I cheer, clapping my hands.

Peyton gives me a grin. "You try!"

"Wow, okay," I say, pretending to be nervous. "It's been a while since I hit a ball. I'm not as good as you are, that's for sure."

"That's 'cause my dad taught me a lot," she says confidently. "Don't worry, I'll help you." Her adorable face makes me smile in return. And for the next half hour, we take turns hitting the ball, then switch to tossing it gently to each other before she gets distracted by a board game sitting on a table. We play that, then Peyton decides it's movie time.

Finally, two hours later, her eyelids are drooping as I turn off the TV. "Come on, kiddo. It's late. We gotta get you to bed," I say quietly.

Instead of standing up, Peyton lifts her arms up, and my heart swells at the gesture. Trying to ignore the moisture in my eyes from this sweet little girl, I pick her up, but when she rests her head on my shoulder, her arms wrapped around my neck, I feel one tear escape.

Carrying her to her bedroom, I help her into pajamas and her bathroom routine. Once she's settled in bed, her eyes barely open, I sit next to her. "Thanks for being so much fun, Peyton."

"You're fun, too, Willow. Can we play again soon?" she asks sleepily.

I nod. "I'd really like that."

"My daddy says he really likes you. I do, too."

Leaning down, I press a gentle kiss to the top of her head. "I really like you and your daddy, as well. Sleep tight, kiddo."

Her eyes flutter closed, and I watch her breathing settle into a slow, steady rhythm. The easy sleep of a child. I stay there for several minutes, watching her, filled with longing to have more nights like this.

Because I wasn't entirely honest with her. I don't just like her and her dad. I love them.

When I head back downstairs, I come to an abrupt stop at the entry to the kitchen. Ronan's mom is there, in a bathrobe, her face pale and drawn, getting something out of the fridge.

"Pam, hi," I say when she notices me. I know Ronan said his mom was home sick, but I didn't expect to find her in the kitchen. And since I don't know if Ronan ever got around to telling her about us, I have an idea what she thinks about me being here with her precious granddaughter.

"Hi, Willow," she says with a wan smile. "Sorry to intrude, I just wanted to get one of Ronan's electrolyte drinks."

"That's okay," I say, making my way into the kitchen. "How are you feeling?"

Ronan's mother grimaces. "Not great." She coughs into her elbow to punctuate the statement. "Whatever this bug is, it came on fast. I just hope Ronan and Peyton don't catch it. Which is why I won't linger."

Drink in hand, she shuffles toward the back door, then pauses and looks back at me. "Thank you for coming to help tonight. My granddaughter was thrilled to know you were coming back."

"Oh, it was nothing," I stammer, feeling the weight of her gaze on me. I may not have grown up with a mom of my own, but I've spent enough time around Tori to sense when a mother is about to stand up for her kid.

But to my surprise, Pam doesn't have anything bad to say.

"My son and granddaughter are happy. Very happy. And I'm no fool, I know it's not just because they enjoy living here or that the team is doing well this season. It's because of you. When we moved out here, I could see immediately that Ronan had changed. There was a hopefulness to him I hadn't seen before. He might think he was fooling me with his 'late nights with the team,' but here's the thing. Mothers always know. He was going to see you."

I open my mouth to apologize, but she beats me to it.

"I'm not upset that he didn't tell me the truth. Your relationship is none of my business. Except to say, thank you. Thank you for helping him see that he deserves to be happy and loved. To have someone take care of him the way he always takes care of everyone else." Her head tilts to the side thoughtfully. "Don't hold back your feelings, Willow. Something tells me you deserve your happily ever after just as much as he does."

With one last small smile, Pam walks back out to her guest house, leaving me with my heart beating wildly.

It's still racing an hour later when the front door unlocks and Ronan walks in to find me sitting at the kitchen counter with a cup of chamomile tea in my hand.

"Hey, Cherry. How did everything go?" he asks, kissing the top of my head.

I spin around on the stool and watch him shrug off his suit jacket and loosen his tie.

"I love you."

His hands freeze. Slowly, he shifts toward me, eyes bright with hope and love. "What was that?"

I swallow and offer a tremulous smile. "I love you, Ronan. You and your daughter. I love you both. More than I ever thought possible. I'm sorry it took me a while to say it back, but I was scared. Only I think it wasn't loving you that scared me. I've realized that loving you doesn't mean losing who I am. Because you love me for who I am, and you won't let me lose that."

A smile creases his face as his eyes close and his head tips back slightly. After a second, he looks back at me, fire in his gaze as he lifts me off my stool and into his arms, kissing me deeply, making me dizzy with the intensity of emotion I feel reverberating through him.

Pulling back slightly, he rests his forehead on mine, his hands locked tight around me. "I love you, Willow. Fucking hell, do I love you. You're everything I want, everything I need, and everything I never thought I could have. And I swear to you, for as long as you'll have me, I'll never let you forget that you complete me in a way no one else ever could." His broken whisper has my eyes welling up with happy tears once again.

Tears that quickly dissipate when Ronan steps back and unbuttons his shirt, shrugging it off to the floor.

"I want to make love to you, Willow. Can I do that?"

"Yes."

Chapter Thirty-Six

Ronan

She loves me.

"Heads up, Sin!"

I turn at Rhett's shout, just in time to reach up and catch the ball about to smack me in the face. "What kind of aim is that, man?" I call out.

"Fuck off, bro. If you weren't too busy moonin' about Willow, you'd have heard Coach say we're about to take infield," he replies good-naturedly.

Sure enough, I glance around to see everyone's shifted in position, and I'm the dumbass off in la-la land.

"Shit. Sorry, Darling."

Having two days without a game isn't a common occurrence during the season, especially this close to All-Star break. After taking yesterday completely off, we need a solid practice today to make sure we're ready to kick some ass tomorrow.

It's a glorious fucking day, made all the better by the knowledge that somewhere in the stadium is the woman I made love to last night. The woman who finally confessed her love for me.

"It's fine, man. I'd probably be distracted, too, if a woman like Willow was warmin' my bed each night."

I glower at Rhett. "Careful." Of course, he doesn't know the shitty truth that I actually haven't had Willow in my bed each night — or ever. Last night was the first time she set foot in my bedroom, for fuck's sake. But there's not a chance in hell I'm letting the guys know that. I'd rather they didn't talk about her like that at all.

"Sorry. We all love Willow. You're alright, too, I guess," he continues with an unrepentant wink. "Just sayin', she's out of your league. Willow Lawson is —"

"Willow Lawson is what?" Her sharply amused voice reaches us, and I turn to see her striding across the field, one of her camera guys trailing after. "Hey, baby," she murmurs, surprising me by kissing my cheek. Then she turns, arms crossed, and stares at Rhett. "You were saying?"

He has the decency to look bashful, and I just grin as I wait for my woman to tear him a new one.

"Nothing bad, Wills. Just tellin' our boy Sin he better treat you right or he's in deep shit."

Willow's face softens. "Aww, Rhett. You big teddy bear. Thanks, but I can handle my relationship myself." She leans into my side, one hand coming up to rest on my chest. "If Ronan messes up, I'll just withhold orgasms till he makes it right."

The guys' raucous laughter surrounds us as she pivots on one foot and looks up at me, her eyes sultry with desire. "That backward hat and your ass in those pants is doing something to me, Ronan Sinclair," she murmurs for my ears only. "You're a distraction, looking this good."

I kiss her quickly, my eyes on Coach, who's probably not loving the fact that my attention isn't on practice but on the woman in my arms. "You're one to talk, Cherry. Get your beautiful self away from me before I decide the team can practice without me while I go taste your sweet pussy in your office."

"Is that a threat or a promise?" she teases, backing away with a wink. Without letting me respond, she turns back to the guys and waves her camera guy over. "Ignore us, we just need some B-roll for socials."

Willow moves to walk away, but I grab her hand, pulling her back in for one more kiss. "I'll see you after practice?" She nods, and I get in a tap on her ass as she leaves, earning a smirk over her shoulder.

"You're a lucky man, Sin," Rhett calls out as we move back into position to continue practice.

I just grin. "Trust me, I know."

When practice finishes, I follow the guys through the dugout into the locker room. We're all hot and sweaty, even with it being a light practice. Summer has come to Vancouver, that's for sure.

"Sin, what's the plan for tonight? You wining and dining our Willow?" Monty calls out from his shower stall as I walk into my own.

"No, I gotta get home. My mom was pretty sick the other day. She's feeling a bit better, but not great, so I gotta take over kid duty."

"You need a babysitter? My younger sister loves kids. She just moved back to town to finish her degree to be a kindergarten teacher," Kai shouts over the general chatter and spray of water.

"Thanks, man," I reply, quickly showering off. It's not just because of Mom and Peyton that I'm in a hurry. I want to stop by Willow's office for a minute to give her something before I go. "If you think she'd be interested, that would be awesome."

"Evie's here?" Rhett says sharply, and I look over to see him staring at Kai. "She's in town?"

There's something about his tone of voice, but I don't have time to wonder what it is. Wrapping my towel around my waist, I hustle back into the main locker room and over to my locker. Pulling on my underwear so I can drop my towel, I tune out the conversations, thinking ahead to not just my gift for Willow, but to home, where I'm hoping Peyton hasn't tired my mom out yet. I'll definitely be texting Kai later to get his sister's info.

Between wanting to take Willow out for "wining and dining," as Monty called it, plus to allow my mom a break every now and then, I need some help.

Once dressed, I tug on my hat, grab my bag and the gift bag for Willow, and make my way up to the executive floors. The halls are quiet, with most of the staff having left for the day. Coach kept us here for an extended stretching session after practice, seeing as tomorrow is game day.

I walk swiftly to Willow's office, relieved to see the light on and the door open. She waited for me. Knocking softly on the frame, I grin when she looks up with a smile.

"Hey, I was starting to wonder how long Coach would keep you guys," she says, pushing away from her desk and coming around to meet me as I step in and close the door behind me, turning the lock. Her eyes drop to my hand when I do so, and the corner of her lips tip up in a knowing smirk.

I hug her with one arm, keeping the other behind my back. "Yeah, he worked us hard, then had us do a long cooldown. Need to be ready for tomorrow."

"You'll dominate the Eagles," she says confidently. "Their star pitcher is out with a shoulder injury, and they don't have the roster of talent we've got."

I lean in and kiss the tip of her nose. "Well, if you say we're gonna win, then, of course, we will." I pull my arm out from behind my back. "Especially if you're wearing this."

Willow takes the bag, looking from it to me. "Wearing..." Her face is a mixture of curiosity and happiness. She knows what's in the bag, and her reaction is already better than I could have imagined.

I shrug. "Now that everyone knows, I thought maybe you'd wear my name."

She lifts the jersey out with a look of wonder. "Ronan," she murmurs, looking at my last name written across the back. Her eyes meet mine. "I've never worn a player's jersey before. Just generic team shirts, never a specific player."

Well, fuck. Now I've got a hard-on.

"Good," I growl, cradling her face in my hands. I kiss her again, and her arms come around my neck, the jersey still clutched in one hand. "Because my name is the only name you should ever wear."

She pulls it on over her shirt, and holy shit, that does something to me. "Goddamn, woman. You look good in that."

She pulls her hair out from the collar as I rub my hand over my jaw, still trying to process the sheer perfection of what stands before me. My dick is painfully hard just from seeing her wear my name.

This is why I locked the door.

I push her backward until she's leaning against her desk and tangle my hand in her hair while I ravage her lips. Teeth grazing, tongues tangling, I push my hips into hers so she can tell just what it does to me seeing her in my jersey. Tearing away from her lips is hard, but I need more. "I need you," I growl, dropping to my knees. "Fuck, I need your pussy on my mouth while you wear my name, Cherry."

I look up at her for permission and see her nod. Spinning my cap around to the back, her eyes darken as I give her a wolfish grin. Then, I'm yanking down her pants and pressing my face into her sweet pussy.

Her tight grip on my shoulders is almost amusing. As if I would want to move even an inch from where I am right now.

And when she comes just minutes later, her hands gripping my shoulders and her breathless moans filling my ears, I know. She's mine. And I'm hers. And someday, it won't be my name on that jersey she's wearing.

It'll be *our* name.

Chapter Thirty-Seven

Willow

The stadium is packed, every seat filled with enthusiastic Tridents fans, and a few Eagle fans, as well. The atmosphere is electric, with the hot July sun shining down, music pumping, and everyone ready for a great ball game.

Nervously, I smooth my hands down the front of the jersey Ronan gave me.

I don't think he realizes how big of a deal this is for me. Wearing his jersey where anyone and everyone can see it is taking our relationship public in a much bigger way than just the other players and Tridents staff knowing about us.

I'm the new head of media relations. I run the press conferences. There's bound to be questions. Yet, I feel ready to face them, knowing I've got my man, my uncle, and my team ready to support me. Aside from a little teasing, the guys haven't seemed to care in the slightest that I'm dating Ronan. And my own team is just so happy to have Lydia out of the way, I don't think they'd mind if I was dating every single player all at one time.

"You look good, darling girl."

I look up to see Uncle Mike standing in the doorway of my office, a soft smile on his face. He walks in and places his hands on my shoulders.

"Your dad would be so happy to see you like this. In love with a good man, I mean."

Crap. My eyes start to feel damp. "He'd like Ronan, I think."

"I know he would." Uncle Mike pulls me in for a hug. "He'll treat you right, Wills. And if he doesn't, I'll sever his contract and send him packing."

I choke out a laugh and clutch him tighter. "Don't do that, the team needs him."

"Well, I don't give a shit what the team needs. I need *you* to be happy."

I look up at my dad's best friend, the man who practically helped raise me. The man who has helped me build the life I've always wanted. "Thanks, Uncle Mike. For everything."

"You've earned it. You deserve every happiness." He drops his hands and tilts his head toward the door. "Ready to watch the game?"

I give him a watery smile and a nod, and we make our way up to Uncle Mike's suite where Pam and Peyton are waiting, thanks to a personal invite from Uncle Mike to watch the game from here. I find them sitting in the lower level of the box, where they've got the perfect view of home plate.

"Hello, ladies," I say brightly. Peyton bounces out of her seat and throws herself into my arms.

"Hi, Willow! Look, we're matching." She proudly sticks her thumb at her chest, showing off her own Sinclair jersey. She leads me over to her grandmother, who gives me a welcoming smile.

"Can I get either of you anything? We can have snacks brought up from concession if you don't like what's here," I say, suddenly nervous. First the matching jersey with his daughter, now I'm watching the game with his mom and his daughter in my uncle's box. Maybe it shouldn't feel like such a serious step, but it does to me.

This is the first game in years I'm not officially working. And clearly, Pam can tell I'm at a loss.

"Just sit down and relax, dear. We've got all the snacks we could possibly want." Pam indicates the seat on the other side of Peyton.

I sit down just in time for the players to hit the field. The cheer that goes up around the stadium is deafening, and Peyton and Pam join in as Ronan jogs over to first base. He looks up, scanning the boxes until he sees us, and even from this distance, I see his face light up.

"Daddy!" Peyton screams, waving wildly. She grabs my hand. "There he is!"

I give him a wave, smaller than Peyton's, but there's no shrinking my grin. *There he is.*

The game is fast-paced, and as I predicted, the Tridents pull off an easy win. Ronan scores two runs, and I'm pretty sure Peyton has no voice left by the end with how much she was cheering and screaming.

To my surprise, when we part ways — me to grab my bag from my office and Pam to take Peyton home — I get a hug goodbye from both of them.

"Thanks for watching the game with us, sweetheart, it was lovely to spend some time with you."

"I had a great time," I answer honestly. "It was nice to just watch the game and not be worrying so much about what I need to do for work."

Pam laughs. "I can only imagine. What are your plans for tonight?"

Out of nowhere, I feel my cheeks heat up with a blush. Because the plans I wish I had involve her son in my bed.

Instead, I reply, "Oh, probably not much. Go home and get ready for tomorrow."

She just nods and takes Peyton's hand. "Alright, well, don't let us hold you up. Have a lovely night." The enigmatic smile on her face puzzles me slightly, but as soon as they're gone, I dismiss it.

When an unexpected knock on my apartment door occurs less than half an hour after I get home from the game, I find myself frowning at it. I'm tired and just want to go to bed. And I didn't miss a call from someone trying to buzz in, so I'm also a bit baffled as to who it is. Belting my satin robe even tighter around my middle, I pad over to the door and look through the peephole.

Then I'm throwing open the deadbolt, wrenching open the door, and hurling myself into the open and ready arms of my boyfriend.

"You're here?" I gasp in between kisses. He carries us inside, not missing a beat between closing and locking my door. "Is that a bag?" I look down at the medium-sized duffle he just set down.

Ronan just grins, his hands still clutching my ass as I cling to him like a spider monkey. "Yeah, I was hoping you wouldn't be opposed to a sleepover?"

I stare at him, trying to catch up mentally to what he just said. "Like, all night?"

He nods and starts moving in the direction of my bedroom. "All. Night. I got home, and Mom looked at me and told me to get out." He chuckles. "It's a little weird, my mom kicking me out of my own house so I can spend the night with my girlfriend, but I'm not going to complain."

We reach my bedroom, and I wriggle out of his arms, keeping mine looped around his neck. "You're telling me Pam Sinclair is playing cupid?"

His hands come to the tie of my robe, and he slowly starts pulling it undone. "Mm-hmm."

He pushes my robe off my shoulders, letting the satin garment fall to the floor, leaving me in a skimpy set of sleep shorts and a tank top. My nipples are already hard pebbles, and I'm guessing there's a damp spot on my shorts. The way this man turns me on should be criminal. His lips find my collarbone, brushing feather light kisses across my bare skin.

"I think I love your mom," I gasp, my head falling to one side as his lips trail back up my neck. He tugs my earlobe between his teeth before kissing his way over my cheek and landing on my mouth. I come alive under his kiss. There's no way to ever get enough, but tonight, maybe we can try.

"We're not talking about my mom right now, Cherry." His voice is a mixture of amusement and barely controlled lust. Suddenly, I'm airborne again, then dumped on my bed. Ronan steps back and quickly strips off his clothes before coming back over me, kissing his way up from the waistband of my shorts, lifting my tank up and off as he goes.

"We've got all night. All night for me to make you come on my tongue, and then on my cock. Over and over again. I want to worship your fucking perfect body and make it so you never forget you're mine. All you have to decide is which one you want first. Tongue or cock."

"Decisions, decisions," I murmur as he toys with my nipple, rolling it between his fingers and thumb. "I choose...tongue."

"Excellent choice." His lips wrap around one nipple and he sucks, hard, making me cry out as my fingers find purchase in his hair. He lavishes attention on one breast before moving to the other, his hands roaming my body. I can feel his cock, heavy and long, with only my satin shorts as a barrier. And I don't want anything between us. Squirming underneath him, I try to push them off, but he grabs my hands and pulls them up above my head.

"Don't move."

He slowly trails his hands down my sides, but I do as he says and keep my hands over my head. Slowly, agonizingly so, he drags my shorts down to my feet and tosses them behind him. I'm already breathing heavy with anticipation, the lust-filled looks he's giving me making my head spin. How is it possible that every time we're together, it's hotter? Somehow more intense, more powerful than the last?

I don't know if there's an answer to that question. And right now, with his lips kissing their way up from my ankle to my knee, then tickling the inside of my thigh, I don't fucking care.

His breath ghosts across my core, where I know I'm already drenched with desire.

"Mmm. All this for me? Good thing I'm hungry." He gives me a wicked grin before flattening his tongue up my slit, making my back arch off the bed.

My hands come down, and he stops, lifting his head. "What did I say about those hands?"

I whimper, but put my hands back above my head, clutching the pillow in a death grip. His tongue lands on me again, and my hips start to rock. One arm comes up and bands over me, holding me still.

"Oh, fuck, Ronan, I need to move," I cry out in protest, my toes curling into the mattress. He's only just begun, but I'm already desperate. Needy. Ready to come.

"No, you don't. You need to lie back and let me devour you, Willow. That's what you need to do," he growls against my flesh. "Let go and let me take care of you."

Jesus Christ, this man.

Chapter Thirty-Eight

Ronan

Her taste explodes on my tongue as Willow cries out in surrender. I'll never get tired of this. Of her, of us. I continue licking and sucking her clit, my arms tight restraints against her writhing hips, until I feel her body sag under me, the pleasure-fueled tension leaving her. Only then do I press one final kiss to her sex, then start moving up her body, kissing her damp skin.

"That was amazing," she murmurs when I reach her breasts. "Is it my turn now?"

Ignoring that statement, I don't respond. Instead, I nuzzle her skin, letting the rough scratch of my scruff turn her pink. My hands cover her tits, fingers plucking at her nipples. I can't stop toying with her, teasing every last drop of pleasure from her. She'll come again, there's no doubt. The only question is, how soon and how often.

But I need to stop underestimating Willow's determination. Because in a move I honestly don't see coming, her legs wrap around my waist, heels digging into my ass, and with her hands on my chest, she pushes firmly until I give in and flip over.

"I was planning on you having both ways before anything else, you know. My tongue and my cock, remember?" I say, arching my brow.

Her answering smile is so bright, it's almost blinding. "I mean, if you insist." Her hips wiggle from side to side.

I chuckle. "Oh, I abso-fucking-lutely insist, Cherry." But instead of getting straight to it, I find myself pausing, an overwhelming sense of wonder hitting me.

"You're exquisite," I say lowly, running my hands along her thighs that are pinned to my sides. "A fucking goddess among men. How the hell did I get so lucky to call you mine?"

Willow gives me an impish look before leaning down. Her hair falls to form a curtain around us as her breath ghosts across my lips. "Fate."

My laugh is swallowed by her kiss, her tongue plundering my mouth, giving me everything I gave her and more. She starts to grind on me, her already wet core rubbing against my dick, making me impossibly harder. With every move of her hips, it's clear how easy it would be to just slide inside of her bare. But with all the chaos around us lately, we haven't had that discussion.

I can tell she's reached the same observation when she lifts her head. "I need to feel you, Ronan. All of you. If you're mine, then I want it all."

"Fuck, Cherry. I want that, too. You're sure?" I ask, tucking a piece of her hair behind her ear. "Before you, there was no one for a long time."

Willow's hips are still rocking, the movement involuntary, as if her body can't help but seek pleasure even as we have this important conversation.

"I trust you. My annual exam was a couple months ago, all good here. And I've been with other men, but no one since I met you." She leans down and kisses me lightly. "You ruined me for anyone else."

"Good," I grunt as her petite hand reaches between us to grab my cock. Lining us up, she slowly sinks down. "Oh, holy shit." My head presses back into the pillow as the overwhelming sensation of taking her bare hits me in waves. Her wet heat is amplified by a thousand. I swear to God, every nerve ending in my dick is turned on high.

"I feel you. I feel everything," she says, her voice thready with desire. Placing her hands on my chest, she starts to rock back and forth, slowly at first, then picking up speed. I let her be in control, find her own rhythm. Because honestly? Nothing has ever felt this good. And anything she wants, I know I'm gonna want, too.

My fingers dig into the flesh of her hips. Her eyes close as she lifts herself up, bringing her hands to her breasts. Fuck me, watching her play with herself as she chases her release on my cock is the most perfect thing to witness, ever.

"Goddamn, Cherry, your pussy is fucking strangling my cock. Tell me you're close," I grind out as I feel my orgasm looming. Her head bobs up and down in response.

"So close."

I bring my thumb to her clit as she bounces up and down, and she cries out, losing her rhythm. I could watch her come undone every day for the rest of my life and never tire of it. Her hands fall to the bed beside my head, her hair once again tickling my shoulders.

"Ronan, Ronan," she starts to chant as she thrusts herself along my length. "Oh my God. Yes. Yes. Yes!"

Her shriek trails off as I feel her squeezing me so tight my dick throbs. Then I'm grunting out her name as I shudder through my own orgasm, filling her with my release.

Some day, I'd like to make a baby with this woman.

The thought makes me grin like a fool, which Willow notices when she lifts her head from my shoulder where she collapsed, spent.

"What's got you smiling like that?" she asks, tracing my lips with her finger. I can feel myself softening inside of her, but there's no chance I'm going to lose this connection until I have to.

"Just thinking about our future," I answer evasively.

"It's a good one, isn't it?"

I kiss her in response, drawing her face down to mine, pouring everything into the kiss. "It's more than good, Cherry. It's amazing."

Last night was incredible. But nothing beats waking up with Willow in my arms. Her hair tickling my chest, the feeling of her pressed into my side, our legs tangled together, and my hand holding her ass possessively is everything I thought it would be and more.

Not gonna lie, being woken up at 3 am by Willow sucking my dick into her warm, willing mouth was another perk to spending the night with my girlfriend. A really fucking good perk.

But apparently, we managed to forget to close the blinds, so now, the morning sunshine is streaming in, illuminating Willow as she's lying draped over me, my fingers lazily drawing up and down her spine. She wriggles and huffs out a small sigh, and it's so fucking cute, I just smile and kiss the top of her head.

"Mmph. Why are we awake so early," she mumbles into my chest, burrowing in closer. I chuckle, tightening my hold around her.

"Hate to tell you this, Cherry, but it's 10 am."

Willow pushes herself upright, blinking sleepily. "What? It is not. There's no way. I don't sleep in."

My grin widens as I tilt my head over to the alarm clock. "You do when you're up most of the night fucking me."

Willow's throaty chuckle stirs up memories of last night and my dick starts to harden. With her still half sprawled across me, she feels it and arches a brow. "Listen, buddy, you might have the stamina of a twenty-year-old, but I need a little downtime. And a lot of coffee. Especially with the way you ravaged me last night"

"It's not me, it's you. You do this to me," comes my honest answer. Her eye roll is accompanied by the faintest of blushes and a smile that tells me she likes my response. "And you say ravage, I say cherish. Worship. Adore."

"Okay, charmer." She laughs, pushing at my chest to sit up. "What time do you need to be home for Peyton?"

My heart warms that she's thinking of my daughter, even now. "Whenever. Mom has their day all planned with preschool and gymnastics. I'd like to see her before I head to the field for warm-up, though." I reach up and tug her back down, loving how easily she falls back into my arms. "Are you sure I can't cherish, worship, and adore you one more time? For good luck in the game later, of course," I say with a mischievous smirk.

"You don't need to fuck me for good luck, Ronan Sinclair." Willow rolls her eyes.

Taking her by surprise, I roll us so she's underneath me, grabbing one of her legs to draw it up to my hip so I can grind against her. "You're right. I don't need to fuck you. I need to make love to you." When her face softens into that expression of pure love that I finally get to see from her, I know I've won this round. Notching myself to her entrance, I slide into her pussy as if I'm sliding into home.

And when I hit the field later that day, I find her immediately, standing off to the side of the dugout where she's coordinating the media coverage for the day. Walking over, I lean in close to whisper so no one else can hear. "I'm gonna hit a home run because of this morning, Cherry."

Three innings later, I do just that. And as I jog around the bases toward my teammates ready to celebrate, my gaze finds her again. The woman I love as much as I love this game and my daughter. The woman who's smiling back at me just as widely as I'm smiling at her.

"Told you," I call out as I jog off the field toward her, her camera crew, and all the Tridents coaches, players, and staff. And right there, in front of a stadium full of fans, a dugout full of my teammates, and who knows how many others watching, I sweep her off her feet and into my embrace, my lips finding hers.

And the way she gives herself over to our kiss, regardless of who's watching, makes me feel like the luckiest guy alive. Because getting Willow to decide I was worth breaking her rules?

Best play I've ever made.

Epilogue

5 years later

Ronan

I knew deep down when I moved to Vancouver, this was the team that could take it all the way. And we did. It might have taken a few years, but here we are, confetti streaming down onto the diamond and deafening cheers and laughter from the fans, players, and staff. Just in time, too, with my retirement from major league baseball finally here.

Every baseball player dreams of a moment like this. As I hoist the championship trophy above my head, my teammates surrounding me, all I feel is a deep sense of accomplishment and excitement for whatever comes next. My years playing professional ball might be over, but I'm ending things with my team in the best possible way.

As champions.

It's been a long season, hell, it always is with close to two hundred games when you include spring training, postseason, and playoffs. We're all looking forward to some time off, possibly no one more than me. Because in two days, Willow and I leave on our traditional trip back to Hawaii where we've gone every year.

This time the trip will be even longer, with my mom and our kids flying out a week later to join us. After my girl and I get some much-needed alone time. We started talking about trying for another baby soon, and what better place than Hawaii to make that magic happen?

All it takes is the thought of Willow, round with my baby growing inside of her, and my pulse starts to speed up. Then, as if fate once again knows exactly what I want, the crowd in front of me parts slightly and my gaze lands on the woman I love with every fiber of my being. All of a sudden, my attention isn't on the trophy I'm holding or my teammates. It's on the beautiful brunette with our toddler on her hip and our daughter at her side, walking toward me with tears spilling down her cheeks. My mom is with her, and the sight of them has me smiling almost wider than I did when Rhett slid into home, cinching the win for us. That's my whole world, right there.

Proud doesn't even begin to describe how I feel looking at Willow and our family. She's the most incredible woman, and she's inspiring countless other women to work in sports media. Every year, she's invited to the university to give guest lectures to the business department, and last year she was interviewed by an international magazine for a spread on influential women in sports. My powerhouse of a wife is a wonder, and not a day goes by that I'm not in awe of her. And of the love she freely gives me and our family.

I turn to Maverick, who's standing next to me, and hand him the trophy, slapping him on the shoulder with a grin. Truthfully, we wouldn't be here without him, that's for fucking sure. The way he turned things around four years ago made him a force to be reckoned with on the field. Coming back from his injury stronger, and somehow more grounded, was a privilege to witness. I count him as one of my closest friends now.

He takes the trophy from me just in time for our three-year-old, Jett, to lean out from Willow's hold, making grabby hands at me.

"Dada, you won!"

I take the little guy with a grin. "Sure did, buddy."

Peyton also wraps her arms around my waist. "Congrats, Dad."

"Thanks, Rocket." She's tall enough now that it's easy to bend down and kiss the top of her head, even with Jett in my arms. Next year, she'll hit double digits, and as we hit those tween years, I'm so grateful she has Willow as a mom now. Their bond is strong.

Pulling back, my not-so-little girl gives me an impish grin. "But it's a good thing you're retiring. You're getting slow, rounding the bases in your old age."

Before I can give her crap for that remark, she takes off, over to Monty and Lark.

Willow's soft laugh reaches me as her hand comes to my shoulder, and I turn slightly to face the love of my life.

"Ignore her, babe. You were fast."

I chuckle as I lean in and kiss her forehead. "Nah, she's right. My knees aren't what they used to be."

"Still good enough to win, though."

I nod, and my smile grows. "That's true. We did it."

"Yeah, you did," she replies with a smile, rising up on her toes to kiss me again. Jett's squirming to be let down, but he's a wild one, and in this crowd, there's not a chance I'll let him go free.

"Dada, let gooooo," he protests, breaking Willow and I apart. My beautiful wife just shakes her head and gestures to take him back.

"Here, I'll take him. We'll go join Peyton and Auntie Lark. You've got interviews."

"You're not the head of media relations right this second, Willow, enjoy this moment with your husband. I'll take my grandson," Mom interjects from behind me, and I spin around to pull her in for a hug.

"Mom." My voice cracks as the other woman who has done more for me than I could ever repay her for takes my son. "Thank you."

Two words that don't say near enough, but as always, she gets it. "You're welcome, Ronan, but you don't need to thank me. It's an honour to be your mother and watch the man you've become. I love you, honey." We hug again, then she takes Jett and walks over to Peyton, Lark, and Monty. And finally, I'm alone with my wife. Well, as alone as I can be standing on a baseball diamond full of Tridents and their families.

"I'm so proud of you," Willow says, and just like that, I'm choked up again.

Pulling her into my arms, I hold her tight and just soak in the moment. This day is one I'll never forget. It's in my top ten of all time, for sure. Right up there with signing my first major league contract, Peyton's birth, marrying Willow, and

Jett's birth, along with a few other perfect moments in time, all of which include my family.

Because even as I take in the sounds of celebration surrounding us, I know that as amazing as today is, it would be nothing without the woman in my arms.

She's my wife, my family, my everything.

I kiss the top of her head again, and she tilts her head up to meet my lips.

Then, the love of my life says the only words that could make this day go from top ten of all time to top five.

"By the way, I'm pregnant again."

Acknowledgements

There is not a chance this book would exist without my author bestie and sports expert, Chelle Sloan. Thank you for your patience, your encouragement, your humour, and your friendship.

Starting a new series is scary... but so many amazing people helped keep me going when I wasn't sure I could write a sports romance. THANK YOU to every single one of you. My dream team, Kelly, Erica, Jess and Andrea... and Meg and Caroline for your input. Chris, editor extraordinaire for making it shine. Carolina, my brain, always keeping me on track. Roxie and Theresa for loving my crazy and handling hours of voice memos.

And Vana. The Christina to my Meredith. For the hours of brainstorming driving through Tennessee. I adore you.

About Julia Jarrett

Julia Jarrett is a busy mother of two boys, a happy wife to her real-life book boyfriend and the owner of two rescue dogs, one from Guatemala and another one from Taiwan. She lives on the West Coast of Canada and when she isn't writing contemporary romance novels full of relatable heroines and swoon-worthy heroes, she's probably drinking tea (or wine) and reading.

For a complete listing of Julia Jarrett books please visit
www.authorjuliajarrett.com/books

Follow Julia:

Instagram @juliajarrettauthor
Facebook Reader Group: Julia Jarrett's Nutty Muffins
TikTok @julia.jarrett.author

Printed in Great Britain
by Amazon

43596073R00172